Reawakened

Denise Dowdell-Stent

Awakening, by Carmen Willcox

To share the cup
that binds—

To bind the lives
that will be true
for all of Time.

What will be hence
or was before—

Of no concern can be
for the two
who share
the cup that binds.

The cup will live
and live on long,
For both that share it
Live in One, Eternal Time

1

14 months after the *wedding*

Shrill screams reverberated through Vala's head as though bouncing off the walls of her skull and penetrating her brain. Her eyes shot open and she sat bolt upright in bed, perspiration dripping from her brow, stinging her eyes. Elvar, disturbed by the sudden commotion, sluggishly opened his eyes and yawned.

"What is it, my love?" Elvar said, pushing damp locks of Vala's hair away from her face. "Have you had another vision?"

"Not a 'vision' in the strictest sense of the word," Vala replied. "I didn't see anything—just heard screaming—a sense of pure terror and complete helplessness."

"I am sorry," Elvar stroked Vala's cheek lovingly. "It must be very frustrating and frightening for you."

Vala looked into her husband's eyes and saw his concern for her reflected back. She cupped Elvar's face in her hands, touching her forehead and nose to his, kissing him slowly and softly. As Vala's tongue darted into his mouth, Elvar felt his desire igniting. His hands moved under her pyjama top, and the feel of Vala's soft skin intensified his passion for her. In response, Vala deepened her kisses as heat rose in her body, her nerves tingling with electricity and anticipation. She promptly pulled Elvar's T-shirt over his head and helped him remove her top, pressing her bare skin to his. Vala shrugged off her pyjama bottoms, and Elvar pulled her on top as he lowered his boxers. Vala gasped as their bodies joined and rapturous pleasure rippled through every cell of her body. Elvar moaned quietly as Vala's movements brought him ever closer to ecstatic release. Vala felt Elvar reaching an apex, and her own body responded in kind.

Through her haze of pleasure, Vala heard the sound of soft footsteps on her bedroom carpet. A startled cry from Elvar abruptly shook Vala from her euphoria. She turned her head, and a small scream escaped her lips as a tall figure stood not more than a few feet away from the bed. Vala quickly pulled the duvet up to protect their modesty, though she realised it was rather too late for that now.

"Tarrys!" Vala shrieked.

Tarrys grimaced in embarrassment, a red flush rising from his neck and colouring his face.

"I am sorry, Sister," Tarrys began. "I did not mean to intrude at such an inopportune moment, but I had no choice!"

Vala steadied her breath and looked at her brother, taking in his highly distressed expression.

"What is it, Tarrys?" Elvar asked as he hitched up his boxers under the duvet.

"It is Gweneira," Tarrys said, his voice rising. "There is something wrong! She is writhing in agony and haemorrhaging. I think she might be in premature labour. Derryth cannot stop it. Please, Vala, come with me, you have to help her."

"Of course we will come!" Vala assured her brother. "Though if you wouldn't mind ducking into the bathroom for a minute so we can …"

"Of course," Tarrys agreed, promptly stepping into the en suite bathroom and closing the door.

Vala and Elvar dressed quickly and with little conversation. Vala sighed deeply as a mixture of anxiety and uncertainty washed over her.

"If anyone can help her, it is you," Elvar squeezed Vala's hand reassuringly and kissed the top of her head.

"Tarrys," Vala called out softly, "you can come out now."

Vala looked up at her brother, noticing his dishevelled auburn hair, unshaven face, and red-rimmed eyes. Her heart ached for him and she pulled Tarrys into a fierce hug.

"I will do my absolute best, Tarrys," Vala assured him.

In the year that had passed since she met Elvar and learnt of her fae heritage, Vala's abilities had grown exponentially. One of her favourite new skills was mastering the ability to manipulate air currents, allowing her to fly.

"We will have to travel quite fast," Tarrys stated, as all three of them found an inconspicuous area outside Vala's shared house to ascend into the air. "It would probably be better if you stay in between us both and hold each of our hands in your own as I very much doubt that you are accustomed to travelling at such speeds."

"Please, Vala," Elvar asked. "It can be disorientating and quite a head rush. We only wish to keep you safe."

"Seriously, guys!" Vala said laughing. "Do you actually hear me disagreeing? I am *not* going to argue against that one!"

Vala was thankful that the crisp night air was at least still tonight, as she did not enjoy navigating against turbulence. A quick check around the perimeter of the house revealed that no one was likely to see them and they promptly ascended high into the night sky.

Once they had reached a significant altitude, Elvar looked at Vala and smiled, kissing her cheek and taking her hand in his. Tarrys took Vala's other hand and nodded at Elvar.

"Vala, beloved," Elvar squeezed her hand, "we need to gain speed pretty quickly. I would advise you to close your eyes and hold on tight. You are in for quite a ride!"

Vala did as Elvar instructed, listening as the rapidly increasing air current whistled in her ears. The chilled breeze caressed her skin in an icy embrace, its glacial fingers whipping through her hair.

"You weren't kidding—this is really fast!" Vala barely managed to get the words out.

"Are you okay?" Elvar asked with concern.

"It's strangely exhilarating, though I'm not sure if my stomach agrees!"

They continued for an hour before dropping speed, and as Vala's stomach lurched, she realised that they were losing altitude too. Before long, an unfamiliar river and fields came into view, leaving Vala wondering where they were.

"It is time to alight, Vala," Tarrys said softly, lightly tugging on her hand to emphasise his intention.

"But where are we?" Vala asked in bewilderment, as all she could see was a line of trees, the river, and endless fields. "There's no stone circle here."

"Not a circle—no," Elvar confirmed. "There are two very inconspicuous standing stones, which I believe are referred to in this realm as Robin Hood and Little John. In answer to your question, we are situated close to the River Nene, near the village of Alwalton, west of Peterborough."

Elvar and Tarrys alighted softly on the tall grass below, with Vala still between them.

"A little underwhelming!" Vala said, laughing.

"No matter," Tarrys replied. "It will take us to where we need to go."

Upon crossing into Avalonia, it was a very short walk to the woodland home Gweneira shared with her husband, Tarrys. Their peaceful journey was soon shattered by the sounds of distressed crying coming from the house, piercing the still of the night outside.

As was custom in Candalia, the three of them promptly removed their footwear at the door and rushed up the stairs to the master bedroom. Vala looked anxiously upon her friend and sister-in-law; she had never before seen anyone look so unwell. Gweneira's skin had taken on a much paler pallor than usual, which stood in contrast to the red flush on her cheeks. She was clothed in a light-cotton nightgown that was saturated in sweat and clung to Gweneira's clammy skin. A patch of blood had stained the nightgown and spread onto the bed sheets below.

Gweneira drew a shuddering breath and turned her head slowly in Vala's direction, looking at her imploringly and reaching out with her hand. Vala took Gweneira's hand in hers and squeezed. She had always been extra receptive to others' emotions, and the distress in the room was overwhelming her.

"I need you all out!" Vala said as calmly as possible. "You too, Tarrys."

Tarrys nodded his assent and led the others to wait downstairs with him.

"I will try my best, Gwen," Vala assured her, "but I need you to really concentrate on calming down. Try flowing the pain from your body—let it ebb away."

Vala placed her hands on Gweneira's swollen belly, feeling the unease of the unborn child beneath her hands. Vala focussed all her attention into forming a connection with the baby and was now also aware that Gweneira's energy had shifted somewhat into a slightly more relaxed state. Feelings of fear, no, more like terror, Vala thought, filtered through her. The feelings were accompanied by flashes of colour, strange metallic tastes, and loud noises. Vala allowed the disturbed emotions to flow into her before channelling them back out into the ground beneath her to neutralise them. She concentrated her efforts into sending the baby strong sensations of love and serenity, trying to instil a sense of security to make it feel safe. Having meticulously pored over the medical textbooks Gweneira had lent her, Vala had realised that Gweneira had suffered a mild placental abruption. She brought her attention to the rupture— visualising Gweneira's placenta fusing to the uterine wall— and channelled her energies as pure white light emanated from the palms of her hands. Thanks to her healing efforts, it immediately reattached and healed. Vala inhaled deeply, then allowed her breath to slowly escape through her mouth. The baby's movements had slowed, and Vala registered the sense of relief flooding through Gweneira's body. Vala palpably felt the baby relax and return to a content, happy state.

"It's okay, Gwen," Vala reached for her hand and smiled. "You suffered a mild placental abruption, which is why you were in so much pain and bleeding. The placenta's now reattached to your womb, and the baby is fine."

"Thank you, Vala!" Gweneira exclaimed, pulling her into a fierce hug. "I am forever indebted to you. First you saved my cousin's life and now my unborn child's. You are amazing—beyond words!"

"You would have done the same for me," Vala replied, yawning. "It is important for you to rest for the remaining duration of your pregnancy though—nothing more exertive than walking. But for now, a warm bath is in order."

Although exhausted from her healing efforts, Vala had learnt of ways to rapidly replenish some of her lost energy. She did not need to sleep it off as she had done in the past.

"Tarrys, Elvar, Father, come up please!" Vala called out.

Tarrys appeared first, his face stricken with anxiety. He was closely flanked by Derryth and Elvar, who looked pensive but not as fretful as his brother-in-law.

"How is she?" Tarrys asked nervously.

"*She* is quite fine, my love!" Gweneira answered cheerfully. "As is our baby, thanks to your sister, and now we are both quite well!"

Tarrys looked upon Vala in awe, his face lined with tears. He walked over to envelop her in a tight embrace.

"Words will never express how grateful I am that you came into our lives, sweet sister. I have known you such a short time, yet I love you dearly and only regret that we have missed out on so much time together."

"I love you too, Tarrys," Vala replied, choking back a sob.

"That was quite remarkable!" Derryth said, squeezing Vala's shoulder. "You have surpassed me, Daughter. I have never before seen a more powerful healer."

"Thank you," Vala replied quietly.

"Well, Gwen, I shall leave you in Vala's capable hands and be heading home," Derryth said, kissing Gweneira on the cheek.

After Derryth's departure, everyone was quiet for a short time, allowing their emotions to settle, before Vala broke the silence.

"Okay guys," Vala began. "Tarrys, you can help me bathe Gwen whilst Elvar gets some fresh bed linen."

With Tarrys' help, Vala took Gweneira to the bathroom, supporting her weight carefully between them. Once inside, Vala closed the door and Tarrys helped his wife undress while Vala ran the bath.

"I've put in a few drops of lavender oil, Gwen, to help you relax," Vala said, helping Gweneira into the bath. "Whilst you get comfortable, I'm just going to nip out for a quick recharge."

"Absolutely!" Gweneira replied, motioning for Vala to leave. "Take as much time as you need."

Vala sat on a chair in Gweneira and Tarrys' bedroom, easing back into the plush, soft cushioning. She planted her feet firmly on the ground and took three slow, deep breaths. Closing her eyes, Vala imagined a golden ball of light just above her head and glowing silver-white strands connecting her to the earth below.

It was imperative after a healing not only to replenish her energy reserves, but to cleanse herself of other accumulated energies—to reunite them with their rightful owner, and to disperse any unwanted energies into the ground below to be cleansed and purified.

Vala scanned her body, paying particular attention to its sensations or discomfort—anything that indicated an area of concentrated energy—and then differentiating her own unique energy signature from that of another.

Having identified the extraneous energy, Vala felt a tingle in her fingertips and a sensation of heat in her solar plexus, which quickly spread out to her hands and feet. Grateful for the release, she channelled the displaced energies through her body's meridians and out through her feet into the ground for purification.

Feeling a fresh levity within herself, Vala knew the process was complete and focussed on regaining her lost energies, allowing the golden ball of light to restore her and connect her to the universe and all the love that surrounded her.

Though still a little tired, Vala felt considerably better and returned to the bathroom.

Although she had had time to grow accustomed to the fae lifestyle, Vala still found herself awestruck on occasion; fae bathrooms, at least the ones she had seen, tended to have this effect on her. Gweneira and Tarrys' bathroom was particularly beautiful. Because they were afforded a considerable degree of privacy due to their secluded woodland location, it allowed for a more adventurous design. The walls were curved and made from a special prismatic glass. Sitting in the large, sunken circular bath, it was possible to rest back and enjoy a panorama of the lush forest outside.

Gweneira sank deep into the bath, with just her head above water, and sighed.

"I have been thinking, Tarrys," Gweneira began. "In my absence, I would like my apprentice, Lann, to undertake my duties under Derryth's supervision. I feel this is something he is ready for, and if he ever needs help, Derryth will be there."

"Of course, my love," Tarrys replied. "I shall make the necessary arrangements in the morning."

Vala rubbed her eyes and yawned, running her fingers through her long auburn hair, repeatedly twirling a lock of it between them.

"You must stay here tonight, Sister, with Elvar of course," Tarrys said, gently touching Vala's arm. "It is important you rest well after such a healing."

"But I have uni tomorrow!"

"I will get word to your institute of study. I shall do so personally. You must not resume your studies tomorrow; the toll on your mind and body will be too great," Tarrys insisted.

2

Vala awoke the next day to find that Elvar was no longer beside her. She yawned, stretched, and inhaled deeply, hoping it would clear her head. Vala felt that her brain was resisting all efforts to awaken; it was like a thick blanket of fog had settled over it, making it difficult for her to focus or even think coherently. She padded to the bathroom and repeatedly splashed cold water over her face. Feeling slightly more enlivened, Vala dressed quickly and ran a brush through her hair before heading down.

"Good afternoon, beloved," Elvar walked over to his wife, lifting her gently off her feet and spinning Vala in his arms.

"Afternoon? What time is it?"

"Just past one o'clock," Gweneira replied warmly. "I am afraid it is too late for breakfast now, but you can join us for lunch."

"Who's cooking?" Vala asked, looking towards the kitchen. "You need to rest, Gwen, I'm more than well enough to take over."

"No need," Gweneira assured her. "Tarrys is making Manchun and Konchi nut muffins and hot tea."

Vala leaned back on the sofa and snuggled up to Elvar. She rested her head on his chest, listening to the soothing, steady beat of his heart. For a moment, Vala thought of what had happened fifteen months ago when Elvar's lifeless body had lain in her lap, his heart no longer beating. But she had revived him, and he was now healthy and robust, as though nothing had happened. Elvar had only once talked about his experience of dying—how he had felt as though he were floating out of his body, the sensation of invisible hands pulling him towards something unknown. However, he had felt a far more powerful force tugging him back into his body: it was Vala, it would always be Vala. His soulmate, his Eternal

Beloved. She would always be Elvar's reason for living, and he knew she felt the same way about him.

"So, you have the day off?" Vala gently murmured in Elvar's ear, her breath warm against his skin, sending a pleasant tingling down his spine.

"I do," Elvar whispered back, his lips grazing Vala's ear as he spoke, "but on this occasion, and as much as I want to—and I really, really want to—I cannot. Tarrys has a surprise for you."

"A surprise?" Vala exclaimed more loudly than she had intended.

"Did I hear the word 'surprise'?" Tarrys said, smiling and carrying a large plate of muffins to the table.

Vala inhaled the enticing sweet aroma from the muffins, and her stomach rumbled loudly.

"Elvar tells me you have a surprise for me?"

"I do indeed, sweet sister."

"Well," Vala prompted, "what is it?"

"Now, if I told you that, it would no longer be a surprise," Tarrys teased. "However, what I will tell you is that you and I shall be taking a little excursion today whilst Elvar watches over Gwen."

"Not even a clue?"

"Absolutely not!" Tarrys retorted. "You will have to be patient, but I can promise you it is something very special. Now, if you would all like to be seated, lunch is served."

Tarrys waited for the others to be seated at the table before bringing in a tray with mugs and a steaming pot of sweetened Malvi spiced tea.

Vala bit into the muffin, savouring the sweet, nutty taste, and the warm, moist but slightly crumbly texture. She washed it down with a sip of hot tea, enjoying the soothing flow of liquid as it warmed her throat.

"Are you feeling all right, Gwen?" Vala asked anxiously.

"Yes!" Gwen said cheerfully. "I am completely well, you need not worry. Besides, Elvar will be with me should any problems arise, though I do not anticipate that they will do so."

Tarrys smiled at Vala as she finished the last bite of her muffin.

"We should depart now. There is somewhere and something I need to show you."

3

As Vala stepped outside, she was met by a warm breeze and the aromatic fragrance of lavender and roses. She had always found the scent of lavender to be quite somnifacient and avoided inhaling deeply for fear of it lulling her into sleepiness. Whatever her brother had planned, Vala wanted to be very much awake for it.

The woodland surrounding Gweneira and Tarrys' home had a calm ambience—a sharp contrast, Vala remembered, from fifteen months ago when the Spindler's minions, and other infernal entities, infested the usually peaceful area. Sunlight trickled through the gaps in the branches, illuminating some areas and creating ever-changing dancing shadow shapes in others. Vala drew in a long breath of air; unlike the garden, it was infused with the smell of pine and other native trees, which were more stimulating than soporific. Unfortunately, Vala had been walking in an almost trance-like state and was startled when her foot crunched a large twig.

"You are in a rather contemplative mood today, Sister," Tarrys commented, laughing at Vala's reaction. "Is something on your mind?"

"Many things are on my mind, Tarrys, that is the problem."

"We have become very close this past year, have we not?" Tarrys replied softly. "You can talk to me about anything."

"I haven't really sorted it out in my own mind yet," Vala admitted.

"A lot of the time when we think we are troubled by many different things, it is really not all the other trivial issues that we are worried about, but one central problem that branches out. Sometimes, the other worries are merely a distraction—our mind's way of diverting our attention from the main issue—a coping mechanism, if you will."

"Are you speaking to me as a psychologist or as a brother?"

"As your brother. Always," Tarrys assured her. "My profession is merely a helpful aid—nothing more."

Tarrys held his hand out to Vala as they reached a sharp incline with a succession of rocks set into the earth and fashioned into rudimentary steps. Vala took her brother's hand as they started to climb, keeping one step in front of him. Unlike Vala, Tarrys had inherited his father's tall physique, and his long legs were an asset at times like these. It was a long, steep passage uphill, and Vala was gasping for breath as they reached the top; her breath was further taken away when she scanned the view before her. They had reached a verdant valley, blooming with wildflowers and herbaceous plants. Honey-scented pollen tickled Vala's nose, and she fought the urge to sneeze. It was a glowing, living, and breathing prismatic panorama, and other than Paradise Falls—which would always be most special to her—the most beautiful place Vala had ever seen.

Tarrys led them to a spot under a purple-and-white-striped tree, offering some shade from the sun, and removed a covering from his bag.

"Please, be seated, Sister."

Vala removed her boots and sat on the covering, stretching out her legs and resting contentedly back on her arms.

"This is a lovely surprise." Vala smiled at her brother.

"Yes, it is lovely here," Tarrys replied, sitting beside her, "but it is not your surprise—all in good time. Firstly, Sister, please impart what is vexing you so."

"I'm afraid to say it," Vala said quietly. "I'm afraid that if I do, it will make it more real, and then I will have to face it, and I am not sure that I am ready to."

Tarrys placed a comforting arm around her and she settled her head on his shoulder. As they touched, Tarrys involuntarily shuddered, and Vala looked at him to see a flicker of confusion cross his face.

"I think I can feel it!" Tarrys said in astonishment. "I can feel your emotions! It is like the first time that we touched and shared all those memories—it must happen at times of heightened emotion." "Can you read what I am thinking about?" Vala asked.

"Not exactly," Tarrys ran his hand through his wavy auburn hair. "Though I am seeing your university—seeing you in a library making notes."

"I haven't even told Elvar yet," Vala said.

"I will not disclose anything you tell me, though as Elvar is your husband and Eternal Beloved, I strongly suggest that you talk to him too. So please, Vala, the suspense is too much. Just tell me!"

"Okay, okay!" Vala laughed. "It's to do with uni, so those images you saw in my head were pertinent. You know that in addition to the degree I am taking there, Gwen has also been mentoring me as a healer."

"Yes," Tarrys returned impatiently, "continue please!"

"For quite some time now, I have been feeling unhappy at Cambridge. Don't get me wrong, the people are great, and the course is interesting and thought provoking, it's just that it doesn't feel right anymore. It doesn't feel like my true path."

"But your work as a healer does?" Tarrys ventured.

"Yes," Vala said, sighing. "But I worked so hard to get into Cambridge and our parents are so proud of what I've achieved—how can I let them down? They would be so disappointed if I didn't get my degree. It's what I've been working towards for so many years."

"This may seem rather simplistic, but you must do what makes you happy—what you intuit is right for you." Tarrys gently squeezed Vala's shoulder. "I very much doubt that anything you do now would be as big a shock to them as when they found out you had married Elvar. However, they not only came to terms with it, but now fully embrace the situation, as they can see how happy he makes you. If you are happy, Vala, Mother and Father will be happy too—they may simply need time to adjust. And goodness! They have adjusted so well to your marriage, and then chancing upon me again, I am sure this will not be overly difficult."

"Should I finish Lent term first?" Vala asked.

"If it helps bring you closure, then yes, but as I said before, let your heart guide you. You already know what to do, you just need the confidence to see it through."

Tarrys reached into his bag and extracted a deep-blue crystal decanter and two matching crystal goblets.

"Here," Tarrys handed Vala one of the goblets and filled it with an amber liquid. "Drink this, it will help with what we are about to do."

"What *are* we about to do? And how will this concoction help?" Vala raised an eyebrow as she sipped from the goblet.

"*What* we are about to do is your surprise, and the elixir helps to sharpen and amplify psychic ability—just watch."

Tarrys closed his eyes, and a look of pure serenity washed over him. Vala watched her brother expectantly, restive to know what was happening. For a few minutes, nothing appeared to change; Tarrys' breathing remained slow and steady, his countenance calm and quiet. The silence was soon broken, however, and Vala looked away from her brother as she felt the ground vibrate from what sounded like hooves pounding the earth. She continued to look ahead as a beautiful black stallion galloped up to them, stopping a few yards in front of them and whinnying softly. Tarrys walked over to the stallion, smiling broadly and patting the horse gently on its nuzzle.

"Vala, this is my dear horse Wildfire," Tarrys inclined his head reverently, then looked at his horse. "And, Wildfire, this is my very special, talented, and lovely sister, Vala."

Vala stepped closer to the stallion. "Honoured to meet you, Wildfire— though my brother's description of me is greatly exaggerated!"

Vala tentatively reached out to stroke Wildfire's mane but was a little afraid.

"He will not hurt you," Tarrys assured her, "go ahead."

Vala softly stroked Wildfire's mane; it was deep ebony black, and it surprised her, as the texture was soft and silky, not coarse and dry like those of horses in the human realm. It evoked a calm in Vala and a feeling of complete safety and trust. When she looked into the animal's eyes, she could see the very core of its being: its intelligence, empathy, and gentleness, yet still with an edge of wildness. Vala sensed this was Wildfire's freedom—an unrestricted life with the wind running through his mane and the fresh scent of nature infusing his being. However, what struck Vala the most was the obvious connection between her brother and his horse—their mutual love and loyalty for each other. It was the same for Elvar and her other fae family members—the unbreakable soul connection between the fae and their horses.

"It is time now," Tarrys said, touching Vala's shoulder. "I need you to stand back a little, close your eyes, and focus. Let all other thoughts, sounds, and stimuli fade into the background." "What am I meant to do?" Vala asked nervously.

"You are going to bring forth your very own horse. He or she is already destined for you—you just need to call."

"And how do I do that?"

"As I instructed," Tarrys said. "But once you are focussed, place both your hands over your Iridiscus crystal, and your horse will come to you."

Vala closed her eyes and did her best to clear her mind.

I have done so on many *occasions*, she told herself, *this is no different.*

Gradually all Vala's extraneous thoughts slipped away; she had learnt through experience never to forcefully push thoughts away as they had a tendency to come back with a vengeance. She allowed all the sights, sounds, aromas—all external stimuli—to simply fade away, till all she could hear was the rhythmic sonancy of her own breathing. Once completely centred, Vala clasped her hands over the Iridiscus necklace that Elvar had given her when they had first met. But instead of concentrating on contacting anyone specific, she simply channelled her energy, particularly her feelings of love, into it.

Vala stood still with her eyes closed. For several minutes there was almost no change, but then, almost imperceptibly, the air warmed around her face and a soft breeze brushed over her fingers causing them to tingle. A moment later, a soft drumming sound resonated through the earth, gradually becoming more prominent until it was clear that it was originating from another horse.

Vala opened her eyes to find a chestnut-brown horse with a large white marking on its face standing about two feet away from her. It lowered its head and made a quiet contented noise. Vala closed the distance between herself and the horse, gently wrapping her arms around its neck, resting her head on it as she did so. She was overcome with an intense feeling of love and a need to protect this beautiful creature; strongest of all, though, was the intense and profound understanding and connection between them—it had been instant.

"Her colouring is the same as our hair!" Tarrys laughed. "She is a beautiful horse and will no doubt serve you well."

"She's smaller than both your and Elvar's horses," Vala remarked. "It feels really amazing, Tarrys, thank you."

"You are most welcome," Tarrys replied. "To be honest, I am honoured that I got to fulfil at least one traditional brotherly duty. I was afraid that Elvar might beat me to it."

"I'm glad too!" Vala admitted. "I'm rather enjoying having a big brother—I just wish we could get back all those lost years."

"We cannot go back, Vala, we can only move forward. And, God willing, we have many, many years together yet."

"So, do I get to ride her?"

"Of course," Tarrys returned. "Just a trot today, though, we are not to travel at speed."

"Absolutely!"

"Later," Tarrys said, "we can take her back with us and get you fitted for a saddle. All our saddles are formed specifically to work synergistically with the horse and the rider—both must find it a
proper and comfortable fit. Now, let us go riding!"

Vala levitated a few feet above the ground, enabling her to mount the horse with ease. She placed her hands on the base of its neck, leaning forward slightly.

"Um, Tarrys?"

"What is it, Sister?" Tarrys smiled, looking at Vala quizzically.

"How do I avoid falling off when there are no reigns?" Vala bit her lip nervously.

"You have a connection to your horse, Vala, it knows your intent: where you want to go, how fast you wish to ride," Tarrys replied. "As for falling off, you will not fall. The fae have an enhanced sense of balance, and whilst you and I are partly human too, we are thankfully still blessed with that particular attribute!"

Vala eased back a little and let her arms rest at her sides as Tarrys mounted Wildfire.

"Are you ready?"

Vala nodded in agreement.

"Then let our journey commence!" Tarrys exclaimed. "Incidentally, what is her name?"

"Dream," Vala replied automatically. "Goodness! I'm not even sure why I said that."

"Your horse already has a name that equates to the meaning of the name you spoke. It was merely communicated to you in an understandable form."

Vala gently patted Dream's side, and sensing her intention, the horse started trotting slowly forward. Tarrys kept pace by her side. They were both quiet for some time as Tarrys allowed Vala to fully embrace her new experience and connection with Dream. Reaching the edge of the valley, they slowly descended into the glade below, now much darker than when they had entered it earlier that afternoon.

"Tarrys?" Vala glanced at her brother. "I've been meaning to ask you something for ages but haven't quite known how."

"Well, I am truly intrigued, so you simply must ask me now."

"How long have you known you were adopted?"

Tarrys exhaled deeply and brushed his fingers through his hair.

"I have known for as long as I can remember," Tarrys replied. "My parents, my adoptive parents that is, told me when I was just an infant. They told me that I had been gifted to them by very kind people who wanted them to have a child to raise, as they were unable to have one of their own. They said I was their miracle baby and had been bestowed upon them with much love. When I was older, they explained that my birth parents had been very young and did not feel they could provide a stable home environment, so they gave me to them so that I might have a happy and content home life. I never knew of you, though. If I had, I would have undoubtedly searched for you."

Vala started to reply but was distracted by a rustle in a nearby tree, followed by the sharp sound of snapping twigs. Dream snorted nervously, and Vala felt her heartbeat quicken as the atmosphere palpably and dramatically changed from serene to menacing. At what seemed to be an unnatural speed, a white shape appeared in her peripheral vision, and Vala screamed as a whitish corpse-like arm reached out and grabbed her leg.

Tarrys leapt off his horse and lunged towards the creature, not noticing that Vala had already fallen and was lying motionless on the ground.

"All that you are, all that you have ever been, and all that you are yet to be, unfold at once—for your eyes to behold—for your mind to see!" Tarrys yelled at it fiercely, his hands wrapped around its scrawny neck.

The creature stared at Tarrys, hissing angrily—veins protruding from its wafer-thin skin—white, flaky, and decomposing. Tarrys held his breath in revulsion as the putrid stench of the creature's flesh assaulted his senses and made his stomach lurch in protest.

"You are a Dessicatus!" Tarrys shouted as he loosened his grip, his brow furrowed. "But why? The Spindler is gone. There is no one left to feed you souls! Who sent you?"

The Dessicatus looked Tarrys directly in the eyes and smiled malevolently before disintegrating into a pile of dust.

"Vala!" Tarrys cried in alarm, dusting his hands and running over to her.

Tarrys was not an experienced healer like his wife, but as with all fae or fae/human hybrids, he still possessed a certain level of healing ability. He gently pressed two of his fingers to Vala's neck, checking for a pulse, and was relieved to find one, though it was fainter than he had hoped. Vala's chest was rising and falling, so it was clear she was still breathing. Tarrys had hoped that by now Vala might have regained consciousness, but she had not. He removed his jacket and carefully propped it under her head. The base of Vala's skull had impacted with the rocky steps that led down from the valley. A small rivulet of crimson blood was oozing from her right ear and trickling down her cheek, staining the biscuit-coloured stone beneath her.

"No, Vala! Please!" Tarrys cried fearfully as he felt an icy cold terror snake its way through his veins and into his heart.

Attempting to focus, Tarrys slowly hovered his hand over the length of Vala's body, scanning for damage. He surmised from her injuries that the brunt of the impact had been taken by her head, right elbow, and a few of her ribs.

Tarrys clasped his hand over his Iridiscus crystal and psychically reached out to Derryth. As his crystal began to glow brightly, he knew Derryth had heard him.

"Vala has had an accident, Derryth! She was thrown from her horse. It is very bad! I am bringing her to you now!"

Tarrys patted both their horses and prompted them to return to their homes. He very carefully lifted Vala into his arms, ensuring he was holding her gently but securely, then lifted off into the air at speed, headed for Derryth and Essyeult's home.

Derryth was already waiting for him at the door, as were Elvar and Gweneira.

"What happened to her?" Elvar asked, his voice cracking, his face tear-stained and distraught.

"I am so sorry, Elvar!" Tarrys sobbed. "It is all my fault! What have I done?"

"But how, Tarrys?"

"A Dessicatus attacked whilst we were on horseback—the horse reared."

Derryth quickly took Vala from Tarrys and lay her out on a specially prepared surgical bed.

"I understand your sorrow, boys," Derryth said, "but right now I need to assess Vala's injuries and tend to her promptly. Time is of the essence, and I will need your help—all of you!"

Derryth carefully scanned Vala's body as Tarrys had done, before returning to her head.

"Vala has a cerebral haemorrhage, which has caused an oedema and a haematoma. Our primary objective is to stop the bleeding and alleviate the pressure around her brain."

"I will bring the Cerabruxis serum," Gweneira said calmly. "Maiwen, come with me to get the cleaning fluid, we will be needing a lot."

"She will awaken, Father?" Elvar asked anxiously, clutching Vala's hand.

"I have stopped the bleeding, Elvar, and the Cerabruxis will alleviate the swelling around the brain. After that, I will conduct further healing, but I am sorry, son, I cannot assure you that Vala will awaken. I can only guarantee that she will not suffer lasting damage if she does regain consciousness." Derryth placed an arm around Elvar's shoulders.

"Dear God, please!" Elvar sobbed, a torrent of tears streaming down his face. "Father, you have to heal her. I cannot exist without Vala!"

"I will do all that I can, son." Derryth sighed. "Send loving thoughts to her, pray for Vala."

"Maybe I could send her some of my own healing energy?" Elvar suggested in hope.

"Before any of us do anything further, we need to clean her up. I have not yet closed the laceration at the back of her head—it needs to be thoroughly sterilised," Derryth said. "Elvar, find a comfortable loose gown for Vala and some fresh linen. Essyeult—"

"Sorry," Gweneira interrupted. "I have the Cerabruxis serum, Uncle, should I administer it now?"

"Yes, Gwen," Derryth began, "but as soon as it is done, I would like you and Tarrys to head home."

"But I need to be with my sister!" Tarrys protested.

"Your wife needs to rest, Tarrys, and there are more than enough of us to care for Vala here. I promise that I shall be in touch the moment there is any change in her condition."

"Very well," Tarrys returned. "The very moment, though!"

Gweneira and Tarrys left, each planting a kiss laced with a small amount of healing energy on Vala's cheek.

"Essyeult," Derryth said, turning to his wife, "Laoli and Patrick need to be informed. I will entrust that task to you, whilst Elvar and Maiwen help me tend to Vala."

"I will do it expeditiously, my love," Essyeult replied. "Undoubtedly, they will be returning with me."

"I will prepare the large guest room after I have helped with Vala," Maiwen said, squeezing her brother's hand and kissing him on the cheek.

"Thank you, Maiwen, you are a good daughter and sister." Essyeult hugged her. "I will be back soon. Take special care of your brother, he needs you now more than ever."

Derryth promptly healed the fracture in Vala's elbow and the cracks in her ribs before Elvar and Maiwen assisted him in cleaning Vala and changing her soiled clothes. He carefully sanitised the laceration at the back of her head and proceeded to close the cut, leaving only a faint pink scar.

"What now, Father?" Elvar asked impatiently.

"We wait."

An uncomfortable silence ensued until Maiwen jumped up, speaking in a forced jovial tone.

"Right then! I shall be preparing the guest bedrooms."

She placed a hand on her brother's shoulder, then spoke in a more subdued tone.

"I am here for you if you need me brother. She will awaken—have faith."

Elvar rested his head next to Vala's, the tip of his nose touching hers. He took solace in feeling her warm breath against his skin and gently pressed his lips to hers; as he did so, he passed a powerful current of healing energy into Vala's body, willing her to come back to him with every fibre of his being.

"Please, Vala," Elvar whispered in her ear, "I cannot continue my life without you. I *will* not."

Elvar tenderly stroked back a lock of Vala's hair, sighing unhappily. And then he heard a murmur, almost indiscernible, but he was sure he had not imagined it.

"Vala?" Elvar placed her hand in his and gently squeezed.

Vala murmured something incomprehensible and her eyelids flickered.

Derryth produced a light from his medical kit.

"Vala?" Derryth carefully lifted her upper eyelids and shone the light into her eyes. Her pupils were instantly responsive.

Vala's eyes flickered open once again and opened, her vision gradually sharpening as indiscernible shapes became clearer, and she was finally able to focus on her surroundings.

"Elvar?" she said, her voice barely above a whisper.

"I am here, beloved!" Elvar knelt down beside Vala, his face level with her.

"What's happened to me? I feel strange."

"There was an accident; you were attacked. Do you remember anything?"

"Yes," Vala said, her voice growing stronger. "Tarrys and I were on our way back. I have a horse, Elvar!"

"Yes, my love," Elvar said, stroking Vala's cheek, "but do you remember the accident?"

"I noticed the forest had grown a little quiet and the atmosphere felt wrong somehow, but before I had a chance to ask Tarrys about it, this putrid thing came at me ... grabbing my ankle ... it looked like a zombie, all white with rotting flesh. I thought ..." Vala's voice faltered as tears trailed over her cheeks.

"It is okay, you are safe now," Elvar gently raised Vala's upper body and held her to him.

"I thought it was going to devour me, that I would never see you again. I saw its milky eyes, cold and empty, but then I was falling and everything went black—only it didn't stay that way."

"We can talk later," Elvar's lips grazed her cheek, his breath tickling her ear. "You must rest now."

"I need to perform a more detailed examination of Vala," Derryth interrupted. "After that, assuming all is well, we can move her to your bedroom, son. I am sure she will find it a much more pleasant environment to recuperate and receive visitors."

As Derryth was checking her reflexes, Essyeult returned with her parents.

"Sugar Plum!" Laoli said loudly, rushing to her daughter's side. "You have awoken, thank God!"

"We were so ..." Patrick choked back a sob and kissed the top of his daughter's head. "Never mind. I am overjoyed that you're okay!"

"I'm glad you're here," Vala said, smiling and taking each of her parents' hands.

"I shall take Vala to our bedroom now," Elvar said, tenderly brushing her cheek with the back of his hand. "It will be more comfortable for her there."

"May we join you, Elvar?" Laoli asked, placing a hand on his shoulder.

"Of course," Elvar replied, reddening a little. "I did not mean to imply that you were not welcome. Vala and I would very much enjoy your company."

Elvar carefully lifted her into his arms. She turned her head, nestling into the warmth of his chest and breathing in his comforting scent. In spite of Vala's overwhelming tiredness, she felt her body tingle in response to Elvar's closeness, and a familiar yearning took hold.

"Actually, can you give us a moment alone?" Vala said turning to her parents. "Elvar will let you know when I'm ready."

Laoli looked knowingly at her daughter and smiled coyly.

"Remember, it is imperative that you rest at this time, your body must have time to recover from such an ordeal."

Elvar looked between mother and daughter curiously, before fixing Vala with a probing stare and whispering, "What are you up to?" "Take me upstairs and I'll tell you," Vala whispered back, impatient for Elvar to deliver her to their room.

Elvar briskly, but carefully, scaled the stairs and laid her down on their bed. The sun had now set and a deep purple light filtered through the window casting amorphous, yet mesmerising patterns on the bedroom wall. Vala stared at them for a moment, her mind discerning the shape of a rabbit, but at the same time, trying to collate her thoughts. Although she and Elvar had been together for some time, Vala still felt a little shy with expressing matters of a sexual nature.

"Vala?" Elvar said, kneeling beside her.

Vala pulled his head down towards hers and engaged Elvar in a hungry kiss, feeling her desire for him pulsate fervently through her veins.

"Make love to me," Vala murmured, her hands under his shirt, running over his smooth warm skin.

Elvar sighed. "I cannot. Please do not ask that of me."

"Please, Elvar! I'm fine, honestly. I thought I would die today, that we would be parted, I need to feel you close to me—within me."

Elvar sighed again, raking his hands through his hair in frustration.

"I will not risk it," Elvar replied firmly. "In a few days, I promise. Just not now. However ..."

Vala felt her heartbeat accelerate as Elvar sat on the bed and placed one of her legs across his lap. He leaned forward and planted gentle kisses along the length of one inner thigh, then the other. Elvar paused for a moment, feeling his body arouse, then breathed out slowly, the vapour of his breath hot and damp between Vala's legs. A small murmur of pleasure escaped her lips as she felt Elvar's finger brush over her most intimate area. A further cry followed as his tongue flicked over the same area, sending sparks of ecstasy throughout her body.

Elvar needed to stop now before their passion escalated further. He moved Vala's leg from his lap and lay down beside her, enveloping her in his arms. Vala sighed contentedly, neither one of them speaking until she finally broke the silence.

"That was lovely," Vala said grinning, and kissed Elvar lightly.

"Glad to be of service!" Elvar replied, chuckling. "Though I think it is time to call your parents up."

4

Night seemed to come quickly, and Vala fell into a restful sleep. She stirred slightly as a faint breeze circulated around her, causing the tiny hairs on her arms to stand on end. A tingling static charge tickled her forehead before moving to her scalp, creating a prickling sensation within her hair follicles. Vala reflexively scratched her head, the action disturbing her slumber as she gradually awakened. Her eyes flickered open blearily, taking several attempts before opening fully. Something felt different. Vala continued to stare into the darkness, keeping her breathing slow and steady, attempting to tune into the change of energy within the room. A rapid succession of tiny bright lights in a myriad of colours flashed in front of her, sparkling and shimmering like tiny stars. Startled, Vala attempted to sit up, but was unable to. She tried again; her efforts unavailed. It was as though she were tied to the bed by an invisible binding, unable to escape. A deep primal terror arose within Vala and she opened her mouth to scream. No sound emerged. She was trapped. Before she had time to contemplate her next actions, Vala's eyes involuntarily closed, the flickering lights still visible from beneath her eyelids. She tried to force her eyes open, but some vexatious force kept her from doing so, and an intoxicating haze seeped through her consciousness, trickling into her neural pathways and—*Where am I?*

A rushing vertiginous feeling seized Vala, the air around her moving so fast that she found it hard to breathe. As suddenly as it had started, it stopped. Finally, Vala was able to open her eyes and breathe normally, though her head still felt woozy. As her eyes adjusted to the darkness around her, Vala inhaled deeply; the air was effused with the scent of something familiar. *Jasmine*, Vala thought as her mind started to still. Vala realised that she was curled on the ground and that her nightgown was saturated with something very wet. She looked down to see a blanket of lush, dewy, verdant grass lying beneath her. Her head now felt steady and she carefully sat up, hugging her knees to her chest. Her surroundings were still very dark, though a thick white mist prevailed, rising several feet from the ground and obscuring Vala's vision. She stood, the mist swirling around her. There were tall, spindly white trees, the wood striated with a network of silver veins. Sprouting from the branches were heart-shaped silver leaves that glistened in the moonlight. A little way ahead was an imposing white colossus with Corinthian-style columns depicting foliage, flora, and tiny winged birds at the top of each. The length of the columns had diagonal fluting and the entire building was composed of a brilliant white alabaster flecked through with sparkling variegations. In the ante of the building was a large decorative arch, embellished with birds and butterflies. Above it was a sizeable oval baroque window with silvered edging and a simple red rose centred within three concentric circles, engraved into the glass pane. The atrium of the building was flanked by extending chambers, one on each side, both of them with a substantial semicircular arched window. Like the fae architecture of Avalonia, the grandiose building had four organic-looking leafy spires from each of its four cornices, which interwove with each other and extended into the sky, disappearing into the misty ether above. Vala gazed up at the sky; above the layer of mist was a strata of swirling violet clouds.

Lost in her thoughts, Vala was startled by a touch to her arm. "Vala?"

It could not be, but it certainly appeared to be! Vala looked incredulously at the girl standing before her. "Amalia?"

"Yes, Vala, it is I," the girl replied softly.

"But how?" Vala asked. "Where are we? I thought you had crossed over, that you were at peace."

"We are in Elsorriden," Amalia explained. "It is an intermediary plane between the earthly realms and the afterlife—a resting place for souls that have not crossed over for whatever reason. I summoned you, assisted by the Celestia."

"But why *didn't* you cross over?"

"Because I need help in finding ..." Amalia stopped as Vala clutched her head. "Vala, what is wrong?"

Vala crumpled to the ground, disoriented and vertiginous; it was much like the sensation she experienced before arriving at this creepy place. The tiny lights reappeared and Vala was surrounded by a cyclonic tunnel of wind. Through the ether, she heard Amalia's voice.

"Vala, be careful! You are in very grave danger!"

Vala felt a strong magnetic pull as though gravity was reasserting itself and found herself back in her bed. Elvar was awake, an alarmed expression on his face.

"Vala?" Elvar said loudly, gently shaking her shoulder. "Are you all right? I could not rouse you. I thought—"

"I am okay," Vala assured him, wrapping her arms around his neck. "Physically at least!"

"You would not wake," Elvar explained. "I felt something ... I cannot quite explain, but something felt amiss and I awoke to check on you. You were still breathing, but ..." Elvar faltered, his voice catching, tears coursing down his cheeks.

"Don't cry, Elvar," Vala wiped away his tears with her thumbs and cupped his face in her hands. "I was somewhere else with ... with Amalia."

"Amalia? But how? We released her spirit from the amulet—we watched her shimmer and pass into the light!"

"Well it seems she stepped out of it," Vala replied. "She was in a place in-between—Heaven, I guess, and the earthly planes—somewhere known as Elsorriden. I was taken there by the Celestia. I think—"

"The tiny lights? You saw them?"

"Yes."

"Very few of us have ever seen them," Elvar said. "They are messengers between the living and the dead. They open a passageway between dimensions, taking the living to Elsorriden and returning them when the purpose of their visit has been fulfilled. Those tiny winged entities depicted in many of our paintings—those represent the Celestia—it is thought that is their true appearance."

"Amalia said she summoned me," Vala said. "She didn't get to finish whatever she wanted to tell me. Something pulled me back here prematurely."

"That would probably be me," Elvar admitted. "You must have sensed my distress on some level, as will have the Celestia, so you were returned early."

"Do you think she will summon me again?"

"Vala," Elvar said, his brow crossed, "calling upon the Celestia is never a decision taken lightly. If Amalia requested an audience with you, the gravity of—"

"That much is apparent. Her last words to me were that I was in very grave danger."

5

Vala was awoken the next morning with a tender kiss on the cheek and a tray of assorted foods.

"Good morning, beloved," Elvar said, smiling warmly. "I thought I would bring breakfast to you today so that you may rest a little longer."

"Thank you," Vala replied, yawning. "That is a lot of food though!"

"You need the nourishment, my love," Elvar said. "There are also drafts of Ferriliqium, Branalium, and Neuromithium to aid your recovery."

"Neuromithium?"

"It is an elixir designed to have a calming effect on the neurons after a cranial trauma such as yours. The Ferriliqium, of course, helps replenish lost blood, and the Branalium to restore energy."

Vala looked down at the plate of food before her: fresh Silanchi berries, half an Uquilico fruit, toasted Savima bread with Chavalet cheese, and a steaming bowl of Amarivir porridge: a mixture of grains, fruits, and nuts sweetened with honey. To wash it all down was a mug of hot chocolate with Chando pods. In spite of her protestations, Vala's stomach grumbled hungrily, imploring her to eat.

"Unfortunately I cannot stay with you today," Elvar said. "I have an important examination. If I pass, I shall move onto the next level of Mastery in Spells. However, I believe your parents are here still and Mother and Father will also be here to help you."

"Don't worry about me," Vala said, kissing him. "I will be fine. Now go kick ass in that exam!"

"Kick ass?" Elvar asked, his brow knitted. "I do not understand what you mean. Why would I wish to kick an ass? Asses are docile, gentle animals—I would not wish one any harm."

Vala fell into a fit of giggles, choking on a mouthful of hot chocolate.

"Your humour evades me at times, my love," Elvar admitted.

"Elvar," Vala said, her voice quivering, "it is an expression that means to go do something amazing! Oh, and *ass* is referring to a person's behind, as in *arse*, not the animal!"

"You are a strange girl, beloved," Elvar said, shaking his head in confusion, "but I do love you more than anything in the universe."

"I love you too," Vala said, resting her head under his chin. "Now in words you understand, the best of luck. I will say a special prayer for you."

After Elvar had left, Vala drifted into a light sleep, only to be awoken by a loud knock on the door. Her curiosity piqued, she quietly made her way to the top of the stairs and sat down inconspicuously, watching.

Maiwen opened the door to a tall, muscular handsome boy with sandy blond hair and eyes so blue that Vala could see their intensity from her vantage point.

Maiwen said nothing for a moment, her eyes transfixed to the boy in front of her. She could not think at all. Her heartbeat thundered so loudly that she was sure the boy must be able to hear it. Finally, he broke the silence.

"Good morning, my lady," the boy said. "I am Lann, Master Oakley's apprentice."

"Hello, Lann," Maiwen replied, her voice finally returning. "I am Maiwen, Master Oakley's daughter. Please do step inside."

Removing his shoes, Lann followed Maiwen into the lounge.

"Father," Maiwen said, gesturing towards Derryth. "Lann is here to see you."

Derryth smiled warmly at Lann and invited him to sit down.

"This is a wonderful opportunity for you to truly excel, Lann. As you know, you will be undertaking Gweneira's duties, under my watchful eye of course!"

"I am very honoured to have been chosen, Master Oakley," Lann said, flushing a little under Derryth's gaze. "I will endeavour to meet your undoubtedly high expectations of me."

"You were selected, Lann, because you are my most promising senior student, and I am confident that you will not let me down," Derryth said.

"Now, may I offer you some refreshment before we go to the mixing rooms? Today's assignment will be preparing vials of Nonceptium elixir. As you are aware, there will be varying degrees of potency to create, so it is imperative that you remain focussed on the task at hand."

Lann smiled nervously, anxiously rubbing an imaginary spot on his trousers.

"What would you like to drink, Lann?" Maiwen said, smiling brightly at him. "We have Alushi nectar, Mirisum or Silanchi juice, Avanis—"

"I will have the Avanis please, my lady. I believe it is good for concentration," Lann answered nervously, glancing at Maiwen and smiling in spite of his nerves.

Maiwen hurried to the kitchen to prepare the Avanis and returned promptly, handing over the drink. She sat opposite Lann, covertly looking up at him every so often, blushing when his eyes met hers.

"So, Lann," Maiwen said, breaking the tension, "how many years of study do you have left?"

"I am twenty years old, so I have another year before I am fully qualified," Lann replied. "And you, my lady, have you specialised yet?"

"Yes, I am in my first year of botany and alchemy."

"So, you must be sixteen or thereabouts?" Lann said, his eyes locking with hers.

"I am indeed sixteen." Maiwen twisted a lock of hair around her finger.

Derryth looked between his daughter and Lann, his brow furrowing.

"All right then!" Derryth said, standing. "We should head to the mixing rooms, Lann."

"Mother is taking a bath," Maiwen said, pre-empting her father's next words.

"You know me too well, Daughter!" Derryth said, laughing.

Derryth called out, bidding his wife farewell, before he and Lann made their way to the front door. As Lann approached the door, Maiwen boldly reached out for his hand.

"It was a pleasure meeting you," Maiwen said, gazing up at him.

"Likewise, my lady," Lann replied, smiling. "I hope that our paths cross again soon."

As the door closed, Maiwen let out an excited squeal and rushed upstairs, only to find Vala on the top step. Maiwen's face burned hotly and she exhaled a shaky breath.

"Would I be correct in presuming that you bore witness to all of that?"

"Every minute detail!" Vala said, grinning. "Wow, you're crushing on that guy big time!"

"Crushing?" Maiwen said. "I do not understand."

"It means you are infatuated with him—you fancy him, right?"

"Please," Maiwen begged, an edge of desperation creeping into her voice, "do not tell Elvar, nor Mother or Father. I am not sure they would approve."

"Let's go to my room and talk," Vala offered. "But first, I might need a little help standing, I'm feeling a bit wobbly."

Maiwen helped Vala to her feet and followed her to her room. Vala sat on the bed, patting the space beside her. Maiwen sat, looking at Vala shyly.

"You will not tell?" Maiwen repeated anxiously.

"Your feelings are your own business, Maiwen," Vala reassured her. "It is not my place to tell anyone else, but if I am asked—"

"I know," Maiwen stated, "you will have no choice."

"Why are you so worried that your family won't approve?" Vala asked. "Is it the age gap?"

"Mainly, yes," Maiwen replied. "Though it hardly matters; what is four years after all?"

"I agree, four years doesn't seem like a lot, but you are sixteen, Maiwen, and Lann is a grown man; he is older than both your brother and me."

"Why should that matter?" Maiwen argued.

"Have you had any romantic experience?"

"Do you mean, have I had any suitors?"

"Near enough, I suppose," Vala said. "What I'm trying to impress is that Lann may have prior experience, romantically speaking, and because of that, he may have certain expectations."

"Yes," Maiwen stated, "I know there may have been others, but I felt something special between us—a spark. Maybe he is my Eternal Beloved. Maybe we are destined for each other."

"If that is the case, then no one will be able to keep you apart," Vala said before sighing deeply. "Just be sure before you give yourself to him completely."

"Were you sure?" Maiwen asked, her gaze fixed on Vala. "When you gave your virginity to my brother—were you sure that he was the one, your Eternal Beloved?"

"I was completely sure!" Vala said, her cheeks aflame, unconsciously curling a lock of hair between her fingers, feeling uncomfortable with the direction their conversation had taken. "I was also just a few months shy of eighteen. You are just sixteen, Maiwen—it makes a difference."

"Well, maybe I am ready now!" Maiwen replied indignantly and left the room.

6

Maiwen had grown increasingly restless since her conversation with Vala. Not at class today, she had an assignment to gather and document various herbs. However, her mind was preoccupied with thoughts of Lann and she was unable to focus. Sighing, she picked up her herb basket, deciding on a plan that would both allow her to finish her assignment and see if Lann returned her feelings.

As Maiwen approached the mixing rooms, she felt an electric tingle throughout her body and a thrilling rush of desire smouldering in her belly. Inhaling deeply, she tentatively knocked on the door.

"My lady!" Lann said, opening the door. "I was not expecting to see you again so soon. How can I be of assistance to you?"

"I, um, just wanted to find out how you are, um, how things are going on your first day?" Maiwen said, her face crimson. "May I come in?"

"Yes, of course," Lann answered. "I have been preparing batches of Nonceptium elixir and am now in the process of labelling several vials ready for collection."

Maiwen left her shoes outside and stepped inside the room, surreptitiously wiping her balmy palms on the back of her dress.

"So, um," Lann started hesitantly, "you are not in class today?"

"No, I have to collect and reference herbs. I collected several specimens on my way here. I thought maybe you would have some medicinal samples that you could show me?"

Lann looked at Maiwen intently, his gaze scanning her, taking in her heart-shaped face and violet eyes, her long tumbling dark curls, before moving down—noticing the way the stretchy silk fabric of her red dress clung to the contours of her breasts.

This is going to be trouble, Lann thought. *She is my master's daughter, and yet so beautiful, so very, very beautiful.*

"We could go to the storing room in a moment," Lann offered. "We have a wide variety of herbs that would no doubt be useful for your assignment. I cannot give you much in quantity, but I can tell you a fair bit about their properties and usage in medicine. There is also a study area in the room, somewhere we can sit and talk if you would like? I just need a moment to finish labelling these vials."

"That sounds good!" Maiwen said, feeling as though her body was ablaze and that her heart might explode at any moment. "One condition, though."

"And that is?" Lann asked, smiling flirtatiously.

"That you call me Maiwen."

"I think I can manage that," Lann replied, "Maiwen."

*

Elvar rubbed his temples; it had been a tough examination, and he was thankful that he had prepared well for it. This was usually the time he took for lunch, but his tutor had given the class the remainder of the day off, and Elvar needed to collect his vial of Nonceptium elixir before heading home.

He arrived at the mixing rooms and tapped on the door lightly. Receiving no answer, he tapped again more loudly. Still no answer.

"Lann," Elvar called out loudly. "It is Elvar—I have a collection to make."

Elvar grew puzzled at the lack of response and decided to step inside. As he removed his sneakers, he noticed another pair on the mat that did not belong to Lann—a pair of red shoes that looked very much like Maiwen's.

"Lann?"

He made his way down to the storing room and opened the door.

"No! It cannot be!" Elvar took a sharp intake of breath, feeling a surge of anger rise through him.

There, on the sofa in the study area, was Lann locked in a passionate embrace with his sister, his hands rubbing over her breasts. "What the hell are you doing with my sister?" Elvar shouted.

Both Lann and Maiwen stopped and turned, startled by the sudden intrusion. For a moment, neither spoke.

"Elvar!" Maiwen said, feeling hot tears surfacing. "Please do not be angered. Lann and I—"

"Just get away from him, Maiwen!" Elvar interjected. "And go wherever it is you should be right now. We will talk later."

Maiwen looked at her brother imploringly, searching for any show of empathy, but finding none.

"Go!"

Tears flowed over her cheeks. She discretely adjusted her clothing and compliantly left, too shocked by her brother's outburst to risk angering him further.

"I believe I asked you a question, Lann!" Elvar said, his jaw tightening.

"I am sorry you feel this way," Lann said, a trickle of perspiration running down his forehead. "I like Maiwen very much. I was hoping to ask Master Oakley for permission to court your sister."

"She is sixteen!" Elvar retorted. "Four years younger than you, Lann. She is not ready for a ... for a ..." Elvar felt his face reddening and stalled for a moment, considering his words.

"She is not ready for *that* kind of relationship." Elvar sighed, covering his face with his hands.

"No disrespect intended, Elvar," Lann replied, his voice quaking a little, "but your wife was seventeen when you married her, barely older than Maiwen."

"Vala was almost eighteen!" Elvar replied angrily.

"Please," Lann pleaded. "I will not dishonour Maiwen—my intentions are serious. I would not influence her into doing anything she was not ready for."

"But how would you not have such expectations?" Elvar countered, though his previous anger was now dissipating and transmuting into something else that he couldn't quite discern. "There have been others for you—you have bedded other girls, have you not?"

"Yes," Lann admitted, sighing in frustration. "There have been two others, but this feels different! I feel a strong connection with Maiwen."

"I do not believe my father will consent to this," Elvar replied. "However, I also believe that there is little to be gained in further discussion at this point."

"Of course," Lann replied, sighing once again.

"I would like to go home now," Elvar said tersely. "May I have the Nonceptium elixir I came for?"

Lann stood up, gesturing for Elvar to return to the mixing rooms.

"I do hope that this will not be injurious to our friendship?" Lann asked, passing Elvar the Nonceptium elixir.

"I am tired," Elvar replied. "This is a lot to process."

Lann nodded in resignation, and Elvar quietly left, eager to reach home and the comfort of Vala's arms.

7

In spite of protestations from both her and Elvar's parents, Vala insisted on sitting at the bottom of the stairs, expectantly awaiting Elvar. She did not have to wait long as the front door swung open and Elvar walked in, looking up in surprise to see Vala waiting there.

"I could sense you," Vala explained, putting her arms around his neck and brushing her lips against his. "I could also feel something else, something troubling."

"There is something," Elvar said, touching his head to hers, "but I need to shower first and then we can talk."

Vala sat on their bed, patiently waiting. She had contemplated joining him in the shower but intuited that he needed some time alone. As Vala contemplated the nature of Elvar's unhappy countenance, he walked into their bedroom, a towel around his waist, his glossy dark hair slicked back and dripping with water. Irritated by the water droplets running down his face, he removed the towel and rubbed it over his hair. Elvar lay back on the bed next to Vala and stared at the ceiling. Vala lay next to him, resting her head on his chest.

"I am not sure where to begin," Elvar said, rubbing his hands over his face. "I thought that we were over the worst after you destroyed the Spindler, but now, the Dessicatus attack and your dream encounter with Amalia. I have a very bad feeling that we are facing another storm, and that last year we were merely in the eye of it, protected from whatever new menace is awaiting us. And now Maiwen ..."

"I am afraid too," Vala admitted, "but until we know more, the most I can do is be as well prepared as possible. I have been learning some new defensive spells; I haven't actually tried them out on anyone, though they certainly work well on some pretty big inanimate objects, and I'm not so bad if I say so myself! Maybe I should ask Tarrys to join me, perhaps we could combine our energies for a more consolidated, powerful effect. And regarding Maiwen, I have some notion of why you might be upset, but—"

"You know! For how long?"

"Calm down! She only told me this morning," Vala said. "I don't think it's anything more than a crush, and it's not like anything's happened!"

"You have not seen her since, obviously."

"Since what?" Vala asked. "What's happened?"

"I caught them together," Elvar said, exhaling deeply, the corners of his mouth turning down. "They were in the storing room on the sofa, kissing passionately, and his hands were all over her—" Elvar's voice caught, unable to continue.

"She is sixteen, Elvar," Vala said gently. "She's not a little girl anymore. I know that for a long time my parents were uncomfortable with the idea of us having sex."

"No!" Elvar said, sitting up suddenly. "I will not permit Lann to take my sister's virtue! We were older, Vala. Besides which, he is older than Maiwen. He has had ... others."

"Talk to Maiwen then," Vala advised, "but don't preach to her or it will have the opposite effect. I did not sense anything dishonourable in Lann's intent or disposition, and anyway, isn't he your friend?"

"Yes," Elvar said sadly. "But seeing him with my sister like that—it was difficult. I do not know how to act around him now."

Vala leaned over Elvar, softly planting a kiss on his lips and gently threading her fingers through his damp hair. He returned her embrace, lightly at first, his tongue meeting hers as he explored her mouth, then more fervidly as his desire took hold. Elvar pulled her on top of him, his heart beating fiercely as his hands ran under her top, his fingers pressing into her shoulders. Feeling his arousal pressing against her, Vala lifted her skirt and wriggled out of her undergarments.

"I want you so much," Elvar said breathlessly, "but we cannot do this. We need to stop now, or in a moment neither of us will be able to and it will be too late."

"We've made love nearly every day since our first time together," Vala said, heart hammering and body aching to join with Elvar's.

"I know," Elvar said, carefully lifting Vala off him. "And we will again, but right now, we are both going to get dressed, and when Maiwen returns, we shall call a family meeting."

8

Maiwen returned late afternoon, carrying a basket of herbs. She glanced at Elvar as she ascended the stairs and bolted to her room, slamming the door. Elvar raced after her, knocking on her door.

"Maiwen? We need to talk. All of us."

"Go away!" Maiwen shouted. "I do not wish to talk with you. Leave me alone—I have homework to complete."

"This is not just about Lann," Elvar explained, trying to maintain calm. "We are having a family meeting over dinner. Gwen and Tarrys will be joining us too."

"All this because of Lann?" Maiwen replied incredulously.

"Of course not!" Elvar said, a note of irritation creeping into his voice. "I believe that we are in danger again. If not all of us, then certainly Vala."

The door opened a crack and Maiwen peeked out.

"Come in," she said quietly. "Tell me what has happened."

*

They all gathered at the dining table a few hours later, Derryth bringing forth platters of Zimfi fritters, spiced Linvi sautéed with Ginsil root, Maravi compote, and Savima bread. Vala adored Zimfi fritters; they reminded her of aubergine, only more flavoursome and purple throughout. Gweneira said grace, and as Vala passed the basket of bread to each of them, she wondered when the *family meeting* would start and what they could realistically resolve with such sparse information. She did not have to wait long.

"I believe we are facing an undoubtedly grave situation," Essyeult said. "Before, at least, we knew the source of the threat. This time, it is an unseen danger."

"Vala has been visited by the Celestia," Laoli continued. "This is a rare occurrence and not to be taken lightly. It is likely ..."

Laoli looked at her daughter, a cold sliver of fear slaking through her body. She stroked Vala's cheek and sighed.

"It is likely that you will receive another visitation, Sugar Plum, as Amalia did not finish conveying her message to you."

"Vala tells me that she has been practising some new defensive spells," Elvar offered, glancing at Tarrys. "She has not had the opportunity to demonstrate them on a living target, so maybe you and I could volunteer for that, Tarrys?"

"I don't know," Vala said hesitantly. "I could hurt you accidentally."

"We are of a strong constitution, Sister," Tarrys replied, smiling warmly at her. "And you will not harm us if that is not your intent, which of course it will not be."

"What have you been learning?" Maiwen asked, distracted from her own troubles.

"Maybe I should show you all after dinner?"

"No, Vala," Derryth interjected. "Not just yet. You will need some days to recover your strength."

"Not all the danger *is* unseen of course," Tarrys said, his eyes meeting Vala's. "The Dessicatus that attacked Vala yesterday—why are the Spindler's minions on the prowl if they are no longer procuring souls for the Spindler? And why with the victim awake? Why Vala?"

Elvar reached for Vala's hand and clasped it firmly within his own.

"I will not let anyone harm you, beloved."

For a while, no one spoke. Everyone continued eating, uncertain of what action could be taken.

"What if there is another?" Maiwen suggested. "Another like the Spindler. Are there not ancient texts detailing a stealer of souls?"

"There are indeed, Daughter," Essyeult confirmed. "However, until we have more information at our disposal, there is precious little we can do. I suggest that we wait for a further visitation and that all of us refine and strengthen our defensive magic."

9

An hour after dinner had passed, Vala could barely keep her eyes open. She rested her head into the nook of Elvar's neck and closed her eyes. Elvar tenderly kissed her head and gathered her into his arms.

"Vala is fatigued," Elvar said. "If you will please excuse us, we must retire to bed now. Goodnight to you all. And, Maiwen, we shall speak again in the morning."

Maiwen shot a furtive glance at her brother and shook her head imperceptibly.

"Goodnight, Son and Daughter," Essyeult replied. "Sleep well and do not worry. A rested mind is essential for what lies ahead."

"Goodnight, Elvar and Vala," Gweneira said. "I am sorry that I cannot be of more help in this situation, but my current state has rather significant practical limitations."

"I will take Vala to the library tomorrow," Tarrys offered. "If she is feeling well enough, we can investigate if there is a way of combining our abilities."

Elvar nodded in agreement and carried Vala up the stairs to their room. She was already soundly asleep. He carefully removed her clothes and placed the coverlet over her prone form. As Elvar was undressing, it occurred to him that Vala would likely receive another visit from the Celestia. Not wishing her the embarrassment of being naked for such an encounter, he gently propped her up and slipped her nightgown over her head, struggling to guide it past her hips. Vala stirred and opened her eyes.

"I am sorry, my love, I did not wish to disturb you," Elvar said quietly.

"It's okay," Vala mumbled sleepily, pulling her nightgown down. "Goodnight, Elvar."

"Goodnight," Elvar replied, softly kissing her, "and good luck!"

Vala was not sure how long she had been asleep when she felt a familiar tingling over her scalp. She was immediately roused from sleep and opened her eyes to see the tiny bright lights flashing before her. As before, her body was temporarily incapacitated, but this time, knowing what was happening, she succumbed to the situation and tried to relax. Her eyes were forced closed, and Vala felt a vorticular current surround her. Her lungs struggled to draw breath as the air whirled around her tempestuously. The dizzying sensation stopped and the air stilled. The aroma of jasmine wafted in the air, and she looked around, recognising her surroundings as the crepuscular world of Elsorriden.

"Amalia?" Vala called out, rising to her feet.

A blur of motion moved towards her, mingling with the prevalent mist, which extended as far as Vala could see. The movement stopped, and the nebulous, hazy shape sharpened to reveal the form of Amalia. Looking at her more closely this time, Vala realised that Amalia appeared more corporeal on this plane, as solid as Vala herself.

"I am glad the Celestia were able to reach you, Vala," Amalia said. "I was concerned when you were so abruptly pulled away from here last time."

"It was Elvar," Vala explained. "I had suffered a severe head injury earlier that day and he thought—"

"I understand," Amalia smiled knowingly. "The love between the two of you is very special—you are fortunate to have Elvar as your Eternal Beloved."

"Did you have ..." Vala started, not wishing to pry, but curious nonetheless, "someone special?"

"No," Amalia replied quietly. "If I had met my Eternal Beloved, I would have stayed in the light, despite my sister's absence. The only bond as powerful as that is the one experienced between parent and child."

"You warned me I was in grave danger?" Vala said, unsure of how much time she had in this place.

"Yes," Amalia said, already moving towards the white palatial edifice before them. "Please come inside, I need to show you something."

Vala followed Amalia through a large arched doorway carved into the atrium of the building. Amalia invoked the incantation for light, and the entrance immediately illuminated. Expecting to see the familiar fae frescoes that she had grown accustomed to, Vala was taken aback; adorning the curved walls and ceiling were painted images of her and Elvar. And not just her and Elvar, but babies playing together on a picnic mat, surrounded by both her and Elvar's parents, Maiwen, Lann, Gweneira, Tarrys, Jelly, and Max. As with the other frescoes, the images were animated, and Vala could hear the figures in the painting talking softly and laughing. She could even detect the distinct aroma of grass and wildflowers, feeling a gentle breeze ripple through her hair.

"What you are seeing is personal to you," Amalia explained. "I cannot see the images before you. What you see is a representation of one possible future scenario—how things could be should events unfold a certain way."

Vala nodded in acceptance, though her thoughts dwelled on the dark-haired baby with soft curls and deep green eyes—so much like her own, so much like the baby she had seen in her vision over a year ago.

They soon reached a capacious, airy room with a domed clear ceiling, which revealed the strange, swirling dark skies above. The walls were lined with rows of books and shelves extending to the centre of the room, housing yet more books. In the area of the room not occupied with books, were tables and seating. Amalia led Vala to one of the unoccupied tables and gestured for her to be seated.

"These tomes contain a monumental wealth of knowledge," Amalia said, making a sweeping motion with her arm to indicate the numerous books. "There are a number covering the subject of foreseers."

"Foreseers?"

"Those who experience potential future events," Amalia continued. "Those like you and me. There are ways, there are methods to induce such visions, though it is not something to be undertaken lightly and not something I would recommend a living soul participate in, as the consequences could be fatal. As I explained, it is only in the most desperate of situations that such a decision be warranted."

"And you decided to do it?" Vala said. "You underwent whatever it was to induce a vision?"

"I am no longer living," Amalia said. "I know it posed no danger to me, so yes, I induced a vision, as I felt something was terribly wrong. You see, like you, Vala, I have presentiment, and I had to find the cause of it."

"And?"

"It was an incomplete vision," Amalia replied, an edge of frustration in her voice. "I saw you and Elvar, your companions, Jelly and Max, and others I did not recognise in the Avalonian woodland.
There was a girl there, a girl wielding the sword, the sword bequeathed to Arthur by Merlin—Excalibur. She is full of fury towards you, though I do not know the reason. She attempts to attack you."

"And then?" Vala asked cautiously. "What happens to me?"

"I do not know," Amalia admitted. "My vision ends there, and I cannot force any additional premonitions. They always conclude before I am ..."

"It's all right, Amalia," Vala rested her hand over Amalia's. "What did the girl look like? Will I have a way of knowing who she is before I happen upon her?"

"She is at least a head above you in height," Amalia said, "and of exceptional beauty, with long ebony curls and eyes that ... they are neither blue nor green, somewhere in between. They hold a great sadness, though, but also a familiarity that I cannot quite ... it does not matter. In my vision, she is wearing a light-blue gown with shoulder straps, but no sleeves and a silken blue sash around her waist."

"Then surely now that I know her appearance I can pre-empt an encounter, perhaps avoiding it altogether? Or even if I can't avoid it, I can use soul-mirroring?"

"I am not certain," Amalia sighed, setting her face in her hands. "Like you, Vala, this girl possesses immense power. I am not sure that you *can* defeat her unaided."

Vala anxiously knotted the strands of hair that she had been twisting together around her finger, forming a tight noose, watching as her finger turned white from the restricted circulation.

"What would you suggest?" Vala asked.

"Although many others before you have attempted to do so," Amalia replied, "I believe that you should attempt to find the one man who will almost certainly have the power to help you."

"And who would that be?" Vala asked curiously. "Merlin."

10

"Elvar?" Vala gently shook Elvar's shoulder to wake him.

Dawn had not yet broken, and the pervasive darkness felt ominous and premonitory. The tiny hairs on Vala's arms prickled as Elvar stirred and forced open one eye.

"What is wrong?"

"I saw Amalia again," Vala explained. "I'm sorry to wake you, but this is really important."

Vala recounted most of her experience with Amalia, stopping before reaching the part about Merlin.

"Then the threat is much greater than we ever imagined," Elvar said, rubbing his temples.

"There is something else," Vala continued. "Amalia believes that there is someone who can help us. She thinks that we should find Merlin."

"Merlin?" Elvar repeated incredulously. "Amalia may be right that he remains in the realm of the living, but others have sought him out—many, many others—ever since his disappearance."

"Amalia said that his family's Iridiscus crystals were found in Merlin's home after their disappearance: Merlin's and his wife,
Nimeva's, were found in their bed. And their young daughter's—
Merevina's tiny bracelet—was found in her cot."

"Yes," Elvar said, a little impatiently. "I know the story well, but how does this help us in any way?"

"The crystals are kept in the castle," Vala said. "Amalia advised we speak to the Queen and gain permission to borrow them. She believes that because I have such strong empathic and premonitory abilities, I might be a guide to Merlin and his family, that maybe I will see or sense something."

"But what if you do not have any immediate visions?"

"We have to try," Vala said softly. "She—Amalia, that is—suggested we go to Merlin's last known location, his home in the valleys of Cavania."

"To see if you can sense anything, that maybe something there will trigger a vision?"

"That's the idea," Vala said, yawning.

"You need to rest now," Elvar said, stroking her hair. "We can talk more about this in the morning."

"Tarrys and I didn't go to the library," Vala said sleepily. "We were going to go after your exam."

"I know," Elvar replied, touching Vala's cheek. "I am afraid I was rather distracted by your revelations from Amalia, and then Maiwen."

"It doesn't matter," Vala said, placing her hand over Elvar's. "You can take me tomorrow."

"I will, my love," Elvar said, touching his nose to hers, "that is a promise."

*

Vala awoke to the sound of raised voices and the clamouring of dishes below her and Elvar's room. Elvar was no longer beside her, in fact, she could hear his voice mingled with those of his family downstairs. Vala stretched before carefully standing and walking to the dressing table to retrieve her hairbrush. She tugged the hairbrush through her slightly tangled hair and went to the bathroom to wash. On the way out, she bumped into Laoli, who was carrying a breakfast tray.

"What's all the noise about? And why the tray? Did you have breakfast up here?"

"I felt it necessary to afford the Oakleys some privacy with Maiwen," Laoli answered. She smiled and shook her head.

"But why are they arguing?" Vala pressed, suspecting she knew the reason, but wanting confirmation before volunteering any information.

"Maiwen's choice of suitor is causing some tension," Laoli replied.

"Because he's older?"

"That is the primary reason," Laoli confirmed. "They are concerned that he might have certain *expectations* of her that she is not yet ready for."

"Well, I'm going down there!" Vala said. "I'm hungry, and Elvar and I are due to go to the library today."

"You are a braver lady than I!" Laoli returned, grinning and shaking her head.

11

Vala loved the Avalonian library; it was a beautiful building with an organic structure, characteristic of fae architecture. The façade was a chalky white with pale green striations throughout, with curved windows and a circular window above the entrance. It had a high roofline with spindly branch-like spires that interwove with the tree branches. The interior was welcoming and homely, with plush velveteen sofas and rounded coffee tables constructed from the purple-flecked white Viaspan wood that Vala knew to be customary in both fae homes and public buildings. There was a sectioned-off area for quiet study on the third floor—this was also the area that housed the books on defensive magic that they needed.

"Why can't these buildings have elevators?" Vala complained when they were halfway up the second flight of stairs.

"It is not necessary," Elvar said simply. "There is nothing wrong with your legs, my love. I do not understand your protestations."

"I hate long flights of stairs," Vala said indignantly. "They make my legs ache like nothing else."

"I could carry you?"

"Um, no thank you!" Vala turned and grinned at him. "That would attract a lot of unnecessary attention."

Elvar checked that they were alone, then pulled Vala to him, engaging her in a deep kiss. Vala entangled her fingers in his silky hair before pulling her body into his. An intense tingle started in her abdomen and worked its way down. Vala pulled away, gasping as she tried to catch her breath.

"We have to stop," Vala said, her face flushed, "now!"

Elvar released her, his face also reddened, his breathing fast and shuddery.

"I am sorry," Elvar said, closing his eyes for a moment to regain composure. "I did not mean to ... I mean to say ..."

Elvar ran his hands over his face in frustration and groaned.

"I just really needed to kiss you," he finally said, voice catching.

"The problem with that," Vala said, a small smile tugging at the corners of her mouth, "is that we never manage to stop at the kissing stage."

She placed her hand in Elvar's, and they continued up the long flight of stairs, finally ascending the last steps to the third floor.

The library shelves were decorated with ornate floral carvings, and Vala absentmindedly traced her fingers over part of them as Elvar searched for the selection of books they needed.

A short while later, Elvar tapped Vala on the shoulder. She had been gazing out of the large circular window and was startled by Elvar's touch.

"I think we have what we need," Elvar said, brushing a stray lock of hair from her face. "Sorry if I startled you."

"Okay," Vala said, trying to feign enthusiasm as she looked at the pile of books under Elvar's arm. "Let's get to it!"

Contrary to Vala's expectations, the thick tome she was poring over was surprisingly interesting, full of powerful defensive spells, and in certain cases, case histories of their practical application.

"Elvar?" Vala said, touching his hand. "I think I've found one I'd like to try."

Elvar looked at her expectantly, and she continued.

"It's the Aeroexpulsion spell," Vala said, feeling a rush of excitement. "Mastered successfully by only a small number of people due to the sharpened focus and energy needed to create such a powerful force. The most famous example being my great, however many times, grandmother Guinevere during the Spindler's attack on Amalia."

"Please do not take offense, my love," Elvar said softly, "but perhaps we should start with something less demanding?"

"Are you saying I won't be able to do it?"

"No," Elvar replied, "of course not. I know you possess immense power, but perhaps this is something we should build up to rather than dive in at the deep end."

"Maybe I like diving!" Vala replied, feeling a growing irritation.

"I have found an absolutely indispensable spell that I had completely forgotten about," Elvar said, attempting to placate her. "These things tend to slip the mind when not faced with insidious threats on a regular basis."

"Well?" Vala replied impatiently.

"*Me defende integumento magico,*" Elvar replied. "It's a magical barrier spell to protect us from an impending threat."

"Well, if we can do that, is the other stuff even necessary?" Vala said. "Unless, of course, we need to eliminate the threat, and there's the soul-mirroring for that."

"Unfortunately," Elvar said, placing his hand over hers, "the shield cannot hold for long, as it requires considerable energy expenditure from the spell caster." "How long?" Vala pressed.

"Five to ten minutes," Elvar ventured. "It is hard to estimate and depends greatly on the person invoking it."

"In that case, I am definitely pressing ahead with the Aeroexpulsion spell."

"As you wish, my love," Elvar relented. "I will do my best to assist you. Actually ..."

Elvar lowered his voice to barely above a whisper and looked at Vala intently. She instinctively tilted her head forward so that her forehead met with his.

"I have been working on devising my own defensive spell. We are all required to formulate a spell for our final-year assessment. I cannot remember the last time anyone chose defensive magic, but after what happened ..."

"What does it involve?" Vala asked, her heart quickening.

"It's a disabling spell," Elvar explained. "Ironically, the idea had been brewing ever since I showed you the Fountain of Love Truth—before we even knew of a threat. It works on the principle of neurodisruption."

"Care to elaborate?"

"It temporarily interferes with various lobes in the brain, causing, if you will, a short circuit in the neuro-transmittance between certain receptors. In this instance, the parts of the brain involved in sight and sound."

"That's pretty scary," Vala said, squeezing his hand.

"It is meant to be, and only to be used in the direst of circumstances, though I fear it may be warranted. I will do anything to protect you, Vala. *Anything.*"

"I know," Vala replied, her lips grazing his. "And I would do the same for you."

Neither moved for some time—both content with just being in each other's company and enjoying the intimacy of the moment and their close proximity.

Vala's heart skipped a beat as she looked up and her gaze locked with Elvar's. An intense love swelled in her heart, and she knew that although Amalia had presaged the threat to Vala, that she would willingly give her life for Elvar's if it became necessary.

Elvar met Vala's gaze, his being consumed with an overwhelming sense of love and the need to protect her from whatever wished her harm. He placed his hands on either side of her face and gently kissed her.

"I will never let any harm befall you, my love," Elvar said.

Their noses touched, and his warm breath tickled her lips.

"Now, we should have lunch, and after, start putting these spells into practice."

Elvar had brought her to a grassy lowland not far from their house. The area was surrounded by a copse of trees but had little in terms of flora or fauna, just a large expanse of land—perfect for spell practice. The weather, as was often the case in Candalia, was temperate and comfortable; however, a few pregnant rain clouds hovered, threatening to unload their burden at any moment.

Vala rubbed her bare arms as she felt the tiny hairs on them rising as a static charge buzzed around her.

She looked ahead at the objects that Elvar had placed approximately twelve feet in front of her: a table with a ceramic jug, a wooden chest, an empty freestanding bookshelf, and an armoire that Tarrys had helped Elvar carry to the field.

"We will all be working on this one," Tarrys said, smiling supportively at his sister. "But as this Aeroexpulsion spell was your idea, you should do the honours."

Vala closed her eyes and slowed her breathing, blocking out all distractions. She focussed on her breath, listening to the inhalation and exhalation of air, feeling her chest rise and fall to its rhythmic sonancy and allowing her mind to calm. According to the book, it was important to create a baseline state of neutrality before starting the spell, as the emotions required to succeed would be intense and needed to build up fast rather than cumulatively.

Upon opening her eyes, Vala stared at the table ahead. She quickly cast her mind back to how she had felt when learning of her parents' abduction by the Spindler. A surge of energy rose from deep within her solar plexus. Vala outstretched her arms and concentrated on moving that internal energy outward towards her intended target—the vase. Within seconds, the vase was jettisoned at great velocity to a distance of at least twenty feet where it collided with a tree branch and smashed.

Vala let out an excited whoop before turning to see the shocked faces of Elvar and her brother.

"Do neither of you have anything to say?" Vala said, looking at them expectantly.

"A word of advice, brother," Tarrys said, placing a hand on Elvar's shoulder. "*Always* let her win any future arguments!"

Vala playfully punched Tarrys' arm, then softly kissed Elvar's cheek.

"You haven't said anything, Elvar." Vala looked at him quizzically. "I was not prepared for that," Elvar admitted, his voice rather muted. "That is an immensely difficult spell to master—channelling one's energies in such a way—it does not usually have such a pronounced effect, particularly the first time."

"I think *pronounced* is something of an understatement!" Tarrys said, laughing. "Remind me never to get on the wrong side of you, Sister!"

"Well, you're my brother," Vala countered, "so surely you must possess similar abilities."

"I am not certain if it quite works that way," Tarrys replied. "However, I am willing to give it a try, though the vase is obviously a lost cause!"

"There's the table," Vala said, grinning.

Tarrys sighed but closed his eyes, emptying his mind of all preoccupying thoughts and used a centring technique that he had taught his patients. However, although necessary, it felt uncomfortable sifting through memories to pinpoint one that emoted a strong enough negative response. For the most part, Tarrys' life had been happy, but there were of course, troubling recollections—two of them very recent. He briefly thought about his adoption, he could not remember ever not knowing, but when old enough to process the implications—that had been a difficult time for a while. Though he never doubted his adoptive parents' love for him, he wondered about his biological parents and had sometimes felt sad that they had been unable to find a way to keep him.

More recently, there was the dreadful twisting knot of fear Tarrys had felt upon arriving home one day to find Gwen had left to seek out the Spindler—his fear had further augmented with each day she was gone. Although Gwen had kept in touch via the Iridiscus crystal, Tarrys had been faced with the very real possibility of losing his soulmate. Then there was Gwen's pregnancy; both he and Gwen had been overjoyed to discover she was expecting, but this happiness was suddenly shattered when Gwen suffered the placental abruption. Although Vala had put things right again, it continued to haunt him, a constant shadow would hang over them until the baby was born.

Tarrys chose to channel all these emotions simultaneously, allowing them to course through his body, expelling them through his fingertips towards the table, opening his eyes as he did so. The table was propelled upwards by approximately eight feet, dramatically breaking apart and splintering into tiny shards.

"OMG!" Vala said, laughing nervously. "What the hell were you thinking about, Tarrys?"

"Ostensibly every negative episode I have ever experienced," Tarrys replied, feeling shocked at what he had done.

"The two of you make quite a formidable force," Elvar said, smiling. "Though you might want to reign in some of that emotion, brother—the idea being to attenuate our attacker's strength, not obliterate it!"

Tarrys exhaled a shaky breath and raked his fingers through his hair nervously.

"Point taken," Tarrys said, a few errant tears escaping as he felt an unexpected release after discharging such a large amount of stored negative emotions. "However, that was quite a cathartic experience. I feel strangely lighter."

"Maybe this could have a therapeutic application for your patients?" Vala suggested.

"Yes, um, maybe not!" Tarrys said, laughing.

Elvar groaned, looking between the remaining objects. He intuitively felt that Vala and her brother possessed prodigious abilities that he could not hope to emulate.

"My turn to try, I suppose," Elvar said, looking to Vala for encouragement.

"You will be fine," Vala assured him, feeling Elvar's apprehension.Elvar decided on the bookshelf as his intended target, then closed his eyes. There were very few negative incidents in his repertoire of memories, but four very recent ones stood out: the time when Keela had drugged them all and he had been unable to reach Vala—he had seen her in anguish over his apparently lifeless body but had been powerless to communicate with her. Another time was when Vala had faced down the Spindler, shortly before the Spindler turned his wrath on Elvar for interfering. He had felt pure terror over the possibility of what the Spindler might do to his beloved, and pure anger at the Spindler for forcing them into that situation by abducting Vala's parents and causing her such pain.

More recently on his mind was facing the possibility of losing Vala during that terrible accident caused by the Dessicatus several days ago—he could now truly empathise with how Vala had felt when the Spindler had left him for dead. Although not nearly as grievous, but still irritating was his sister's dalliance with Lann. Seeing her in such a sexually provocative situation with a friend of his—a friend older than Elvar no less—it was just too much.

Elvar cleared his mind, channelling his emotions into his fingertips as Vala and Tarrys had done, and secreted the energy towards the bookshelf.

He opened his eyes as he watched the bookshelf shudder violently, move back a few feet, and fall to the ground.

"Not quite as impressive as the two of you," Elvar said, feeling disappointed at his lack of adroitness.

"You did well," Vala said, feeling Elvar's sense of dejection permeate her as she pulled him into a hug.

"I feel so useless," Elvar said, his voice catching. "I am meant to protect you, but I am obviously lacking the aptitude that both you and your brother possess."

"We protect each other," Vala said, pressing her forehead to Elvar's. "I am naturally adept at certain things as is Tarrys because of what we are, but you have many other skills. And, besides, there's that other spell you've been working on."

"Which is not one I can really practice," Elvar replied. "Anyway, you might as well try your hand at taking down the chest and armoire. If you are not too fatigued, that is?"

"I think I can give it a go," Vala said, feeling confident from her earlier accomplishment.

Vala shrugged her shoulders, pulling them back to release the strain that had accumulated there. She had decided to move both the chest and armoire simultaneously, though this would require a considerable expenditure of energy.

This time, Vala homed in a powerful combination of negative energy: the rage she felt at the Spindler, first for the abduction of her parents, then for killing Elvar, and then the utter devastation and pain she had felt when she thought Elvar had been taken from her. She allowed the energy to stream through her body, projecting it outwards towards the two remaining items of furniture.

Instantaneously, the chest and armoire elevated several feet in the air and shot forward, crashing to the ground upturned, but in one piece.

"Bravo, Sister!" Tarrys said, clapping. "I think you have this one truly mastered!"

"You are amazing," Elvar said, taking Vala's hand and looking deeply into her eyes. "You never cease to amaze me. I cannot believe how far you have come in such a short space of time."

"I'm actually a little tired now," Vala admitted, yawning and resting her head against Elvar's chest.

"I will take you home," Elvar replied. "But first we have a little cleaning up to do."

1 2

Vala felt a tight knot in her stomach as she approached her tutor's office. Though she knew it was the right action to take, quitting her degree was one of the most difficult decisions she had ever had to make. A coil of nausea rose from her stomach, bile burning her throat as she contemplated telling Elvar and her parents. She had not found the courage to tell Elvar, as she was worried he might talk her out of it. And her parents ... her parents would be bitterly disappointed; Vala dreaded telling them the most. She felt that she was betraying them, cheating them out of their dream for her. She realised with irony that had she stayed on this path, her future profession would have been the same as her brother's—they were so much alike—and yet, she felt her true calling lay with healing. Vala felt much more than a sense of satisfaction when she healed—it was like pure joy, elation, and an amazing feeling of purpose. It was what she was destined for, just as she had been destined to be with Elvar.

Vala knocked hesitantly on the door, her heart hammering so loud, she felt sure it must be audible. The door opened, and Vala stepped inside, a trickle of perspiration running down her back.

Afterwards, Vala exhaled a long sigh of relief; it had been an uncomfortable experience, but at the same time had resulted in a more positive outcome than she had anticipated. She had come to an agreement with the tutor that she would finish the remaining few weeks of the Lent term, then if she felt the same after the Easter break, her resignation would be officialised.

As she walked back to her lodgings, the noise of Cambridge traffic and aromas from nearby restaurants invaded her senses, making her head pound, compounding her emotional exhaustion. Vala loved the culture of Cambridge: its museums, galleries, shopping, and numerous eateries brought her a lot of pleasure. She smiled as her mind drifted back to a few weeks earlier; she had had an early morning lecture and Elvar had a free day. They had walked to the Rainbow Vegetarian Café for an early lunch and talked for hours, not about anything of any great importance, but small things, their respective studies, friends, books they were reading; however, it had reinforced Vala's deep connection with Elvar. Once they had eaten, they wandered around the Fitzwilliam Museum; both she and Elvar had a great interest in Egyptology in particular and enjoyed browsing the exhibits there. They later walked back to Vala's lodgings, taking a long, hot shower together. That part made Vala smile the most as she recalled the playful way she and Elvar had lathered each other in soapy suds. His soft hands glided over the surface of her body, and as her hand found his most intimate part, he had suddenly lifted Vala, pulling her into him, Vala wrapping her legs tightly around him as they made love—it had been electrifying. Elvar had carried Vala to her bed after, curling into her, his body warm and comforting as she drifted into a deep restorative sleep.

Vala kicked off her shoes outside her bedroom door and stripped to her underwear, throwing all of her outer clothes into the laundry basket. She made her way to the bathroom, rinsing with mouthwash and splashing her face with cold water. She still felt completely enervated, and a migraine had started to surface. She placed her hands over her temples and released a healing energy into her head, allowing it to relieve her migraine. She climbed into her bed and texted Jelly to see if she was free to talk.

Vala's phone rang and she picked up.

"Hey, Vala!" Jelly said cheerfully. "What's up, babe? I know something's wrong. I may not have your precognitive abilities, but I can still tell when something's not right with you." "I quit," Vala said simply.

"What do you mean *you quit*? What exactly did you quit because I can't imagine you mean that you dropped out of uni?"

"I did," Vala confirmed. "It just isn't for me, Jelly. I want to be a healer. Besides which, I don't feel I belong here. I want to be in Avalonia with Elvar."

"Oh, Vala, are you sure about this?" Jelly said. "It's a pretty big deal."

"I'm sure."

"Well you've certainly been full of big surprises ever since Elvar entered your life! How did your parents react?" "They don't know," Vala admitted.

"OMG!" Jelly screeched, causing Vala to wince. "Vala! They're gonna freak! What about Elvar? What's his take on this?"

"He doesn't know either."

"You *are* kidding me, right?" Jelly replied. "You guys are so tight you're practically melded together! Why haven't you discussed this with him?"

"I was scared he might try to talk me out of it, and he's the one person who probably could," Vala said, sighing. "I really needed to do this and not lose my nerve."

"Well, if you're sure it's what you want, you have my full support, just as you did when you married Elvar," Jelly said. "What happened to the careful, cautious Vala Pendragon I once knew?" "She grew up," Vala said.

There was a brief pause before Jelly spoke again.

"There's something else, isn't there?"

Vala said nothing for a moment, contemplating her words before deciding upon full disclosure. She told Jelly everything about her meetings with Amalia in Elsorriden and of Amalia's premonition.

"Did she have any suggestions on what we can do?" Jelly pressed, anxiety twisting in her stomach.

When Vala didn't reply, Jelly asked again.

"She believes that our best bet is to find Merlin by procuring the amulets I told you about."

"Then I'm coming with you, and I'm sure Max will want to too."

"No!" Vala said emphatically. "It could be dangerous if we encounter whoever it is that intends to harm me."

"Like a little bit of peril stopped us before!" Jelly said, laughing in disbelief. "Listen to me, this is not up for debate, non-negotiable, okay? Max and I will accompany you."

"I won't be going straightaway," Vala said. "I need to assist with the birth of Gwen's baby; she's due in a few weeks, at the start of the Easter hols."

"Well then, that settles it!" Jelly declared. "Assuming she's more or less on time, Max and I will be on our Easter break. Perfect timing!"

*

Vala was startled awake by a hand on her shoulder. After her discussion with Jelly, she had drifted into a dreamless sleep, and her heart pounded as she forced her eyes open.

"Vala," Elvar said gently, sitting on the bed next to her. "I did not mean to frighten you. Are you all right, my love?"

Vala yawned, her speech slightly slurred. "It's fine, I was just in a very deep sleep."

Elvar pulled up the comforter and snuggled up beside her, hugging her closely to him. Vala placed her arms around his neck and kissed him softly, touching her forehead to his.

"Elvar, there's something I need to tell you," she said, biting her lip.

"Well it is obviously causing you distress, so the sooner you tell me, the better," Elvar replied, stroking her hair.

"I'm scared to," Vala admitted, tightly knitting a lock of hair around her finger.

"How could you possibly be scared to tell me anything?" Elvar asked. "You know my love for you is unconditional—nothing you can say will ever change that."

"I know," Vala said quietly. "It's just that I'm not sure if you will agree with my decision."

"Whatever it is, if you have made a decision based on what feels right for you, then I will fully support it."

"I'm leaving college," Vala said. "Psychology will always be a great passion for me, it is what I have wanted to do ever since I was a child, but things have changed."

"And now you wish to be a healer and live with me in Avalonia?""You know me very well," Vala said, smiling and brushing a finger over Elvar's cheek.

"You are my twin soul," Elvar answered. "So why would you possibly believe that I would not be supportive of your choice?"

"I thought you might try and talk me out of it," Vala confessed, "so I delayed telling you. In fact, please don't be hurt, but—" "You confided in Tarrys, and perhaps Jelly prior to telling me?" "You really do know me well!" Vala exclaimed.

"I am not hurt, beloved," Elvar said, his breath warming Vala's face. "You felt that if my opinion was in conflict with yours, that perhaps I might sway you from resigning your course."

"And I'm supposed to be the one with enhanced intuitive ability!" Vala said, laughing.

"Actually," Elvar said, tracing a finger between her breasts, "it might be a little selfish of me, but I cannot pretend to be unhappy about you living with me permanently in Avalonia. Hopefully, in time, we can have our own home together, and in a few years, maybe—"

"Consider starting our own little family?"

"Yes," Elvar said, planting a trail of hot kisses down her neck, his tongue teasing the hollow of the nape and igniting her body with desire.

"Maybe we should start practising," Vala said breathlessly, hastily pulling off Elvar's top and unzipping his jeans.

Afterwards, Vala lay contentedly in Elvar's arms, feeling protected and safe, as though nothing unpleasant in the world could ever touch her.

"It is your birthday this weekend," Elvar said, caressing the top of Vala's head, "and I have been planning a little surprise ..."

"Do I get to know what this surprise is now?" Vala asked, her curiosity piqued.

"I believe you mentioned having a few free days, though now that you have left college, I am not sure it is pertinent."

"Well, actually, I promised to stay till Easter, so I haven't technically left yet."

"No matter," Elvar said, "but in answer to your question, I am planning to whisk you away for a romantic stay in—" "In where?" Vala asked impatiently.

"Now that would ruin the surprise," Elvar said, tracing his thumb over her cheek.

"But how will I know what to pack if I don't know where we're going?"

"Well, I will tell you that it is in Candalia, and as you know, other than the more alpine regions and a certain other place I care not to dwell upon, we have a perpetually temperate climate," Elvar replied. "However ..."

"Elvar!" Vala raised her voice. "You are being infuriating!"

"However," Elvar continued, his mouth twitching at the corners, "you should most definitely bring that swimsuit I gave you for our anniversary."

"And why is that funny?" Vala demanded, playfully punching Elvar's arm.

"You misunderstand, beloved," Elvar returned, smiling. "I do not find it humorous. I was remembering when you wore it last; how utterly beguiling you looked, the way it clung to your curves, the way it made me want to do this ..."

Vala began to talk, but Elvar silenced her with a passionate kiss, his fingers interlacing with hers and his knee parting her legs.

"I love you," Vala said breathlessly, her body aching for his.

"I love you too, my Eternal Beloved," Elvar replied. "I always have and I always will."

13

It was a few days before Vala's birthday, and she and Elvar were preparing to leave for their mini-vacation. Vala had perfected the art of packing lightly since meeting Elvar, as there was no mechanised transport in Candalia, the only means of travel being direct selfflight—which was virtually impossible with any luggage—foot, boat, or horse. For this particular trip, Vala could see that they would be travelling by horse, as Elvar had harnessed his horse, Cloud, and Vala's horse, Dream, to a small carriage. Vala had realised when Elvar had asked her to summon her horse that they would probably not be holidaying in Avalonia.

It was relatively early in the morning, and there was still a slight chill in the air. Vala shivered and rubbed her arms to generate some warmth. Elvar removed his jacket and she gratefully slipped it on. He then took her hand in his and helped Vala into the carriage. Although the interior of the carriage was fairly basic, Elvar had taken care to pad the seating, and Vala noticed two folded Furlomyn blankets, no doubt for her benefit. Still feeling chilly, she reached for one and draped it over her legs. Elvar loaded their bags onto the seating opposite and sat next to her, placing an arm around her and resting his head on hers.

"Are you feeling warmer, my love?" he asked, breathing into Vala's hair as he kissed the top of her head.

"Much," Vala said, snuggling into Elvar's chest and placing her hand on his thigh. "Especially now that I have you to heat me up." Elvar prompted the horses to depart before turning his attention back to Vala. They were both silent for a while, content merely to be in each other's company. However, for the past few minutes, Vala had been thinking back to her encounters with Amalia and how emphatic she had been that Merlin and his family be found. More specifically, she had been wondering about

Merlin himself and how much of what she knew of the man was steeped in myth or based on fact.

"How much do you know of Merlin?" Vala said, abruptly breaking the silence.

"Where did that come from?" Elvar said, laughing.

"It's been on my mind a lot since Amalia's premonition," Vala admitted. "Just with everything else happening, I hadn't got round to asking you."

"Well," Elvar began, "I know about as much as most fae do, some of which will probably bear some semblance to human accounts. Maybe you should tell me what you know and I will try to fill in the gaps."

"Okay," Vala agreed. "I know that he was, or should I say *is* a powerful fae, married to Nimeva and had one daughter with her: Merevina. Before this, though, he had spent time in the human realm as Arthur's advisor and protector for him and Guinevere. Merlin also had a home in the valleys of Cavania, which was his last known location before he and his family mysteriously disappeared, never to be seen again. He was chiefly responsible for Arthur's success in procuring Excalibur. Oh, and he created the Fountain of Love Truth."

"Merlin was, is, one of the most powerful fae in our history—the provenance of many of our spells, including most of our defensive magic is owed to Merlin. As I said to you at the time, we do not know for certain if the Fountain of Love Truth is imbued with that rather alarming enchantment or if it was merely his way of discouraging temerity.

"Merlin was, however, Arthur's most trusted advisor and his closest friend—they were actually of a similar age. Merlin was a great seer and had known since childhood that Arthur would make a great king. So, as you also know, he affected and influenced certain key moments to ensure Arthur's victory.

"Part of your human mythology that Arthur is *the once and future king*, was a term coined by Merlin—it was something he prophesied. This is where it becomes rather confusing, though, and has fuelled many a debate: according to Merlin, although relations between the fae and human worlds had deteriorated, the rift would one day be healed by two children possessing fae and human blood, a boy and a girl, who would essentially be the true king and queen of the human and fae realms."

"But what does that have to do with Arthur?"

"It is thought that Merlin was either referring to a descendant of Arthur, or that Arthur himself would somehow be restored to the living world."

"Do you know how many descendants Arthur has?" Vala asked. "Other than my immediate family?"

"Less than you might think," Elvar said, chewing on his lip. "And no others with the potency of fae blood to possibly be part of that prophecy. The only descendants with that potential ability are—"

"Me and Tarrys," Vala interjected, nervously twisting a lock of hair around her finger. "Though I hope that he wasn't suggesting that my brother and I reign over two worlds?"

"I do not know, Vala," Elvar said gently, "though I think we have to presume that if Merlin was not referring to you and Tarrys directly, that he certainly must have meant your bloodline."

"Um," Vala said, unsure of how to respond. "I don't really have any comeback to that. It's not exactly ... I don't know what to say ..."

"Do not concern yourself over it, my love," Elvar answered. "Whatever is destined to happen will happen—worrying over something we cannot control is unproductive. Besides which ..."

Elvar ran his finger over Vala's lips and kissed her softly. "I would rather spend the next few days exploring more pleasurable pursuits."

"Elvar?" Vala said, suddenly anxious. "You are sure the horses know where they're going without guidance?"

"They are not like horses in the human realm," Elvar replied. "Our horses have a telepathic connection to us. They will be stopping next in the village of Tevali where we shall have lunch and rest for a while; there is a tavern there with stables so the horses may rest and receive sustenance. So, in the meantime ..."

Elvar kissed Vala hungrily, his hand slipping beneath her bra and cupping her breast.

"You, Mr Oakley," Vala said, running her hand under his T-shirt, "are a very bad boy indeed."

14

They reached the tavern three hours later. Like the other localities Vala had seen in Avalonia, this one was also reminiscent of a Swiss chalet.

"I am just going to tether, feed, and water the horses, my love," Elvar said, climbing out of the carriage. "You rest for a moment, I will be right back."

"I'll be waiting," Vala said, leaning down to kiss him.

Vala sat back and sighed, her thoughts drifting back to Merlin's prophecies. Lost in thought, she was startled when she found a pale girl with long dark hair standing outside her carriage. Not wishing to be rude, Vala opened the carriage door.

"Lady Vala Oakley-Pendragon, I presume?" the girl asked in a flat monotone voice. "Am I correct in my presumption?" "Um, yes," Vala replied nervously.

The girl stared at Vala blankly, and an involuntary shiver snaked down Vala's spine.

"My mistress seeks an audience with you," the girl said, seizing Vala's wrist.

As the girl's fingers locked around her, Vala looked at her in pure terror as the girl's face transmogrified into something truly horrific—it was as though she were looking at a charred skeleton with glowing red orbs for eyes. Vala screamed as the girl tried to pull her from the carriage. She was on the verge of inciting the soul-mirroring incantation when Elvar came running to her side.

"Get away from her!"

The girl glanced at Elvar briefly then ran into the surrounding woodland.

"What the hell happened?" Elvar said, frantically pulling Vala to him and holding her tightly in his arms.

"I don't know," Vala said. "She obviously knew who I was, as she asked for confirmation of my identity. Then she just grabbed me and said her mistress seeks an audience with me."

"This must be whatever, or rather, whomever Amalia was alluding to when she said you were in danger," Elvar said, stroking Vala's hair. "I will not leave you unattended again."

"That could be a little awkward," Vala said, half-smiling, "as I really need to pee!"

"I am not leaving you alone *anywhere*, Vala," Elvar asserted. "It may raise a few eyebrows, but I will accompany you to the ladies' bathroom."

"They'll probably think we're up to something kinky!" Vala said, her face reddening.

"My only concern is to protect you," Elvar replied. "Though I shall have a word with the proprietors to allay any suspicions of my motives."

"That would be a good idea," Vala said, her cheeks aflame.

Vala felt a sense of relief wash over her as they stepped inside the establishment; it was comforting to be in the presence of others at a time like this, even if they were strangers.

Elvar led Vala to a table in the corner of the tavern as he went to find the proprietors. Whilst Elvar was gone, a waitress arrived and handed Vala a menu, leaving another one on the table for Elvar, who glanced over to Vala and smiled.

"Would you like a mug of Kashali tea? You look like you could use it!" the waitress asked, smiling warmly at Vala. "On the house, of course, and one for your ..."

"Husband," Vala said. "And, yes, that sounds lovely—thank you."Elvar returned as the waitress left to give them time to peruse the menu.

"Would you like me to escort you to the bathroom now?" Elvar asked. "The proprietors were very sympathetic to your plight and are more than happy to accommodate my wishes."

"My bladder's pretty much fit to burst!" Vala said through gritted teeth. "So, no complaints from me, let's go!"

Vala stood, then paused for a moment as Elvar looked at her, his brow knitting.

"What is troubling you, my love?"

"Just to check—you weren't planning on actually coming into the cubicle with me, right?"

Elvar laughed, kissing the top of Vala's head.

"That would be a tad *too* much sharing," he said, grinning. "Even by my standards!"

Vala and Elvar returned to their table to find piping hot mugs of Kashali tea with small clouds of sweet flavoured steam rising from the surface of the liquid. Vala took a small sip of the tea, sighing contentedly as the hot spicy liquid warmed her from within.

"Vala," Elvar began, placing his hand over hers, "that girl—her whole countenance—I think she was one of the Spindler's minions, a Dessicatus."

"But the Spindler is dead," Vala replied. "I killed him ... he disintegrated in front of our eyes—not your eyes—but the rest of us saw him die for sure."

"Yes," Elvar said, "he is gone, but obviously his minions—the Dessicatus and others of that ilk—have not. And back to that girl, she said that she would take you to her mistress ..."

"Which would mean that they have a new leader," Vala finished.

"We must be watchful," Elvar said, running a hand through his hair, "but for now, we should put this aside and concentrate on having fun!"

Vala picked up the menu and browsed through the options, trying to ignore the face of the creepy girl, which had imprinted itself on her consciousness.

"Care to share an entrée with me?" Elvar said, looking up from his menu. "There is a sharing platter of Cheriko nuts, Amblets and Verishi pods, drizzled with Anvali nectar."

"I love Amblets!" Vala said, her face lighting up. "Like chocolate drops without the calories! The Verishi pods taste like spicy vanilla, and Cheriko nuts—you know they're my favourite! What are you having for mains?"

"Chandris stew with Savima bread," Elvar said. "And you, my love?"

"Zimbrini bread topped with melted Astris cheese, Dashel root and Caramea and Malami sauce," Vala replied. "And after that, I'm having Uquilico brulée."

"I quite fancy the hot chocolate soufflé spiced with Chando pods," Elvar said as his stomach growled audibly.

The waitress arrived a few minutes after they had made their selection, taking their order and leaving them alone again.

For a prolonged moment, neither Vala nor Elvar spoke. Elvar had Vala's hands in his and was gently rubbing over the backs of them with his thumbs, gazing lovingly into her eyes. Vala returned his gaze, feeling her stomach flutter, and touched her nose to Elvar's.

"We will get through this, Vala," Elvar said softly. "And together we will be triumphant, as we were before."

The waitress arrived with their entrée, and they both tucked in hungrily.

"You know," Vala said after swallowing a mouthful of Cheriko nuts, "maybe the Spindler had a family—a secret family he kept hidden from the world."

"I thought we had agreed not to discuss this right now," Elvar said.

Vala wiped a smear of Anvali nectar from above Elvar's lip and licked her finger.

"But it's playing on my mind," Vala admitted, sighing heavily.

"We know very little of the Spindler and *what* he actually was," Elvar replied. "Many believe he was once an ordinary, if not powerful, fae who somehow became corrupted. But he is so ancient, nobody knows for sure—correct that—*was* ancient."

"But if he did have a family, perhaps they would be seeking revenge? Retribution for the Spindler's death?" Vala ventured. "And as I was the sole perpetrator of that particular act—"

"You bringing an end to the Spindler's nefarious existence is the best thing that has happened to Candalia, and if," Elvar said, cupping Vala's face in his hands, "if there are to be any repercussions, we will face them together."

Vala sighed again but knew nothing would be gained by discussing it further. Elvar leaned forward to kiss her forehead, though like Vala, he was preoccupied with thoughts of the sinister girl, so they finished their entrée in silence.

Their main course arrived, and Elvar decided to make a concerted effort to shift the focus onto something more quotidian.

"You never did tell me," Elvar said, "how Laoli and Patrick took the news of your leaving college?"

"Oh that," Vala said, picking off a piece of Dashel root from her bread and nibbling on it. "Um, I haven't actually told them yet."

"There is little time left," Elvar replied, his eyes fixing on Vala's. "Do you not think you should do it *before* you actually leave?"

"I will," Vala said, casting her eyes down. "I just wanted to have these few days with you before having to face them."

"I believe you are underestimating their capacity for empathy and compassion," Elvar said. "I am certain that they will understand your reasons and be supportive of you, even if it does come as a shock in the initial instance."

"I know," Vala said, guiding a string of cheese into her mouth. "I just feel like I'm smashing all the dreams they had for me, and the idea of hurting them again is awful."

"I do understand," Elvar replied, "but it is better not to defer it for too much longer. It will be a more painful process for you and will upset them more if they know you were withholding this from them."

As their empty plates were taken away, Elvar got up and sat next to Vala, who was seated on the opposite side. He placed an arm around her, and she rested her head under his chin.

"I love you, sweet beloved," Elvar murmured, his breath tickling the top of Vala's head. "Let me help you forget all this, if only for a while."

15

After their meal, Elvar led Vala to the horses, taking some time to commune with them before resuming their journey. The horses were sentient and intelligent animals, deeply disturbed by Vala's encounter with the creepy girl. Elvar taught Vala a meditation technique for calming her horse as Elvar employed the same method on his, coaxing the animals back to the carriage.

Vala felt a wave of drowsiness wash over her and snuggled up to Elvar, pulling the blanket over her legs. She closed her eyes, letting the rhythmic motion of the carriage lull her into sleep. Elvar gazed out through the window for a while, his eyes glazing and eyelids growing heavy as they crossed into a long stretch of farmland. Before long, Elvar too had drifted into a deep slumber, his head resting on Vala's.

Vala knew she had been trapped in yet another nightmarish vision, but as she opened her eyes, it slipped away from her as she grappled to hold onto fragments of the images, dissolving into the depths of her subconscious.

The air had grown crisper, and Vala forced her eyes to open fully, inhaling a lungful of cool air. The sun was now setting, and it cast a mesmerising palette of colours in the sky: shades of intense orange, coral, and turquoise swirls that blended into cerulean and indigopurple. They had passed into another town now, notably different from the other fae dwellings Vala had grown accustomed to. She gently nudged Elvar awake.

"Where are we?" she asked as she continued to gaze out.

Elvar yawned and rubbed his eyes, his vision slowly focussing as he looked out the window.

"We are in Castaria," Elvar replied. "We have reached Moredonia."Vala opened the window on her side of the carriage and leant out, taking in her new surroundings. The homes they passed were the most unusual she had seen yet. Each dwelling was made from crystalline rock, irregular in shape and roughly carved to accommodate rooms and openings. The rock seemed to Vala to be some sort of quartz and possibly another mineral, in many variants and hues. Some looked like rose quartz, others a smoky grey; others like amethyst, citrine, topaz, sapphire, and one that was much more opaque, resembling jade with unusual red striations running through it.

The windows were oblong on the horizontal, with a slight convexity that complemented the natural curve of the façade, each one framed by a delicate coppery edging, with a decorative curlicue offset from the centre of each side. The glass itself had a prismatic iridescence, which reminded Vala of soap bubbles. The doors had an ornate coppery shutter with decorative floral patterns, leaves, and curlicues, behind which was the door itself, comprised of a slightly more opaque, cloudy version of the shimmering glass. The rooftops were at once both beautiful and strange: from each sprung a large, opaline crystalline structure, sculpted into a flower with curved, concave petals. Vala watched, mesmerised as the petals gently rotated in the breeze.

"What are they?" she asked, pointing at the flower structures.

"Moredonia is a slightly windier region due to its proximity to the sea," Elvar answered. "The petals act as sails and provide an energy source to each home. The centre, a form of which is on all Candalian homes, provides solar energy for less windy days."

Vala leaned her head on Elvar's shoulder and sighed. Her surroundings were breathtaking and she had always adored being close to the sea. However, she could not quite shake the uneasiness from her earlier encounter with the creepy girl, and a sense of disquieting anxiety knotted in her stomach. When Vala gave in to the discomfiting thoughts, her chest would tighten in response, so she made a concerted effort to keep her mind focussed on the here and now.

Elvar broke Vala's reverie, giving her a gentle nudge. "Look, my love," he said, indicating at the horizon.

Vala looked ahead at the sparkling azure strip on the horizon, the Moredonian Sea. Even from a distance, she could see the gentle waves rippling, the late-afternoon sunbeams sparkling across the water like effervescent starlight and captivating Vala's attention as she stared ahead of her.

"Feeling a little zoned out, beloved?" Elvar said, stroking Vala's cheek.

"Mmm ..." Vala replied, "a bit. I'm just—"

"I know," Elvar said. "I am feeling it too. However, we are away from it all right now and we must try to forget, if just for a while."

The horses came to a stop, and Elvar opened the door to their carriage, beckoning Vala to follow him. As Vala stepped out, a slightly perfumed and salty aroma filled her nostrils, leaving a briny tang in her mouth. The ground beneath her comprised rounded crystal cobblestones scattered liberally with white sand. A low wall made from the same crystal cobblestones stood to the left of Vala, just about reaching her waist height. She peered over it, observing that they were on a promontory approximately twenty feet above the ocean. Below her was a sandy white beach, the tiny white grains interblended with iridescent pink and blue crystals. It was truly stunning and contrasted perfectly with the aquamarine ocean that gently lapped the shoreline.

"It is quite something, is it not?" Elvar commented, placing an arm around Vala's shoulders. "We can take a walk down there later if you wish?"

"That would be nice," Vala replied, yawning.

"You need to rest," Elvar said. "I will take our bags inside."

"Inside?"

"The beach house," Elvar said, his mouth twitching at the corners. "Where we are residing for the week?"

"Oh," Vala said, smiling. "Right, the beach house!"

She turned around, noticing a short boardwalk that led up to a wooden beach house, constructed from the white wood with purple striations, which Vala had since learned came from the Viaspa tree, native to the

Avalonian woodland. The top of the house was encased in a large glass dome, piquing Vala's curiosity.

"What is that?" Vala asked, pointing to the dome.

"An observatory," Elvar replied. "I will show you at nightfall." "This house isn't anything like the others here," Vala said.

"No," Elvar confirmed. "My father built it, hence the Viaspan wood and different architectural style."

Elvar took Vala's hand and led her around the boardwalk to the front of the house, which overlooked the sea. He quietly spoke an incantation, and the door opened. They stepped inside, removing their shoes on the mat and walking into a large room with a Viaspan floor and walls, an enormous, irregularly shaped, honey-coloured Furlomyn rug, and an impressive fireplace surrounded by a curved off-white sofa. On the far side of the room was an open-plan kitchen area, and to the left, a staircase leading to the second floor.

In spite of her tiredness, Vala felt an excited buzz infuse her body and a pleasurable tingle at the anticipation of spending some quality alone time with Elvar.

"Would you like to explore upstairs?" Elvar asked, squeezing Vala's hand.

"Please!" Vala said excitedly.

"After you," Elvar said, gesturing for Vala to go ahead of him.

Vala ascended the oak wood staircase slowly, committing all the details of her surroundings to memory.

At the top of the stairs was a wide, capacious landing with large glass doors leading to a balcony that overlooked the sea. A total of eight chairs had been placed there, four around a circular table on the landing, and four outside on the balcony, also arranged around a table in the centre.

Vala peeked through the glass doors, taking in the view outside for a moment before moving on to a room on her right.

"This is usually Maiwen's room," Elvar said.

Vala lightly placed her hand on the sky blue wall, silently watching painted images of soft white clouds idling by. Butterflies, bees, and birds fluttered in and around the clouds in an unending, but seemingly random pattern. She was briefly startled by a soft neighing sound as a unicorn skipped into view, having appeared to be hidden within one of the larger clouds.

"I've never thought of asking before," Vala said, a little hesitantly, "but are unicorns real?"

"In all honesty, I do not know," Elvar admitted. "There have been stories of sightings, though nobody I know has ever seen one; if they do exist, they are certainly a rarity."

"Would you like to see my bedroom now?" Elvar said, pulling on Vala's hand.

Elvar's room, in contrast to Maiwen's, and much in line with his room in Avalonia, was very minimalistic. The walls were a stormy blue-grey colour with what looked like a Celtic symbol adorning the main wall.

"What does that symbol represent?" Vala asked, her finger tracing its outline—a pattern of concentric circles. The outer circle filled with interconnecting leaves, the middle with an intricate lattice, and the innermost one with a prominent star. *Possibly the sun*, Vala thought as she awaited Elvar's response.

"It is the Meridia Absolutas," Elvar explained. "The outer ring of leaves represents our affinity with nature and how our natural world sustains and nurtures us, the middle ring with the latticework represents our connection to each other, and the central ring represents the Great Divine or God, depicted as the sun."

"It's beautiful," Vala said, resting her head on Elvar's shoulder.

She looked around at the rest of the room: a Viaspan wood wardrobe stood in the far-right corner of the room, a simple dresser and full-length mirror in the centre, and a single bed with just a white sheet and pillow in the opposite corner.

"Your bed doesn't look big enough for two," Vala said, looking up at Elvar.

"We are not sleeping in here," Elvar said, looking down at Vala and brushing his lips against hers.

"Your parents' room?" Vala asked, feeling a little perturbed by the thought.

"*Our* room for the duration of this vacation," Elvar returned, prompting Vala to follow him into the remaining bedroom.

As Vala walked into the master bedroom, she gasped, then squealed with delight at the truly resplendent environment.

The walls were adorned with a lush forest scene, complete with birdsong and the distant sound of a babbling brook, which she spied between the trees in the far background. The trees were set against a currently sunset sky, and a fresh, pure aroma infused the air as the leaves gently rustled in an enchanted breeze. In the centre of the room was a king size bed, covered with a silken midnight-blue comforter, with matching sheets and sumptuous pillows.

"This is friggin' awesome!" Vala exclaimed, sitting on the edge of the bed and bouncing slightly. "It reminds me of Max's bedroom from *Where the Wild Things Are*."

"I have absolutely no idea what you are referring to, but I shall take your word for it!" Elvar replied. "However, I can tell you that the birdsong you are hearing at present is that of the nightingale."

"It's still a little weird though," Vala said, twisting a lock of hair tightly around her finger.

"What is?" Elvar asked curiously.

"You know," Vala said blushing, "the idea of us *doing it* on your parents' bed."

"It is just a bed, Vala," Elvar replied, cheeks aflame. "Now, swiftly changing the subject, there is one more place to show you. However, you are tired. Rest here for a while and I shall unpack our belongings. I will wake you in an hour or so and show you something truly spectacular."

"Well, I am a bit sleepy," Vala conceded. "Okay. But promise to wake me?"

"I promise."

Vala lay back on the bed and closed her eyes. She hadn't even realised that she had drifted to sleep till she was awoken by a gentle kiss.

"Hey," Elvar said softly, kissing her again. "Time for your surprise."

Vala gasped as Elvar swept her into his arms and carried her over to an area near the far wall—an opening in the forest. He murmured an incantation and carried Vala through the wall before setting her down in front of another stairway. Curious, Vala ascended the steps and found herself in a spacious, glass-domed chamber, with a long telescope and various unfamiliar instruments. Surrounding the telescope was a round metal railing.

"Something to lean on whilst gazing at the stars," Elvar said, reading Vala's thoughts. "Welcome to the observatory."

The sky was now dark and Vala peered through the lens of the telescope, hoping to discern a constellation or two.

"Here," Elvar said, his voice barely above a whisper. "Focus the aperture like this." He carefully turned a ring on the telescope to sharpen the focus.

Elvar's body leaned into Vala's, and a warm tingle spread from below her stomach into her inner thighs and zinged between her legs, generating an ever-growing heat.

Elvar kissed the back of her neck, his breath hot and moist on her skin. Vala shivered, but not from cold. Vala held onto the railing as Elvar pressed against her. His hands moved under her top and over the surface of her bra. She moaned as Elvar's fingers slid under her bra, cupping and gently squeezing her breasts. She heard Elvar's breathing hitch and felt her need for him intensify. Vala reached behind her and rubbed her hand over Elvar's crotch, feeling his arousal beneath her fingers.

Elvar gasped in pleasure and relief as Vala unzipped his jeans, her fingers tantalising and dangerous. He felt a surge of exhilaration through his body as he hastily pulled down Vala's jeans. Vala grasped Elvar's hips, pulling him closer to her, and rubbed herself against him. Almost breathless, Elvar pushed Vala's underwear aside and merged his body with hers. Vala cried out as she felt Elvar move within her. She clutched tightly to the railing as Elvar rocked against her, his movements bringing her closer to rapturous release.

"I love you," Elvar whispered as his pleasure reached an apex, feeling Vala's body respond and shudder against his.

"That was amazing," Vala said breathlessly. "And a little unexpected!"

"A little spontaneity is always a good thing!" Elvar mused, nuzzling the side of Vala's neck. "Which brings me to my next question: how do you fancy a spot of naked stargazing?"

"*Naked*?" Vala repeated, laughing. "Goodness, Mr Oakley, I didn't picture you as the hippy type!"

"*Hippy*?" Elvar said, his brow knitted. "What is *hippy*?"

"Hippies!" Vala said, shaking her head. "You know, the '6os: flower power, tree-hugging, LSD, The Beatles?"

"The '6os?" Elvar replied, growing ever more puzzled. "What are the '6os?"

"The 1960s," Vala said, laughing harder, as she removed her bra, swinging the straps around her finger. "A fair bit of bra-burning too!"

"The human realm will never cease to amaze me in its aptitude for strangeness," Elvar said, also laughing. "But bare-bosomed maidens—now that does not seem like such a bad thing!"

"Hey!" Vala said, throwing her bra at Elvar's face. "The only barebosomed lady you have permission to think about is me!"

"Why would I ever want to think of another when I am already married to such a vision of perfection?" Elvar said, taking Vala into his arms, his hands moving from her waist to her hips as he hooked his thumbs under the elastic of her underwear. "Now, are you ready to get naked with me?"

"You know that means ..."

"That particular one means the same thing in the fae realm," Elvar intercepted, speaking softly into Vala's ear, his breath hot against her skin.

"Oh," Vala said quietly as she melted into his arms.

16

The next morning Elvar woke to find himself alone in their bed. He called out to Vala, but there was no response. He sprang out of bed, and seeing that the bathroom was unoccupied, made his way downstairs, expecting to find Vala there. She was not.

"Vala?" he called out loudly and with a sense of urgency creeping into his voice. "Where are you?"

Elvar raced back upstairs to their bedroom and whispered the incantation enabling him to access the observatory. It was vacant. A surge of adrenaline shot through his veins as panic took hold, and a cold, twisting sensation, filtered through his body.

Hastily, Elvar pulled on some clothes and bolted back downstairs, alarmed and bewildered by Vala's absence. There was a note on the kitchen table—he did not see it.

*

Vala wiggled her toes in the warm sand, the tiny granules soft and comforting against her skin. She turned to her companion and smiled.

"I cannot believe the serendipity, and may I add, pleasure and sheer luck of meeting you, Lady Pendragon, the descendant of Guinevere and Arthur and possible *Chosen One*." The dark-haired boy sitting next to Vala pushed back the hair from his face and flashed her a big smile.

"Serendipity," Vala agreed. "And for the record, it's *Oakley-Pendragon*. But I would rather you call me Vala."

"Of course, my lady" the boy replied ruefully. "*Vala* it is. Oakley? I know of the Oakleys of Avalonia—there is a renowned healer amongst them."

"That would be Derryth, my father-in-law," Vala confirmed, picking up a stray shell and turning it between her fingers.

"I guess that means you are married then?" the boy said, a little crestfallen.

"I'm afraid so, Merridyn," Vala replied. "And happily—for the record."

"Well, I cannot claim to be surprised," Merridyn said, half-smiling. "You are a strikingly beautiful girl! However, we are connected—"

"Yes," Vala said. "You are the descendant of Gawain, son of Morgause and Aravyn—I presume Aravyn was fae, as only Guinevere's and Morgana's lineage is mixed, or at least that is the presumption?"

"That is correct," Merridyn confirmed. "So, these encounters with Amalia?"

"She believes me to be in danger from someone," Vala explained, feeling a twist of anxiety as an image of the mysterious woman flashed into her mind. "I know what she looks like and that she appears to have minions like the ... like the Spindler," Vala trailed off.

"And you have mastered the barrier spell I assume?" Merridyn asked, absentmindedly making a hole in the sand with his finger.

"Um, not quite," Vala admitted, "though I have got rather good at Aeroexpulsion, and Elvar is working on a disabling spell—but as an absolute last resort, as it's rather, um ... extreme."

"The barrier spell only offers a few minutes of protection, but we can practise a little later if you like? I am quite accomplished at it and can hopefully help you out."

"Thanks, Merridyn," Vala said smiling. "I'd like that."

"One request, though," Merridyn said, smiling back. "Call me Merri?"

"As in the Hobbit from *Lord of the Rings*?" Vala said, chuckling.

"I have absolutely no idea what you are talking about!" Merridyn returned, raising an eyebrow. "However, I do know of something that might aid your protection, though ..."

"Though what?" Vala asked impatiently.

"It has been missing for over a thousand years," Merridyn said, frowning. "Do you know of the legend of Gawain and the Green Knight?"

"Not really."

"The human version of events is rather more fantastical than what actually occurred," Merridyn continued. "It involved Gawain accepting a challenge to strike a blow at the Green Knight, who vowed to remain unmoving—an easy target. However, the supposed deal involved the Green Knight, assuming he survived, returning the favour one year hence. Gawain agreed to these terms and swiftly decapitated the Green Knight in one clean blow of his axe. The Green Knight, though, did not die. He picked up his fallen head and reminded Gawain that he was now bound by their treaty and should meet him by the Murmuring Mere, whereupon he would dole out the same measure as had befallen him by Gawain's hand.

"A few days to the date a year later, Gawain, abiding by their entente, set out to meet his fate. On his journey, he met with a friendly innkeeper and his wife. It was purported that the innkeeper's wife bestowed upon Gawain a kiss and a green garter, which would protect him from bodily harm. Gawain then continued his journey to the Murmuring Mere, whereupon he met the Green Knight who delivered three blows to Gawain, the first two missing their target, and the third, lightly cutting him. The Green Knight then reveals that he, himself, was the innkeeper and that it was his wife from whom Gawain received the kiss and protective garter. However, he congratulated Gawain for his bravery, and it was revealed that it had all been a test to see if he was worthy of Elfinhart, a human maiden raised by the fae, with whom Gawain had fallen in love."

"So," Vala said, twisting a few strands of hair around her finger, "what actually happened, and how does this help me?"

"The Green Knight was fae royalty, Prince Bertilak, and he had a sister, Elvinia. She had been courting Gawain secretly but feared her brother's disapproval. Bertilak was not the most sympathetic of characters and had been trying to secure a betrothal for his sister to Prince Amadyr of Cavania—his intention being to keep the royal bloodline *untainted*.

"Anyway, Elvinia and Gawain's union is discovered, and Elvinia pleads with her brother to accept Gawain as her suitor. Somewhat softened by his sister's pleas, Bertilak challenges Gawain to a duel in which the winner will be decided by whoever first draws blood, stating that should Gawain win, he would gain the hand of Elvinia. Elvinia is horrified by this, as she fears her brother will seize the opportunity to eliminate Gawain.

"Elvinia, highly skilled in defensive magic, bestows an enchanted ring upon Gawain that will protect him from bodily harm. Unbeknownst to Elvinia, Bertilak has also used defensive magic and creates a barrier spell, protecting himself from any blows that may be struck against him, albeit for a finite time. The duel commences and Bertilak is perturbed to find Gawain unscathed, as though his blade is missing its mark. They continue fighting, though, and to Bertilak's chagrin, his barrier spell subsides and Gawain delivers a superficial scratch to Bertilak's cheek.

"Bertilak is forced to honour their agreement and allows Elvinia to marry Gawain.

"However, Bertilak makes life unpleasant for them, so when Gawain—during his visits to the human realm—befriends one of Arthur's knights, Perceval, he decides to flee to Camelot with Elvinia, whereupon Perceval introduces Gawain to Arthur, and he becomes one of his most trusted knights."

"Um, Merri," Vala said, wrinkling her nose. "Still not sure where you're going with this?"

"Ah well," Merridyn continued. "The ring I mentioned protects the wearer from bodily harm."

"So where is this ring?"

"Yes," Merridyn replied, his face flushed. "That is the tricky part."

Vala glared at him with a withering look.

"Okay, okay!" Merridyn conceded. "We believe it is hidden, or rather, concealed in plain sight, retrievable by solving a riddle:

Beneath the canopy of palest blue

The second of three

The darkest of two

Within the outer

It resides in plain view."

"Bloody hell, Merri!" Vala exclaimed. "I have absolutely no idea what that means!"

"Unfortunately, neither does anyone else to date," Merridyn said, attempting a smile, but looking ashamed that he had not been more helpful. "I can help you practise the enhanced barrier spell though."

"Fine!" Vala said, playfully punching Merridyn's arm. "Let's do it then."

Merridyn stood, pushing errant dark curls away from his eyes as a light wind picked up. He proffered his hand to Vala, pulling her gently to her feet but continuing to hold her hand.

"It helps initially if we combine energies," Merridyn said, his face crimson. "Which will entail, um, holding hands, if you are okay with that?"

"I guess so," Vala said, feeling a little uncomfortable.

17

Elvar reached the steps leading down to the seafront. Removing his sneakers and socks, he started descending the steps, freezing midway when he caught sight of Vala, her hand clasped within another man's. An unfamiliar feeling stirred within him, a raw heat seething through his veins and bubbling in his stomach. His heart pounded wildly, its sonancy so powerful that it resonated throughout Elvar's entire body. The sensation of heat was suddenly replaced by an icy cold. Elvar's jaw tensed and he clenched his fists, finally forcing his feet to descend the remaining steps.

Vala and Merridyn had their backs to Elvar with their eyes closed in concentration. They did not hear his approach.

Elvar coughed deliberately, at the same time, trying to steady his breathing.

"Excuse me, sir," Elvar said, lightly tapping Merridyn's shoulder as he fought to maintain control of his emotions. "I do not believe I have had the pleasure of making your acquaintance." Merridyn turned, startled by Elvar's touch.

"You must be Elvar," Merridyn said, feeling his cheeks burn. "I am Merridyn Ashwood. It is a pleasure to meet you."

"He was assisting me with the enhanced barrier spell," Vala said, registering Elvar's stony expression. "Look, why don't we all get to know each other better over breakfast?"

"I regret that I cannot accept your kind invitation, Vala," Merridyn replied. "I am already late for work."

"Goodness," Vala said. "Sorry, I didn't realise! What do you do, incidentally?"

"I am Curator of Antiquities at the Museum of Classical History," Merridyn replied. "However, although I will need to take my leave now, I would be honoured to share lunch with you and Elvar, of course, say 1 p.m.?"

"Thank you for the offer," Elvar said tersely, "but I am not sure what our plans—"

"I am quite sure our plans are free," Vala quietly cut in. "We would love to, Merri. Thank you."

Elvar frowned, feeling unsettled and disquieted by Vala's actions. Vala watched Merridyn leave, waiting till he was far enough not to hear.

"Elvar!" Vala said, dispirited by his behaviour. "What is with you? That was bordering on rude!"

"What is with me?" Elvar said, raising his voice. "You were nowhere to be found this morning. I was out of my mind with worry, then I find you ... holding hands with another man!" Elvar's voice shook as he tried to calm himself.

"Elvar Evander Oakley—you're jealous!" Vala said, trying to suppress a giggle.

"And how is that funny?" Elvar demanded, though his anger was fast ebbing away and his mouth twitched slightly.

"Because it's completely misplaced," Vala said softly, touching Elvar's flamed cheek. "You do trust me?" "Unequivocally," Elvar replied.

"Then why?" Vala pressed.

Elvar sighed. "I do not know. It was difficult seeing you in such apparently intimate contact with ... and the easy manner between you both."

"Elvar, you are my Eternal Beloved," Vala said, lightly kissing him. "I could never look at another man that way, nor even entertain the idea."

"I know all this," Elvar said, feeling frustrated. "I did not say it was a logical response—emotions do not follow a code of logic, Vala! Besides, your feelings aside, it was quite clear that he was most enamoured with you."

"He might have shown a fleeting attraction to me, but nothing more than that!" Vala said. "Incidentally, why were you in such a panic about my whereabouts? I left you a note on the kitchen table. I thought you would see it when you went down for breakfast."

"It obviously escaped my attention," Elvar said. "I just panicked!""Come with me," Vala said, taking Elvar's hand and turning left around an outcrop of rocks.

"I am sorry, my love," Elvar said, feeling ashamed as he followed Vala along the beach, a low sinking feeling pooling in the pit of his stomach.

In spite of Elvar's outburst, Vala was feeling much more positive this morning, and though she felt a little ashamed to admit it, she was secretly pleased by Elvar's reaction to seeing her with Merridyn.

"Don't be sorry," Vala said tenderly, as they reached closer inland now at the base of sparkling white cliffs, their tiny mica crystals glinting in the sun. "It shows how much I mean to you. Besides, I'm pretty sure I would have reacted the same way."

Vala led Elvar to the mouth of a grotto, hollowed into one of the cliff fronts. A soft, mauve light emanated from within. She started removing her clothing, leaving it neatly folded on a nearby rock.

"What are you doing?" Elvar asked, raising an eyebrow.

Vala just smiled, so Elvar decided to reciprocate and also remove his clothes, following Vala into the grotto.

"I discovered this place earlier," Vala said. "I thought it rather beautiful and also rather ... secluded." Vala smiled suggestively.

"Was that with Merridyn?" Elvar asked, still feeling a hint of unease.

"No, my silly, jealous boy," Vala returned, trailing a finger down Elvar's chest. "It was before. I woke up early this morning, so I decided to explore the beach. I bumped into Merri on the way back and we just got talking. Right now, though ..."

Vala gently pushed Elvar against the wall of the cave. There was a pool of warm, salty water, which submerged him to waist level, but because Vala was considerably shorter, the water rose much higher and rippled around her breasts. Elvar watched, mesmerised. Vala traced her toe along Elvar's inner thigh, stopping before reaching his most intimate area.

She lifted one leg, sparks igniting in Vala's belly and travelling downwards as she pressed into Elvar, instantly connecting their bodies. Her heartbeat accelerated as Elvar lifted her, his hands grasping her bottom as she pushed and pulled against him, the water making her body feel almost weightless and her movements effortless. A slow burn of energy was sizzling inside Vala, building momentum and intensity— Elvar's occasional gasps of pleasure only serving to heighten the sensation. Elvar groaned, holding Vala's hips tightly against him. She felt him shudder, and her body responded in kind, sending a shockwave of rapturous euphoria throughout her body. She cried out Elvar's name, tugging her fingers through his hair.

First Vala's, then Elvar's Iridiscus pendants glowed. Neither noticed.

"Wow!" Vala said breathlessly. "That was some pretty spectacular make up sex!"

Elvar laughed, trying to catch his breath. "Remind me to argue with you more often!"

18

The Museum of Classical History, although Moredonian, was more typical of Avalonian architecture: an organic-looking structure with a white chalky façade and tall, spindly branch-like spires that entwined with the trees surrounding the building.

Vala and Elvar stepped inside together and were met with an eerie silence.

"Um, Elvar, where is everyone?"

Elvar's brow knitted. "I do not know—something feels amiss."

They continued to walk through the capacious halls of the museum, disregarding the numerous ancient fae relics and treasures displayed in glass cubes and cabinets. Their footsteps echoed loudly on the crystal flooring, the sound amplified by the absence of other people.

"Are you okay to go a little faster?" Elvar asked, tugging on Vala's hand.

Vala nodded in acknowledgement as their walking accelerated to a sprint, following the directions to the museum restaurant.

"Hello?" Vala called out, panting—nausea starting to claw at her stomach.

There was no answer. They continued running till they reached the door of the restaurant. Elvar leaned over, hands resting on his thighs as he waited for his breathing to normalise.

"This is creepy," Vala wheezed, taking in their deserted environment. "Wait!"

A piece of paper taped to one of the doors caught Vala's attention. In dark-blue cursive across the front, was Vala's name. She peeled it off the door and read it aloud.

"*Dear Vala and Elvar,*" Vala began, still trying to catch her breath. "*I tried to contact you both earlier, but although our crystals connected, neither of you answered so I assumed you were both otherwise occupied. However, a council meeting is in session to which all residents of Moredonia have been called. All I know is that it is a matter of grave importance, and I believe it is best that you both convene with us expeditiously.*

Sorry about lunch—I will make it up to you both tomorrow if you are free.

Warmest regards,

Merri X"

"We should go! Now!" Elvar said, grabbing Vala's hand and running back down the corridor.

*

They arrived at the council building, red-faced, sweaty, and gasping for breath. As they pushed open the door to the meeting chamber, all eyes were upon them.

"Um, sorry," Elvar said, turning a deeper shade of crimson. "We only just received word of the meeting."

"Please, my friends," the chairperson said kindly, "be seated. We were just about to begin."

Vala scanned the crowds for Merridyn, spotting him as he waved them over.

"Hi!" Merridyn whispered, a little amused by their flushed appearance. "I saved you both a seat."

"Hey," Vala acknowledged, quickly slipping into the seat next to Merridyn. "Thanks, by the way."

Elvar nodded his head at Merridyn in acknowledgement, but caught himself scowling, so quickly assumed a more neutral expression.

"Fellow Moredonians and visitors to our fine land," the chairperson boomed. "We convene today to bring you tragic and disturbing news. News of such gravity that we have officially declared this a state of emergency."

Hushed, alarmed whispers passed between anxious faces in the crowds as they prepared themselves for what was coming.

"As I was saying," the chairperson vociferated, her voice reverberating off the domed walls. "We received word earlier today of the death of a young man in the Briallania region. This was no natural passing, obviously, as the man involved was barely more than a child at twenty-two years of age. He was discovered in the early hours of this morning by his sister. You can imagine how greatly distressing this was for her, but more so to find her brother's body in a state of undress, lying ossified under his bed coverings."

The chairperson paused for a moment to sip at a glass of water. As she did so, a buzz of hushed but alarmed murmuring resounded through the chamber.

The chairperson deliberately coughed to silence the people before continuing. "We are all painfully aware that this ossification is a characteristic result of the Spindler's soul snatching. However, throughout our recorded history there has only been one of his kind, and thanks to the bravery of this gifted young lady." She stopped and gesticulated towards Vala.

"Please join me, Lady Oakley-Pendragon," the chairperson said.

Vala's heart leapt as her name was called, blood rushing to her face and the palms of her hands perspiring. She shakily rose to her feet, gently prompted by both Elvar and Merridyn, and made her way to the podium.

"It is an honour to meet you, Lady Oakley-Pendragon," the chairperson said in a quieter tone, smiling kindly at Vala. "Because of this amazing young lady, the Spindler has been eradicated. No matter what the threat is that faces us now, we must remember that we do have the power to defeat it!"

A cheer rose through the auditorium, and Vala stood there, feeling self-conscious and uncomfortable from the attention bestowed upon her. Although her face felt fiery hot, her hands and feet had turned icily cold.

"It would be logical to assume," the chairperson said soberly, "that another like the Spindler has arisen. Maybe while the Spindler was alive, he reserved a number of souls for this entity—enough to satiate its needs. We know this is how he managed his minions—that he gave them a minimal number of souls to assimilate, enough to only just sustain their unnatural lifespan. It has never been in a minion's capability to absorb a soul without the Spindler administering it to them in some way. We do not fully understand how this process works, only that the minions have only ever been able to collect souls, not assimilate them. It is possible that one or more of them have somehow developed the faculty to do this, or ... as I mentioned a moment ago, there is another like him."

"Excuse me, Madam Speaker," Vala spoke quietly, lightly touching the chairperson's arm. "May I speak to you privately for a moment?"

"Of course, Lady Oakley-Pendragon," the chairperson replied. "I will call an intermission."

"My dear citizens," the chairperson said, "there will be a thirty minute recess. There are refreshments in the adjacent chamber.
Please do take the time to collect your thoughts. I thank you kindly for your patience."

The chairperson gently rested her hand on Vala's back and led her to another room at the back of the auditorium, politely requesting that Vala remove her shoes upon entering. It was much less formal than Vala was expecting: the walls decorated with animated images of the sea and shoreline—waves rolling gently to land, unfamiliar marine animals frolicking in the water, creating a fine ocean spray with their activity, and seabirds squawking in the powderblue sky. A large cream Furlomyn rug covered the Viaspan wood flooring, and a spacious, plush oval ivory sofa sat in its centre. At the far end of the room was a curved tree-like bookcase with numerous ancient-looking tomes. Vala had not seen anything like it: the wood appeared to be alive with growing leaves and tiny branches. The room smelt of the sea, and in spite of herself, Vala relaxed a little. The chairperson entreated Vala to be seated and then sat beside her.

"Firstly, I must introduce myself," the chairperson said, smiling warmly at Vala. "I am Perravyn Tilawood, and I am most honoured to finally meet you, Lady Oakley-Pendragon."

"Please," Vala said, flushing slightly. "Just call me Vala—it's certainly less of a mouthful and would make me more comfortable."

"Certainly," Perravyn replied, looking at Vala intently. "So what is it that you wish to speak to me about, Vala?"

"Well, regarding the entity that you spoke of ..." Vala's heartbeat rapidly accelerated, and she inhaled deeply, unintentionally exhaling loudly before she continued. "I'm sorry, this is difficult."

"It is all right," Perravyn said softly. "Take your time. I will bring you a glass of water while you collect your thoughts."

Perravyn walked to a corner of the room where a tall cabinet stood, stocked with an array of goblets, glasses, and mugs. She removed a glass from the cabinet and held it under an ornately carved wooden panel in the wall. Vala watched as a gentle stream of water filled the glass. Perravyn brought the water to Vala, placing her hand on Vala's arm.

"As distressing as it must be reliving memories of your encounter with the Spindler, I get the feeling that something else has transpired more recently?"

"There have been some developments," Vala said quietly. "I was summoned by Amalia and brought to Elsorriden."

"The Celestia?" Perravyn looked at Vala in awe.

"Yes," Vala confirmed. "Anyway, I spoke with Amalia; she told me that she hadn't *moved on* because her sister, Nimeva, Merlin, and her niece, Merevina, were not on the other side. She asserted that they must still somehow be on the earthly plane and implored me to seek them out."

"That seems like a heavy responsibility."

"Yes," Vala said, "but the main reason she beseeched me to find them is that I am apparently in very grave danger from someone Amalia believes to be very powerful—a girl. I saw a dark-haired girl in Amalia's vision."

"And you believe this girl is in some way linked to the attack on that poor boy?"

"I forgot to mention," Vala said, "I was attacked by a Dessicatus a few weeks ago. It pulled me from my horse ..." Vala's voice caught and a tear ran down her cheek.

Perravyn felt the blood drain from her face, but prompted her to continue, gently brushing Vala's tear away with her thumb.

"I was badly injured," Vala continued. "My brother destroyed the Dessicatus, mirroring spell, but the fall left me comatose till I was healed by Elvar and his father. After that, things went back to normal until our journey here. Elvar had parked our carriage outside a tavern and had left briefly to attend to our horses. While he was gone ..." Vala felt her heart palpitate and nausea rise to her stomach.

"Breathe deeply, Vala," Perravyn instructed.

"I was alone in the carriage when a girl approached me. As soon as she was sure of my identity, she grabbed my wrist and said that her mistress sought an audience with me. When I looked at her again, her face was hideously deformed—skeletal and rotting, her skin charred."

"The Dessicati have only ever attacked when sent out to gather souls for the Spindler, and always under the cover of night whilst their victims slept—never in broad daylight!" Perravyn exclaimed, clearly shocked by Vala's account. "You were right to tell me, Vala. As I mentioned before, unless one or more of them have developed the ability to assimilate souls, they are doing the bidding of another—another like the Spindler."

"But how could we not have known before?" Vala said. "If there is another like him, why are there no reports of sightings? The Spindler, in spite of all his help, still procured souls directly. Surely this other ... whatever it is ... would be compelled to do the same?"

"We know very little about the Spindler," Perravyn said. "You, Elvar, and your companions, are the only ones, other than Guinevere, to have survived an encounter with the Spindler. We know next to nothing of his origins, though it has been suggested that he was once fae and that something happened to darken his soul, something terrible that catalysed his descent into evil."

"Amalia seems to think that my soul-mirroring ability won't be enough this time," Vala said, sighing.

"Yes," Perravyn conceded, "that is rather more worrying. However, we can only take whatever preventative measures that are at our disposal. Do you truly intend to seek out Merlin and his family?"

"As soon as my sister-in-law has her baby," Vala replied. "Yes, I do."

"And where does one begin on such a quest?"

"We intend to procure their amulets from the Royal household first," Vala said. "But unless they guide us elsewhere, we will start with Merlin's home in Cavania."

"I truly hope you are successful in your endeavour," Perravyn said. "And, please, keep in touch."

Perravyn smiled and clasped Vala's hand between hers. "You are a very special girl, Vala. Do not lose sight of that. I must return to address my people now."

"Do you intend to divulge what I told you?" Vala asked.

"I think it best not to cause further alarm," Perravyn said. "I will give them a description of the girl we believe may be responsible, but no more than that."

Vala returned to her seat between Elvar and Merridyn as Perravyn stepped onto the podium to continue her speech.

"Thank you for your patience," Perravyn said. "It has come to light that the perpetrator of this terrible crime may well be female with dark wavy hair, which of course, in terms of physical appearance, will fit a great deal of us—we cannot exclude the use of a glamour either. However, she is likely to have a very different aura as the Spindler will have done, though what form this will take, we cannot be certain.

"What I can assure you, is that we are doing our very best to provide round the clock protection to all citizens of Candalia. As I speak, royal sentries guard our borders and the borders of our fellow Candalians. This will continue until the threat to us has been eradicated.

"Be vigilant, my people, and should any of you encounter or even see anyone suspicious, please contact either myself or one of the other council members immediately. Do not, I repeat, *do not* approach the suspect yourself. Likewise, as has always been the case, should you spot any of the Spindler's minions, alert us straight away." Perravyn reached for a glass of water and took a large gulp.

"Please now," Perravyn said, skilfully keeping the fear she felt from showing in her voice, "return to your lives and do as you have always done. We are a strong people, capable of overcoming any adversity, and together we shall overcome this threat. With those words, I draw this session to a close; I and the other Council members will be in my private chambers."

Perravyn glanced surreptitiously at Vala and gave her a discreet wave as Elvar gently ushered her out of the building. Once they were outside, Merridyn let out a loud whistle.

"That was rather intense!" Merridyn said. "Though obviously not entirely a surprise."

"Yes," Vala said, closing her eyes for a moment, overcome by exhaustion and feeling unable to say much else.

Elvar looked at his wife, and seeing Vala's fatigue, scooped her into his arms, taking her by surprise. "If you will excuse us, my wife needs to rest."

"*Your wife* can speak for herself!"

"You do look tired, Vala," Merridyn said, lightly touching her arm.

Elvar glared at him, his jaw clenching as his gaze shifted to Merridyn's hand, still resting on Vala's arm.

"I'm absolutely shattered!" Vala admitted. "Though if that offer of lunch tomorrow is still on, we're definitely up for it!" "Absolutely!" Merridyn replied, finally removing his hand from Vala's arm. "It was lovely to meet you, Vala. You too, Elvar."

"Ditto, Merri," Vala said, smiling. "See you at 1 p.m. tomorrow?"

"I look forward to it!"

Elvar exhaled loudly, feeling an uncomfortable heat rising within him. "Goodbye, Mr Ashwood."

He turned his back to Merridyn and ascended with Vala into the air. Vala rested her head on Elvar's shoulder, and they flew back to the beach house in silence. Once inside, Elvar gently lay Vala on their bed.

"You're still jealous," Vala said, yawning.

"I am," Elvar admitted. "I cannot help it! He really likes you, Vala—*really* likes you—and I do not like him touching you."

"Elvar, he knows you're my Eternal Beloved, that we are married, so he must know that he doesn't stand a chance of being with me in that way."

"Maybe so, but as I said earlier, emotions do not follow a logical path," Elvar replied. "And while I know you do not feel that way for him, I am unhappy about him being so openly expressive in his attraction for you."

"I'm too tired for this, Elvar," Vala turned over on her side, curling into a foetal position. "I need to sleep. Wake me up for dinner."

Elvar sighed in resignation, setting an alarm on the clock as he settled down next to her and pulled a Furlomyn blanket over them both.

19

Vala felt the warmth of sunlight on her eyelids and stretched out. For several minutes, she felt disorientated and confused. It had been late afternoon when she fell asleep, and now? She could see through the gauzy curtains that it was clearly morning.

I couldn't have slept all that time! Vala thought, before turning her attentions to Elvar's recumbent form.

"Elvar?" Vala said gently, noticing that he was still fully clothed.

Elvar mumbled incoherently and blearily opened his eyes, blinking a few times before focussing on Vala's face.

"What time is it?" Elvar asked, yawning.

"It's morning," Vala replied, lovingly moving a lock of Elvar's hair from his eyes.

"Morning!" Elvar said, sitting up suddenly. "But how? I set an alarm."

"We must have slept through it," Vala said, rubbing her eyes and pulling Elvar back down to face her.

Elvar stared at her intently, placing a hand on her cheek. "Do you have any idea how much I love you?"

"I have an inkling," Vala said, reciprocating the gesture. "And you know how much I love you, which is why you have no reason to be jealous."

Elvar rubbed his hands over his face, a tight knot forming in his stomach.

"Elvar," Vala said, taking his hand in hers, "I love you. I am in love with you and you alone—I always will be. I am not romantically interested in Merri, I promise. And yes, I do get that it's difficult, I would find it difficult were the situation reversed, but we're young, Elvar, and unless we lock ourselves away from the world, this is bound to happen from time to time."

"You are right, of course," Elvar returned. "As always, my infinitely wise wife."

"Yup, that's me—always right!" Vala said, laughing.

"So, could I interest you in breakfast?" Elvar said, his stomach growls betraying him.

"Hungry much?" Vala said, tickling him.

"Ravenous!" Elvar replied, laughing and trying to evade Vala's tickling.

"Well, if you're cooking," Vala began, "and for clarification, that means you *are* cooking, I would like Misenberry pancakes with Lintelbark syrup."

As Elvar stood over the stove adding to the pile of freshly cooked pancakes, Vala came up behind him and wrapped her arms around his waist. Elvar placed his free hand over hers and smiled. Although the idea of seeing Merridyn again made him slightly uneasy, the twisted knot of ... what was it? Fear perhaps? Whatever it was, it had started to dissipate and he felt more peaceful again.

Vala watched Elvar closely as they sat, eating pancakes in comfortable silence. She had palpably felt Elvar's anxiety, his discomfort over the feelings her acquaintance with Merridyn had stirred. She could sense his internal struggle to stamp out the unfamiliar feelings of jealousy that had arisen—feelings that were at odds with his peaceful, relaxed nature. It pained Vala, an actual tight physical sensation within her heart, knowing that Elvar was suffering. She reached across the table and placed her hand over his, smiling. Elvar looked up and smiled back.

"How are the pancakes?" he asked between mouthfuls.

"Delicious," Vala replied. "Cooking is definitely one of your fortes, as are many things ..." She flashed Elvar a wicked grin.

"Maybe after breakfast I could sharpen my skills at one of those other things?" Elvar said, leaning across the table and placing a gentle kiss on Vala's lips.

Vala darted her tongue over Elvar's bottom lip. "You had a little syrup there," she said, her voice husky.

"Always such a naughty little temptress," Elvar said, his lips still touching hers. "Let me light the fire first—it is a little chilly in here for a romantic atmosphere."

Elvar walked to the fireplace, tossed in a few logs, and quietly said an incantation. Flames sprang to life, licking at the logs, and before long, created a roaring fire. He grabbed a few cushions from the sofa and placed them in front of the fire, inviting Vala to join him. Even though they had made love countless times, Vala still experienced an excited quiver of anticipation in her belly. She lay down beside him. They slowly undressed one another, mouths and hands exploring each other's bodies as though it were undiscovered territory. As their bodies became one, Vala felt a connection between them so powerful that she could no longer tell where she ended and Elvar began.

20

Seeing Vala and Elvar at the entrance to the museum restaurant, Merridyn opened the door and welcomed them inside.

"Good afternoon!" Merridyn said, beaming at Vala and Elvar. "It is wonderful to see you both again."

Merridyn took Vala's hand, bringing it to his lips to kiss lightly. "My lady, how are you feeling today?"

"Much better, thanks," Vala replied. "It is good to see you too, Merri."

"I trust that you are well, Elvar?"

"I am very well, thank you," Elvar said stiffly. "And yourself?"

"Yes," Merridyn said, still smiling. "In spite of the rather tense circumstances, I am in good spirits. Now ..." Merridyn made a sweeping motion towards one of the tables, "please be seated."

Vala squeezed Elvar's hand reassuringly, noting the tense expression on his face as they sat down. She watched him scanning the menu but wondered if he was really taking in anything at all or just using it as a convenient distraction.

"They serve an excellent Marisali here," Merridyn suggested. "It has a perfect synergistic herb and spice blend. I believe they use *Capsicum loralis* spiced honey with Genevis root, Silanchi berries, garlic and fresh Mevelis. You may not be familiar with the last one; it's an herb that grows in the alpine regions of Briallania. It has a sweet, slightly lemony-mint taste."

"You certainly know how to sell it!" Vala said. "I'm impressed with your culinary knowledge. How do you know so much about it?"

"I enjoy cooking!" Merridyn replied, lounging back on his chair and smiling at Vala. "I find it relaxing, therapeutic even. I also asked the chef what ingredients she uses."

"Well, with a pitch like that, how can I possibly not want to try it?" Vala said, smiling back at Merridyn. "How about you, Elvar?"

Vala looked at Elvar. He had barely moved and still seemed overly occupied with studying the menu. He glanced up at Vala and tried to force a smile, but it was strained. She noticed that the tips of his fingers had turned white from gripping the menu so firmly.

Elvar looked back at Vala, watching her expectant gaze. What was he supposed to say? He had been staring at the menu for the entire time Vala and Merridyn had been talking, but he hadn't heard a single word. He hurriedly glanced at his options, although it would be difficult to force down any food when he didn't have much of an appetite.

"I will have some Savima bread with Chavalet, and Misenberry juice to drink," Elvar replied.

"Oh," Merridyn replied. "I thought maybe we could all share a jug of Velinosa between us?"

"I would rather not consume any alcohol just now," Elvar replied tersely.

"Well, I certainly wouldn't mind some," Vala said. "So unless you want us both to get very drunk, wouldn't it be better to share it with us?"

"As you wish, my love," Elvar said, sighing.

Elvar gulped down a large mouthful of wine as they waited for their food to be served, its warming effects relaxing the slightly constricted feeling in his throat and chest.

"So," Merridyn began hesitantly, "I know it is probably none of my business, but yesterday, Vala, when you spoke privately to Perravyn ..."

"It was about my visitations with Amalia," Vala said. "And the encounter with creepy death girl."

"Who was probably a Dessicatus using a glamour," Merridyn replied. "You know, many of us believe that you are one of the Chosen."

"Yes," Vala said, rolling her eyes. "I believe you referred to me as that yesterday. Elvar's filled me in on Merlin's prophecy already."

"Did you mention anything about the Grail, Elvar?" Merridyn asked.

"Sorry, what was that?" Elvar replied, suddenly realising that Merridyn had spoken to him.

"I was just enquiring as to when you spoke to Vala of Merlin's prophecy, whether you had mentioned the Grail?"

"Um, no," Elvar said. "I did not wish to overwhelm Vala with too much information. However, I am sure you have piqued her curiosity now, so be my guest."

"Are you sure you do not mind?" Merridyn asked.

"Go ahead, Mr ... Merri, it is fine," Elvar returned, managing a genuine smile for the first time.

"Yes, Merri," Vala cut in impatiently. "What about the Grail?"

"Firstly," Merridyn began, chewing on his thumb thoughtfully, "the Grail is not an object, nor is it exactly any one thing. The Grail, if you like, is a form of Divine magic that has, up till now, been bestowed by the angelic realm, upon certain key individuals—human and fae—throughout history. However, according to Merlin's prophecy, the full power of the Grail will be, or ..."

Merridyn paused and smiled thoughtfully, locking eyes with Vala.

"Or what?" Vala prompted.

"Or already has been, converged with two souls chosen to unite the fae and human realms."

"And you think that's me?" Vala said, rolling her eyes.

"It might be," Merridyn returned. "Before you and your brother, no one had any clue when or to whom exactly the prophecy might be referring. Tarrys' origins had been kept quiet; we had not known that a fae/human hybrid from Guinevere and Arthur Pendragon's bloodline had been born. When you were born, Vala, again only a select few knew of your existence—those chosen to keep you safe."

"Until the Spindler," Vala said, tightly coiling a lock of hair around her index finger.

"Yes," Merridyn replied. "After that ..."

A waitress arrived at their table carrying a steaming earthenware pot of Marisali Satura, two bowls, spoons, butter, and a platter of bread.

"Your bread and juice will be served in just a moment, sir," the waitress said, looking at Elvar as she inclined her head slightly.

Once Elvar's meal arrived, Merridyn encouraged them both to tuck in, laughing as Vala's stomach rumbled in response.

Vala picked up the ladle and spooned in a modest amount of Marisali before buttering a slice of bread and biting into it—the warm, slightly sweet taste and airy texture mingling with the creamy molten butter. *Delicious!* Vala thought, momentarily distracted by the pleasure it brought.

"So," Merridyn continued between mouthfuls, "as I was saying, after you defeated the Spindler, there was much speculation that you might well be the one, then after it was discovered that you and Tarrys are brother and sister, almost everyone was adamant that the two of you are the ones Merlin prophesised about."

"So what about *Arthur* being the *once and future king*?" Elvar interjected.

"Y-eah," Merridyn drawled. "That is the part that does not quite fit."

"Backtracking a bit," Vala said. "What exactly is the Grail? What is it that's bestowed upon those chosen and converged with their souls?"

"The Grail blessings are all that we know of the Grail thus far," Merridyn explained, sucking in a mouthful of air as he swallowed a spoonful of overly hot Marisali. "Sorry about that! Yes, anyway, the blessings began in the time of Jesus Christ, first amongst his prophets, and then upon various key figures in fae and human history. The blessing itself is given through visitation of a special angel, the Angel of *Pax Aeterna* or *Pax et Lux.*"

"That last one has something to do with light, but I am still not terribly familiar with Latin," Vala said.

"Sorry," Merridyn said, "I did not realise. The first phrase means *eternal peace*, the other *peace and light*. The Angel imparts a special gift, a power to bring about peace where there is dissent and discord: to disseminate the touch of God's love, especially to those most in need, to wherever there is suffering. To give you some idea, Arthur Pendragon was one of those chosen, and in recent human history: Winston Churchill, John F Kennedy, Mahatma Gandhi, Nelson Mandela. The prophesied pair are different though: they have been selected, or will be, to possess a power so great that it will be the catalyst for peace in the human realm and will also heal the rift between the fae and human realms."

Elvar took a bite of his toasted bread before turning to Vala and protectively placing his hand over hers, his gaze fixed upon her. "Are you all right, my love?"

"I'm fine," Vala said, "though I really don't think I'm the saviour of the world! I would know, Merri, if I were destined for something like that."

"She does have a point," Elvar said, squeezing Vala's hand supportively. "Vala possesses considerable intuition."

"Well," Merridyn said, placing a finger on his chin thoughtfully with a challenging glint in his eyes, "maybe the answer lies somewhere in yours and/or your brother's future descendants. Either way, I cannot imagine that you are not directly, or indirectly, the key to the prophecy."

The three of them were quiet for a while as they finished their meal.

"I have been meaning to ask you both something since Vala divulged the plan to search for Merlin: I would be greatly honoured if you would consider me accompanying you on your quest?" Merridyn asked, his voice catching a little as he chewed nervously on his thumb.

"Merri?" Vala said hesitantly. "Are you sure you really want to volunteer? You know what happened on our last mission. It could well be dangerous, especially with the Dessicatus and goodness knows who or what else is at large, not to mention psycho girl!"

"Whom, if Amalia's vision is correct, you are most likely to encounter," Merridyn replied, the corners of his mouth quirking and with a little more enthusiasm than befitted the situation, Vala thought.

"Your bravery is admirable," Elvar offered, "as long as you realise the potential peril involved in such an undertaking?"

"I do," Merridyn replied solemnly. "I believe my knowledge of history and antiquities could be of service to you."

"In which case, we would be honoured to have you on board," Elvar said.

Vala gaped at Elvar in surprise. A smile tugged at the corners of his mouth in response to Vala's expression and he raised one eyebrow at her.

"Thank you!" Merridyn said, beaming at them both. "Thank you! So when do you head back to Avalonia?"

"Vala has to return to the human realm on Wednesday, so we shall be travelling back on Tuesday," Elvar said. "Tomorrow is her birthday. You are most welcome to join us for a celebratory drink at our beach house in the evening."

Although Vala showed no outward sign of surprise, she contemplated what had brought about Elvar's sudden change in attitude towards Merridyn. She leaned back in her chair, wistfully twirling and re-twirling the same lock of hair around her fingers.

"Vala?" Merridyn said, waving a hand in front of her face and breaking her out of her trance.

"Huh?" Vala said as she realised that Merridyn was addressing her. "What was the question?"

"I did not ask one yet!" Merridyn replied, laughing. "I was just wondering if you are happy for me to intrude on your birthday celebrations tomorrow?"

"Don't be silly!" Vala said, touching Merridyn's arm lightly. "You won't be intruding! Besides, we'd like a chance to say goodbye before we depart."

"I would love to then!" Merridyn said, spontaneously squeezing Vala's hand. "So as I am quite certain you are still very young, would it be polite to ask you how old you are?"

Elvar frowned briefly at Merridyn's familiarity with Vala, but he was surprised to find that the uncomfortable feelings passed quickly and that he did not harbour any ill feeling towards Merridyn at all.

"I'm going to be nineteen," Vala said. "My last year as a teenager! So as you've asked me, how old are *you*, Merri?" "I am twenty-two," Merridyn said, smiling.

"Just a year younger than my brother," Vala commented. "I can't wait for you to meet him."

"I look forward to it too," Merridyn said. "Meeting the other half of the dynamic duo—it will be an interesting experience!"

Vala playfully punched Merridyn's arm and laughed. "Shut up!"

2 1

Elvar watched Vala's sleeping form for a while; he never grew tired of looking at her and smiled as he stroked her fanned-out auburn hair, observing her long black lashes flutter as her eyelids moved. *No doubt lost in a* dream, Elvar thought. His eyes followed down, taking in her slender neck, the soft curvature of her voluptuous breasts, her hourglass waist and hips. Elvar felt his body responding and gently kissed her lips, tracing a finger over Vala's chin and down her neck. Her eyes flickered open and Vala rubbed the sleep away, yawning.

"Happy birthday, Eternal Beloved," Elvar said, his voice low and sultry.

Vala turned to face him, returning his kiss as he ran his hands over her curves. She felt his arousal pressing against her. Nerve endings tingled in response and her skin sensitised to his touch—hungry to crush her body to his. As an electrifying throb pulsated between her legs, Vala sat astride Elvar, bringing their bodies together. They moved together in perfect synchronicity till she felt Elvar's body quake and hers respond in kind.

She lay on top of Elvar, her head nestled into his chest, listening to the cadence of his heartbeat: fast at first, but gradually slowing.
He enclosed her in his arms, kissing the top of Vala's head.

"I love you, my gorgeous birthday girl," Elvar said, his voice muffled by her hair. "And I could happily spend the whole day doing this with you—you make me feel amazing—but, I have other plans for you ... for us."

"I love you too," Vala said, tipping her head up to kiss him. "So, what are these other plans? Because I would also be quite partial to a whole day of amazing sex with you."

"Vala!" Elvar said, returning her kiss. "Do not weaken my resolve! I have a special surprise for you, though we could ..."

"What?"

"Well, we could take a shower together first ..."

*

"So why exactly can't I get dressed?" Vala asked, wrapped snugly in a towel after their considerably long shower together.

"You can," Elvar replied. "But just underwear—wait and see."

After Vala had changed into her undergarments, Elvar took her by the hand and patted the bed, prompting her to be seated.

"Close your eyes."

Vala closed her eyes and waited, curious as she heard Elvar's footsteps and a rustling sound.

"You can open them now," Elvar said, sitting beside her on the bed.

As Vala opened her eyes, she was presented with three boxes stacked with the smallest on top in descending size order. Each box was lined with patterned Damask silk, each a different colour: peach, pale yellow, and cream, the colour of her wedding bouquet. All the boxes were tied with an iridescent organza ribbon.

Vala picked up the top box, carefully untying the ribbon and lifting the lid of the box. She pushed away the layers of tissue paper to reveal a necklace, bracelet, and earring set, all crafted from a clear prismatic crystal with a phosphorescent pink glow contained within the centre of each stone.

"Oh wow!" Vala exclaimed in awe, holding the necklace in front of her. "They're beautiful, Elvar! Like diamonds ... only, not."

"Merithius stones," Elvar explained. "Quite rare and found only on the ocean bed, right here in fact. The glow is caused by a phosphorescent mineral—*Tilsus rosaceus*—the Merithius crystal forms around it."

"Thank you, Elvar," Vala said, kissing him lightly before moving on to the next present.

As before, she unwrapped the box carefully and moved aside the tissue paper. Nestled under the wrapping was a pair of shoes: midnight-blue silk with tiny crystalline flowers with equally tiny crystalline leaves.

"They're exquisite!" Vala gushed, pulling them out and wiggling her bare feet into them. "And they fit perfectly. You are amazing ... an amazing, clever, kind and obscenely sexy husband!"

"You are not too shabby yourself, my lady," Elvar replied, laughing.

Vala picked up the final box, laying it across her lap before untying the ribbon. She slowly raised the lid and parted the tissue paper. Vala lifted the midnight silk from the box, gently unfurling it to reveal a stunning dress. Vala held it up against her: it was kneelength, asymmetric one-shouldered, and tapered in at the waist. On the shoulder and hemline were tiny sparkling gems arranged into the same patterns as those on her shoes.

"Oh!" Vala said, hugging Elvar tightly.

"It brings me great pleasure to see your enthused reaction, beloved," Elvar said, cupping Vala's face. "I am certain you will look utterly beguiling in them, though not as beguiling as you look without any attire at all." Elvar flashed her a wicked grin.

"However ..." Elvar continued, intentionally making Vala wait.

"If you don't finish that sentence right now, I may have to tear off those smart clothes you're dressed in and jump your bones again," Vala threatened.

"Okay," Elvar said, laughing, "we cannot be late, so ..."

He pulled out a small box from his jacket pocket and handed it to Vala.

"What's this?" Vala asked, not expecting yet another present.

"Why not find out?" Elvar said, standing behind her, his breath in her hair.

Vala popped open the lid of the box; nestled inside was a silver ring with a jewel in the centre. The metal was thicker where it joined to the gem setting, tapering off to form the band of the ring. The jewel itself was a deep violet-indigo crafted into a rounded square shaped with delicate swirled embellishments.

"It is an Iridiscus ring," Elvar explained, unfastening the Iridiscus pendant that Vala always wore around her neck. "It will work in exactly the same way as your pendant, but gives you the freedom to wear other jewellery."

Vala slipped on the Iridiscus ring; it fit her middle finger perfectly. She held up her hair, allowing Elvar to fasten the new necklace around her neck. Elvar inclined his head and kissed the side of
Vala's neck.

"It looks beautiful on you," Elvar said huskily. "Now, you better get dressed or we will be late for our first engagement."

"Engagement?" Vala asked, her curiosity piqued. "For what? Where?"

"Now that, my dear," Elvar teased, "would spoil the surprise. Just slip your gorgeous body into that dress and um ... maybe dry your hair."

22

Half an hour later, Vala and Elvar stood at the entrance of a dark shaft.

"Fiat lux lucida," Elvar incanted as light flooded the vertical shaft. Vala peered down the long spiralling passageway with wonder. Where on earth could this lead to? The walls were adorned with frescoes depicting the sea—very similar to those in the private Council Chambers: dolphins and other unidentifiable marine life leapt in the painted walls, gulls cawed in the skies, and the waves gently lapped at the shore.

Elvar continued to lead her further inside as they descended the spiral walkway, the constant turns making Vala vertiginous.

"We are almost there," Elvar said, squeezing her shoulder.

"I really hope so!" Vala said, putting her hand over her mouth. "Because I'm on the verge of up-chucking, Elvar. Thank goodness we haven't eaten breakfast yet!"

"My apologies, beloved," Elvar replied, "but it will be worth it."

They approached what appeared to be a wall with a painting of the mouth of the cave that they stood in presently. However, Vala had had enough experience of Candalia to know that walls were often not what they seemed. She heard Elvar whisper a few words as he touched the wall, and his hand passed through. He gently tugged on Vala's hand and she followed him.

The sight that met Vala almost took her breath away—it was as though they were standing on the ocean bed itself. All around them was ocean and marine life: dolphins, starfish, octopi, and other strange creatures, but they were not in the water. It seemed to Vala as though they were contained within a colossal, invisible bubble: an oceanarium without the glass. In the centre of this monumental atrium was a dining area with pale-blue wooden furnishings.

"OMG!" Vala squealed. "This is mind-blowing, Elvar! How does it work?"

"We are standing within a containment field: an invisible shield that is separating us from the sea."

"And how is that barrier kept in place?" Vala asked nervously. "I presume there isn't anything that might just compromise its integrity?"

"No, absolutely not!" Elvar assured her. "It is regularly maintained and checked ... see those?" Elvar indicated towards some small electronic units with flashing lights, situated around the perimeter of the barrier.

Vala nodded.

"Those are ultra-sensitive monitors," Elvar explained. "So you have absolutely nothing to worry about!"

Assured by Elvar's words, Vala continued to step further afield till she reached out and her hands met the barrier. A faint tingle coursed through her fingertips, causing her to instinctively drop her hands to her sides. Vala stood, staring out into the depths of the ocean, captivated by the sights she beheld. Some of the flora and fauna were familiar to her: bottle-nosed dolphins, stingrays, jellyfish, a colourful array of fish and coral. Some of it, however, looked very alien indeed: there were large armoured creatures with a silver metallic sheen and no discernible eyes, some kind of whalelike animal with pink-and-blue marbled skin and a large frill that continually changed colour, rainbow-coloured fern-like plants, and a myriad of translucent tendrilled creatures that emitted an incandescent glow.

"What are all these?" Vala asked in wonder.

"The multi-coloured plants are *Espiritus irideus*—if you look closely, they have a gold sparkle. Those armoured animals are *Mollicidum argentum*—you may see another type, *Mollicidum aurum*—they are a rich gold colour, though somewhat rarer. Those ..." Elvar said, snorting as one of the whale-like creatures swam up to him, observing curiously. "These are very sociable and gentle animals—we call them Marosa. And the little luminescent creatures belong to the *Lucideum genus*, but I do not know what they all are, except for those ones," Elvar indicated towards a group of small translucent, spherical life forms with glowing pink centres.

"That luminescent pink," Vala said, her brow knitted, "it's the same as the Merithius gem."

"That would be because these little animals, *Lucideum rosaceum*, excrete a mineralised substance called *Tilsus rosaceus*, around which the Merithius crystal forms."

"So basically I'm wearing sea creature poo," Vala said dryly.

"Um, well ..." Elvar said, mouth twitching at the corners. "It not like what we ... um, it is not riddled with microbes or anything unpleasant and ..." Elvar started to laugh.

"It is much more attractive, do you not agree?" Elvar continued, openly laughing now.

Vala playfully punched his arm before pulling him into a lingering embrace.

"Thank you, Elvar," Vala said breathlessly, finally breaking contact for air, "for all of this. It's perfect."

"Even with the sea creature poo?" Elvar raised an eyebrow.

"Yes, you muppet!" Vala said, snorting.

"Anyway, you need sustenance, my lady," Elvar said, pulling out one of the chairs and gesturing for Vala to be seated. "We have more to do today, and I would not wish for you to be fatigued so early."

"Fatigued?" Vala repeated, leaning across the table towards Elvar. "Are you planning on engaging me in a little sexercise before lunch?"

Elvar blushed furiously. "You are a wicked girl, Vala Oakley Pendragon—always distracting me with your seductive ways!"

"Like you need much encouragement!"

"I need no encouragement," Elvar said, his thumb brushing her cheek. "Quite the opposite! And now, I really need to focus on something else!"

"So where is everyone else?" Vala asked.

"I hired the oceanarium exclusively for our use," Elvar said, stroking Vala's cheek. "And very shortly, breakfast will be served."

As if on cue, a waiter appeared with a large silver platter laden with a cornucopia of food, a pitcher, and two steaming mugs.

"Enjoy!" the waiter said, bowing in turn to Vala and Elvar. "Please let me know if there is anything else I can bring you."

"Thank you!" Vala said. "I can't imagine that we'll be needing anything else, though."

Vala picked up one of the pastries. "This one doesn't look familiar. What is it?"

"It is a Moredonian delicacy called Zefanea; it is filled with Uquilico puree. The pastry is coated with Alushi nectar and dusted with Minchi nuts and Chando pod shavings," Elvar said, breaking off a piece and placing it in Vala's mouth.

"OMG!" Vala said as she swallowed. "That is out of this world!"

"Out of the human world, maybe!" Elvar replied, smiling. "The rest of the selection, you are probably familiar with, except these."

Elvar picked up a pale blue berry and popped it in Vala's mouth.

"These are Uqualis berries—they grow in vines by the sea front."

"They taste like salted caramel," Vala said thoughtfully. "Thank you again for this, you always make everything so amazing."

"You being part of my life, my twin soul, makes everything amazing for me. I love you, Vala, for always."

"And I, you," Vala replied, touching her nose to Elvar's and popping a berry in his mouth.

23

After Vala and Elvar had finished eating, they observed the marine life for a while. Then Elvar led Vala back up through the shaft into the daylight outside.

"So what's next on the itinerary?" Vala asked excitedly. "Another surprise?"

"Of course," Elvar replied. "What would be the fun in telling you? I hope you are feeling energised after breakfast, though, as we have a little flying ahead of us now."

Elvar twined his fingers with Vala's, and as he elevated above the ground, she took his lead. They ascended into the air, pitched forward, and flew. Vala always felt a tremendous sensation of freedom when flying; after her healing aptitude, it was the one fae ability she loved the most. The aerial view of the ocean was breathtaking, and Vala closed her eyes momentarily, feeling light and unburdened.

After half an hour of flying in companionable silence for the most part, Elvar started to descend, gently tugging Vala down with him. They alighted in front of a chalky-white cave, studded with tiny pieces of glistening mica.

"Where are we?" Vala asked, brushing back her windswept hair.

"If I told you that, it would spoil the surprise," Elvar returned, wiggling his eyebrows up and down, eliciting a giggle from Vala.

"So," Vala said, anticipation needling her. "Are you going to take me inside?"

"Why, of course," Elvar said with a lopsided grin. "But first, this."

He pulled out a swathe of black silk from his pocket and tied it around Vala's eyes.

"Now I'm definitely intrigued!" Vala said as Elvar placed his hands on both of her arms and guided her into the cave.

Without the aid of her sight, Vala's other senses heightened. She listened carefully to the resonant echo of their footsteps as they ventured deep inside, and the sound of Elvar's voice reverberating off the cave walls. Cool, moist air enshrouded Vala, the tiny hairs on her bare arms standing up as she shivered slightly in response to the drop in temperature. Elvar removed his jacket and wrapped it around her shoulders.

"Sorry, Vala," Elvar said softly. "I should have told you to bring a jacket. I forgot how cold the tunnels are."

"It's okay," Vala whispered back. "I'm fine with yours as long as you're not too cold?"

"My arms are already covered," Elvar replied. "I am fine."

As Vala continued walking, the scent of lavender, rose, and other flowers infused the air—flowers mingled with a woody pine aroma. The smell grew more prevalent so that when Vala inhaled, she could taste the floral profusion. Elvar whispered a few words and gently pulled back on her shoulders, prompting her to stop. He removed the blindfold. Vala gasped. They stood under a large hollow, a hollow that Elvar had illuminated, allowing Vala to truly appreciate the spectacle in front of her. All around them were glittering crystals in a multitude of colours and hues: some dark and opaque, others tinted with shades of rose, yellow, blue, green, purple, some metallic, some iridescent, striated with a multitude of colours and patterns—all in different fractal arrangements and sizes—all in great abundance and covering every surface of the cavernous chamber, including the floor they were standing upon. Vala was so awed by the opulent natural wonder, that she could find no words.

"It does take one's breath away, does it not?" Elvar said quietly, his breath warming Vala's ear.

"I've never seen anything like it!" Vala exclaimed, walking over to part of the wall and running her fingers over the surface of the crystals there.

"I believe this cave plays a part in your human Arthurian legend," Elvar said, leaning his back against a wall and wrapping his arms around Vala's waist as she melted into his warmth.

"The Crystal Cave," Vala said. "The one that Merlin was purportedly imprisoned in by Nimue."

"The very one," Elvar replied. "Obviously some grain of truth made its way back to the human realm, insofar that the Crystal Cave does in fact exist. The story of Merlin's imprisonment circulated in the human realm shortly after his disappearance. Nimue is obviously a derivative of his wife's name, Nimeva. The crystals here are all imbued with considerable power. As you can see." Elvar released Vala and walked over to a cluster of indigo-violet crystals.

"These are Iridiscus crystals," Elvar continued. "And these here ..." Elvar touched a cluster of rose quartz, yellow, and blue crystals. "These have protective properties. The green ones right above you are used for purification."

"And what about the metallic ones?" Vala asked, touching one of the golden shimmering stones.

"The gold one is meant to enhance our connection to the universe, enabling us to tap into energies that surround us. The silver one enhances focus and concentration, and the bronze one helps re-establish a feeling of calm when one is feeling panicked and emotions are running high," Elvar explained.

"And this metallic black?" Vala asked.

"Absorbs energies from us that are not our own," Elvar said, touching Vala's hand. "We are permitted to take a selection of crystals, obviously, the metallic ones are very helpful, but with the others, I would suggest picking ones that you are drawn to—that you intuitively feel are right for you. If you include the metallic ones, you may select a further six." Vala hesitated, sighing.

"This is not a test, Vala," Elvar said, smiling reassuringly. "Just close your eyes. I will make sure you do not collide with the walls."

Vala closed her eyes and allowed her mind to filter out all unnecessary distractions, attuning herself to the energies around her. She felt a gentle thrumming sensation pulsate through her body, her fingertips tingling in response. She stepped forward a few feet, and then a few feet more, Elvar watchful that she not injure herself. She turned thirty degrees to her right and reached out, her fingers grazing the surface of several crystals. Vala's fingers settled on a particular cluster, iridescent lilac in colour, and indicated to Elvar that she had made her first selection. Elvar lifted his top to expose a leather sheath attached to his belt. He withdrew a silver knife from it and carefully moved Vala's fingers away so he could extract one of the lilac crystals. Elvar then reached inside one of his trouser pockets and removed a black velveteen drawstring bag, carefully depositing the crystal inside.

Now that Vala had selected her first crystal, having felt an almost magnetic pull to it, she felt more confident in choosing the others, sure that she would be drawn to the crystals that resonated most with her needs and her own energy fields.

In turn, Vala selected a rose quartz crystal, an opalesque one with multi-coloured variegations, an opaque turquoise one with golden glints, a semi-opaque yellow one, and a translucent cerulean gem. "You can open your eyes now," Elvar said as he slipped the final crystal into the velveteen bag. "Here they are!" Elvar jangled the bag in front of Vala, eager to gauge her reaction.

"You are well prepared," Vala said, poking at the bag and lifting Elvar's shirt to see the sheathed knife.

"I always am," Elvar said, grinning, but he was caught off guard as Vala kissed the now-exposed area of Elvar's torso. He yelped in surprise, a deep burning desire stirring as Vala's lips made contact with his bare skin. "Vala ..."

"Yes," Vala said slowly, mouth twitching.

"Not just yet," Elvar pleaded. "You are making me feel ..." Elvar sucked in a breath as Vala's tongue circled his navel.

"Vala," Elvar continued, his voice hitching. "Please stop! We can do this later."

"I wasn't planning on jumping your bones here, silly!" Vala said, snorting. "It wouldn't be too comfortable!"

"Which is why you need to stop!" Elvar said, his skin flushed as he hastily pulled down his shirt.

"Sorry," Vala said, looking into Elvar's eyes. "Just take it as a compliment that I find you so deliciously irresistible."

"You, my beloved," Elvar retorted, "are a provocative little minx. You know I cannot resist your feminine wiles, and yet you continue to tempt me."

"Only because I love you so much," Vala said, her tone more serious. "It's never become ... you know ... the closeness I feel to you, the connection we have when we're making love; it's always amazing ... always as intense as our first time ... always as thrilling."

"I feel the same," Elvar said softly, his voice low. "But right now I have more to show you, and the effect your touch has on my body ..."

"Understood," Vala said. "So, can I see which stones I picked?"

She reached inside the velveteen pouch, pulling out the rose quartz.

"This one augments your connection to those you love," Elvar said. "It aligns you with their innermost feelings, so will no doubt increase your already considerable empathic ability."

Vala reached inside the pouch again, producing the other gems, spreading them out on her palm.

"The metallic one you already know about," Elvar said. "The opalesque crystal, Meridianus, deepens your intuition; the turquoise one is Cimilian for increasing inner confidence and strengthening resolve and self-belief; the lilac one, Trisilium, repels negative energy; the yellow one, Citresea, helps restore equilibrium on all planes: physically, emotionally, spiritually. And the final stone is an interesting choice."

"And why is that?" Vala prompted, her pulse quickening as she awaited an answer.

"Brysillian," Elvar explained. "Connected to the spirit world. It can, under certain conditions, invoke a spirit to come forth, to be brought from Elsorriden to the world of the living."

"So if I wanted to call upon Amalia, I would use this Brysillian crystal?" Vala asked as thoughts collected and formed in her mind.

"Yes," Elvar said, "I suppose so, though you would still need to call upon the Celestia with a specific incantation."

"And that would be?" Vala asked, as she contemplated another meeting with Amalia.

"I will write it down for you later," Elvar said. "I would rather not say it aloud, just in case."

Vala reverently deposited the crystals back inside the pouch, and Elvar placed it inside his pocket for safekeeping.

"Are you ready for your next surprise?" Elvar said with an enigmatic smile.

"Wait," Vala interjected. "I was so absorbed in collecting crystals, I didn't ask you what the floral aroma is?"

"That, my lady, will be revealed very shortly," Elvar said, a trace of a smile turning up the corners of his mouth. "It would be conducive to the element of surprise if you would allow me to blindfold you again."

"Fine," Vala said, rolling her eyes and sighing as Elvar fastened the blindfold around her eyes. "I presume we don't have far to walk if I am to remain blindfolded?"

"Not far at all," Elvar assured her, placing his hands on her arms and guiding her forwards.

As before, Vala's other senses predominated: her hearing and sense of touch became particularly sensitive, her awareness of the tiny currents passing over the surface of her arms sharpened, which were bare again after returning Elvar's jacket. The floral effusion became less obtuse, and Vala was able to differentiate between a myriad of different flora, though she was only able to identify a handful of the omnifarious scents. With her enhanced olfactory sense, Vala could taste the diverse fragrances—it was a peculiar sensation and not one she felt would be tolerable over a lengthy period of time. However, the most unusual feature of her newfound awareness was one of the less tangible senses: her extrasensory perception. Vala's intuitivism, her capacity to read the subtle undertones of her environment, energies, auras—all of it was increasing exponentially the more she allowed herself to be fully immersed in the experience, letting go of distracting conscious thoughts.

"There are some steps here," Elvar said, his voice sounding crisper and louder. "Stand still for a moment. I will walk in ahead of you." Elvar carefully sidestepped around Vala so that he was facing her. With his hands still gripping her arms, he slowly ascended the stone steps, watching his footing so as not to slip. To Vala's relief, there were only five steps. Although she trusted Elvar implicitly, it was disconcerting not being on a level surface without the aid of her sight.

The air had become moist and warm, the medley of floral redolence almost overpowering. Vala sucked in a breath through her mouth to minimise the assault to her nostrils.

"Are you ready?" Elvar said, excited anticipation coiling in his stomach.

"More than!" Vala replied, eager for the blindfold to be removed.

"Just one more thing," Elvar said. "We are standing on a slightly raised platform, so try to stay relatively still."

Elvar removed Vala's blindfold, and she found herself standing in what seemed to be a very unusual arboretum; they were still within a cavernous chamber, but the rock here was completely translucent. *Some kind of clear quartz*, Vala thought.

"What is this place?" Vala said, yet again in complete awe of her surroundings.

"The Quarterlias Arboretum," Elvar announced proudly. "The cave is made from Atherlinious crystal: its transparency allows the light in, but it is also very porous, so water can reach the plants inside. As you can imagine, the soil is very rich in mineral nutrients— ideal for growing plants."

"So can we explore now?" Vala said, tugging on Elvar's hand excitedly.

"First we have to remove our footwear on the platform," Elvar said. "Though I would also advise going barefoot as the Felicia grass is very moist."

Vala peeled off her tights and stepped onto the wide strip of lush green grass that stretched out in front of them like a living carpet. Elvar removed his socks and joined her. The moisture felt cool underfoot, but Vala soon grew accustomed to the feeling and started looking around her. The whole cave was awash with vibrant colour and fragrance. Now that Vala's blindfold had been removed, her olfactory sense had mostly returned to normal, and the bouquet from the flowers was amazing; so many different scents blended, but still discernible from each other in orchestral harmony.

Before she had chosen where to turn her attentions to first, Elvar interwove his fingers with hers and gently led Vala to a profusion of pale-blue roses tinted with the subtlest hint of pink towards their centres. Vala reverently touched one and inhaled, its gentle fragrance filling her senses and at once reminding her of her grandparents' garden in Kealkill.

"This is the Pendragon Rose," Elvar said, his eyes alight with pride.

"Named after Arthur?" Vala ventured.

"Naturally," Elvar confirmed. "Its gentle beauty belies its strength, for this particular variety can withstand frost, heavy rain, and partial drought."

"Except that there aren't any frosts in Candalia," Vala returned. "So how can you be sure of that?"

"You do remember that there is snow sometimes in Briallania, and always in the mountains? Plenty of it on Mount Cavalis too. However, it was Guinevere who cultivated this rose, as a wedding gift to Arthur. She grew it in the human realm successfully, so we know it can withstand such extremes."

"I think I may have seen it before in my grandparents' garden in Kealkill," Vala said, admiring the flower and gently stroking its petals. "So she, Guinevere, meant it to be an embodiment of Arthur's character—so romantic!"

"We believe the rose to be quite rare in the human realm, though it would be logical to presume that there are still incidences of it, probably most likely amongst the fae there," Elvar said, pausing thoughtfully for a moment. "And yes, it is romantic. I am no horticulturalist like Guinevere, but it is certainly Maiwen's area of expertise, so maybe we can come up with something together."

"That would be awesome!" Vala enthused, flinging her arms around Elvar's neck. "My own rose—just, wow! Thank you, Elvar!"

Elvar gathered Vala into his arms, lifting her slightly off the ground and kissing her gently before setting her down.

"So where to next?" Elvar asked, encouraging Vala to take to the lead.

Vala walked over to a plenitude of white lavender, growing in between numerous rocks—the rocks themselves, covered with a blanket of tiny pink flowers. Inhaling deeply, Vala immersed herself in the fresh, clean lavender scent, feeling its soporific effects relax and soothe her. She closed her eyes, surrendering herself to the moment and fully enjoying it. When Vala opened her eyes, her attention shifted to the tiny pink flowers: they had five rounded petals, with sunshine-yellow pollen and stamens in the centre.

"What are these?" Vala asked curiously, brushing a fingertip over one of the flowers.

"Myristium," Elvar replied. "They typically grow in the more alpine regions."

Vala continued to investigate the arboretum, with Elvar happily following her. They could have been almost anywhere and Elvar would still feel the same sense of elation that he always felt in Vala's company. His fingers still twined with Vala's, his thoughts drifted to the comment she had made earlier about *sexercise*. He smiled involuntarily and felt an intense heat rising within him. His face grew hot and his palms sweaty.

Vala was investigating a sunset-orange conical tree flower when she noticed her palms were damp. She reluctantly extricated her hand from Elvar's and waved it about to cool off in the air.

"Sorry," Elvar said ruefully.

"Oh," Vala replied, just noticing Elvar's slightly flustered demeanour. "I thought it was me!"

"Um, no," Elvar admitted. "I was just thinking back to our earlier conversation and um ... imagining—"

"What it would be like to whisk me behind that large bananatype plant and make my toes curl?"

"Something like that!" Elvar said, cheeks aflame. "But we cannot do that, because as much as I would like to, I have another surprise for you."

Elvar led Vala to a sitting area: the seating appeared to be constructed from some unfamiliar organic plant material, it looked to Vala like a pale-green plant husk, perforated with billions of tiny holes. To her surprise, when she sat down, it was soft and spongy, yet still supportive. *Almost like memory foam*, Vala thought, smiling as she settled into it.

"Caniskia husk," Elvar said, sensing Vala's thoughts. "Produced from the pods of the Caniskia tree—indigenous to both Moredonia and Cavania, and far too large to grow in here. We use it in soft furnishings: mattresses, sofas, etc. It is also antimicrobial."

"It's very comfortable," Vala replied, pushing her hand down onto it to test its springiness.

Elvar placed a hand over his Iridiscus pendant, closing his eyes to concentrate. Vala watched quietly as the crystal emitted an indigo glow, indicating that he had made contact with the intended recipient.

"Just wait, Vala," Elvar said, laughing and intercepting Vala's thoughts. "It will not be long—he has been waiting nearby." "Who has?" Vala asked, raising an eyebrow.

"I need to place your blindfold back on, if that is all right with you?" Elvar said, enjoying the intrigue he was creating.

"Very well," Vala replied, sighing dramatically.

Once Vala's blindfold was tied, she nestled under Elvar's arm, resting her head against his chest and enjoying his scent: pinewood mixed with a hint of sea salt. It was always intoxicating, and she breathed it in deeply.

They sat for a while in silence, Vala enjoying that she could just be with Elvar without the need for words, *or sex*, she thought after, a slow smile spreading across her face. Her reverie was broken by the sound of footsteps reverberating throughout the cave—loud and resonant at first, then softer and more muted—the owner of the footsteps had obviously removed his footwear, and Vala could sense his impending approach. The sound stopped abruptly, Vala now aware of a presence directly in front of her.

Elvar removed Vala's blindfold. She looked up to see a tall and— like most fae—handsome young man with green eyes, freckles, and sandy-blond tousled hair. In the man's hands was a fairly large stringed instrument, vaguely resembling a harp. He smiled shyly at Vala.

"Gannlyth Pyrisi," the man said, his eye meeting Vala's as he bowed reverently. "I am deeply honoured to make your acquaintance, Lady Oakley-Pendragon."

Vala stood, holding out her hand for Gannlyth to shake. Instead, he brought her hand to his lips and gently kissed it.

"Pleased to meet you too, Gannlyth," Vala said, smiling warmly. "Please call me Vala, though."

"Greetings, Gannlyth," Elvar said, standing and taking Gannlyth's hand in his. "It is wonderful to see you again after all this time."

Gannlyth grasped Elvar's hand firmly, before pulling him into a fierce hug.

"Gannlyth is a very dear friend," Elvar explained. "We grew up together in Avalonia before his family moved to Moredonia when we were fifteen."

Vala looked at Gannlyth, her brow creasing.

"This may seem like an odd question to ask, but why was he not at our wedding, our second one, that is?"

"Ah yes," Gannlyth said, his cheeks reddening. "Elvar did indeed invite me, and I was all set to depart Moredonia on the eve of your wedding, when, alas, my dear sister, Annlyn, went into labour. I promised I would be there for the birth, so regretfully, I was unable to attend."

"No worries," Vala replied. "I think your sister's situation definitely takes precedence over a wedding—even if it was the most amazing wedding in history—second wedding!"

"Indeed," Gannlyth replied, grinning. "Elvar told me all about it."

"However," Elvar cut in, "in addition to catching up with an old friend, I have invited Gannlyth here for another reason. You see, he is an exceedingly talented Chantaris musician, in great demand throughout Candalia."

Gannlyth placed his instrument on the ground and sat in front of it cross-legged.

As Gannlyth's fingers strummed, plucked and glided over the strings of the Chantaris, music like none Vala had ever heard filled the space around them creating a perfect ambience. It was at once bewitching and captivating, yet lulling and mollescent; a gentle melodic susurration that gradually grew into a rich harmonic sonority, which to Vala's imaginings sounded like a choir of angels, each note like a celestial voice.

"It's beautiful," Vala whispered to Elvar, still entranced by the enchanting music.

Vala felt a palpable change within herself when the music finally came to an end, all her background fears were now quiescent and she felt completely at peace.

"That was stunning! Thank you, Gannlyth," Vala said, clapping. "So emotive and beautiful. Elvar was right, you are quite the musical virtuoso!"

"Thank you, my lady," Gannlyth replied, a crimson blush spreading from his cheeks. "The Chantaris is a very special instrument: it reacts to the energies and emotions of the musician, so each piece is unique. Over time, the Chantaris becomes further attuned to its owner—like a burgeoning relationship that continues to grow over time."

"My lady," Gannlyth continued, his blush spreading to the roots of his hairline, "you must think me most impolite, I forgot to wish you for your birthday!"

"It's fine!" Vala returned, smiling reassuringly at Gannlyth. "You have given me the most beautiful present. I will always remember and treasure this moment."

"That is most kind of you, my lady," Gannlyth replied. "However, I wish you a truly perfect birthday, and if it pleases you, I would be honoured if you and Elvar would join me at my home for lunch?"

"We would love to," Vala enthused, then pursed her lips. "Unless, of course, Elvar has other plans ..."

"Actually, that was part of the plan," Elvar admitted. "Gannlyth had already made the invitation—I said we would be happy to accept as long as you were agreeable."

"Of course I'm agreeable," Vala said. "Why wouldn't I be? And, Gannlyth, please just call me Vala!"

24

After lunch with Gannlyth, Vala and Elvar began a leisurely walk back to the beach house. It was now late in the afternoon, and the low sun painted the sky in broad strokes of rosy pinks and vermillion intermingled with deep yellow hues. The evening temperature in Moredonia was much cooler than Avalonia, and Vala shivered in spite of the warmth provided by Elvar's jacket.

"You are cold, my love," Elvar said, his voice filled with concern. "Let me hold you for a moment so you can absorb some of my body heat."

"You know for optimal sharing of body heat, it works better if both parties are naked," Vala said teasingly, a pleasant tingle stirring in her belly.

"That would be a tad awkward out here!" Elvar replied, his mouth twitching. "Do not worry, we are almost home where I will be more than happy to share all of my body with you!"

The tingle in Vala's belly spread outwards, her nerve endings zinging with anticipation and her heart beating so rapidly she could hear her blood rush.

Once inside the beach house, Elvar ran a hot bath with lavender, chamomile, and zitilia essential oils. Steam filled the bathroom, misting the windows and infusing the air with the soporific herbal aromas. Elvar uttered an incantation, invoking tiny multitudinous orbs of light to appear, magically suspended in the air. He turned off the main light and removed his clothes, folding them neatly on a chair. Elvar felt that a tidy, uncluttered environment was more conducive to creating a relaxing atmosphere, a character trait he shared with Vala, though unlike himself, Vala was a hoarder. Elvar smiled at the paradox: a hoarder who disliked clutter. Somehow, in spite of her many belongings, Vala still managed to be tidy and organised.

"Vala," Elvar called out. "Your oasis of bliss awaits, my love."

Vala padded into the bathroom clad in a fluffy cotton-towelled bathrobe and bare feet. Her face had been cleansed of makeup, and Elvar thought her breathtakingly beautiful. His heartbeat quickened as he closed the space between them, pressed his forehead to hers, and untied her bathrobe, letting it fall to the floor. Vala's breath caught as she ran her hands over Elvar's chest, stopping at his waist. As she did, Elvar laced his fingers with hers and led her into the bath.

The water was hot, but not uncomfortably so, and the herbal vapours swirled around them, chasing away the cold that Vala had felt and replacing it with an intoxicating warmth. She inhaled the humid air and sank deeper into the bath.

"This is sooo good," Vala drawled. "I don't think it could get much better than this."

"I would like to dispute that last claim," Elvar said softly, his lips grazing her ear. "I will demonstrate that this can indeed get better."

Elvar's lips found Vala's, and he kissed her hungrily, his fingers enmeshed in her long wet hair. Momentarily breaking contact, he traced a finger from Vala's lips over her chin and the contours of her collarbone till he reached her breasts. He followed the same route with his tongue, and Vala moaned as Elvar's tongue teased her nipple and his hand stroked down her abdomen to between her legs. Raw energy surged through Vala, enlivening every cell. She pulled Elvar closer, her nails lightly slaking over his back, and wound a leg around his waist. Needing no further prompting, Elvar pressed into Vala and connected their bodies.

An hour later, Vala stretched out lazily in their bed. Elvar had continued her special *spa* experience by treating Vala to a fullbody massage, and now she felt far too relaxed to do anything at all. Sprawled out beside her, Elvar turned to his bedside table and glanced at the alarm clock.

"We have to get ready to welcome Merridyn," Elvar said, thinking that he would have rather spent more time in bed, but they had invited Merridyn over for drinks, and Elvar was not one to shirk obligation.

"Indeed we must," Vala said sighing. "Better get dressed then!"

2 5

Merridyn greeted Vala with a massive grin, flowers tucked under one arm and a gift box in his hand.

"Happy birthday!" Merridyn enthused, hugging Vala and kissing her on the cheek.

"Thank you, Merri," Vala replied. "I'm glad you're here. Come on through."

Merridyn slipped out of his sneakers and followed Vala through to the lounge.

"Good evening, Merri," Elvar said warmly. "Good to see you again. Please be seated."

Vala sat down first and patted a spot next to her, inviting Merridyn to join her.

"These are for you," Merridyn said, handing Vala the flowers and gift.

"Elvar," Vala called out, "please would you put these in water?"

Handing Elvar the flowers, she returned her attentions to Merridyn's gift. It was presented in a small square box, lined in patterned midnight-blue damask and embellished with midnight-blue ribbon and a small cream silk rose in the centre. Vala carefully lifted the lid to reveal an object wrapped in cream silk. She unwrapped the silk, freeing a silver bracelet featuring an oval centrepiece with a small pressed indigo flower, protected by a clear crystal cover. The silver band was inscribed with tiny Latin lettering, and it met with the centre in two delicate swirls: one studded with a lilac Trisilium crystal and the other with the opalesque Meridianus crystal. Vala gently traced her finger over the surface of the bracelet, enjoying the feel of the cool smooth surface of the centre, contrasted with the slightly indented silver band.

Merridyn allowed Vala some time to admire the bracelet before speaking.

Elvar had been watching from the adjoining kitchen area, but was now seated on the other side of Vala, observing with a mixture of curiosity and … what was it? Elvar wasn't entirely sure what other emotion was stirring within him—it wasn't jealousy, but it was an unsettling emotion that he couldn't quite decipher.

"It was my great, great grandmother's," Merridyn said quietly. "The blue flower is a Melisynia—some believe it has protective properties. The Trisilium and Meridianus crystals repel negative energies and increase intuition respectively, and the inscription … the bracelet is inscribed with an ancient protective spell."

"Merri, I can't possibly accept this," Vala said, touched by Merridyn's significant and poignant gift to her. "This is a family heirloom, you should save it for somebody special."

"You are special, Vala," Merridyn blurted, his face flushing.

Elvar shot him a dark look and Merridyn flinched.

"I mean that in an entirely platonic way!" Merridyn quickly added. "I thought maybe you could wear it on your quest, that it may offer you some protection."

Vala registered Merridyn's imploring look and sighed.

"If you are sure, Merri, then thank you very much. It is a very sweet, kind, and thoughtful gesture," Vala said, kissing Merridyn's cheek. "We may not have known each other long, but I already consider you a very dear friend."

"As you are to me, Vala," Merridyn said, blushing again. "Both of you."

"Would you care for a drink, Merri?" Elvar asked quietly, feeling that disquieting feeling surface again.

"That would be most welcome," Merridyn replied, relieved by the change of subject.

"Well, we have quite a selection, so unless you already have something in mind, you may wish to take a look," Elvar replied.

"Do you have any Linsum, perchance?" Merridyn ventured, referring to an alcoholic beverage similar in taste and potency to Bourbon, but slightly sweeter.

"We do indeed," Elvar said. "And what would you like, my love?" Elvar caught Vala's eye and smiled.

"I don't know, surprise me!"

As Elvar prepared their drinks, Vala glanced at Merridyn, who had become rather pensive.

"Are you okay, Merri?" Vala asked, lightly touching his arm. "You seem a little quiet."

"Sorry, yes. Of course!" Merridyn replied, somewhat hurriedly. "I was just lost in thought."

"Maybe this will help!" Elvar said, setting down a tray of drinks.

"Thank you." Merridyn reached for his glass. "So at what time are you planning to depart tomorrow?"

"It is a long journey home," Elvar began, "so we ..."

Elvar stopped abruptly as a sudden cacophony of noise erupted outside: a flock of gulls screeching, a vague rustling sound, and the soft whickering from the horses.

Elvar walked over to the window to look out but could see nothing unusual.

"I think I should go around the back and check that the horses are okay," Elvar said, a flicker of concern crossing his face. "Would you mind staying with Vala, please?" He looked towards Merridyn, who nodded in acknowledgement, then he stepped outside, closing the door behind him.

"I wonder what that was?" Merridyn said, turning to Vala.

Vala sat completely still and wide-eyed, her heart beating at a staccato rhythm, her breathing fast and shallow.

"Vala?" Merridyn said, touching her hand as he took in her terrified countenance. "What is wrong?"

Vala didn't answer—could not answer. She simply stared dead ahead, fear consuming her and seeping into every cell of her body.

"Vala!"

Vala's breathing became erratic and raspy, her eyes glossy and unfocussed. Alarmed by Vala's distressed and unresponsive behaviour, Merridyn shook her shoulders lightly. Not wishing to leave her alone,

Merridyn ran to the door, swung it open and clasped his Iridiscus pendant. Changing his mind at the last moment, Merridyn swept Vala into his arms and ran outside, almost colliding with Elvar.

"What happened?" Elvar asked, bewildered at the sight of Vala's limpid form.

"I do not know!" Merridyn replied, his voice catching. "She suddenly became unresponsive and her breathing laboured. We should get her to Parvys, he is the nearest healer."

Elvar nodded his assent as Merridyn gently placed Vala in Elvar's arms. A confused expression flickered across Vala's face.

"Vala?" Elvar's voice caught. "Can you hear me?"

"I can't breathe properly!" Vala said, her voice high and panicky. "Do not worry, my love, we are taking you to a healer."

Following Merridyn's lead, Elvar ascended into the air with Vala in his arms. The darkness of dusk seemed ominous and oppressive, a thick blanket of anxiety that had settled over them in a suffocating embrace. They flew for only the briefest time, alighting a few minutes later by one of the crystalline houses.

Merridyn knocked on the door, glancing briefly at Vala and sighing. A tall man with dark hair flecked with silver answered the door. He looked at Vala, whose eyes were now closed.

"Bring her inside," the man said.

Elvar and Merridyn kicked off their footwear and followed the man inside the house to a spacious room with an examination couch, a bed, a sofa, and several bookshelves lined with numerous medical and herbology tomes.

"Please lay her down on the couch," the man said, looking at Elvar directly. "You must allay your fears now; I am Parvys, and I have been a healer for 421 years. We will have your wife back to normal very soon."

Elvar gently set Vala down on the examination couch, stroking her hair.

"Would the two of you be so kind as to be seated while I examine ..." Parvys paused. "What is your wife's name, Master Oakley?"

"Vala," Elvar replied, his brow knitted. "How do you know who I am?"

"Ah yes, Lady Pendragon-Oakley, slayer of the Spindler," Parvys replied, a warm smile creasing the corners around his eyes. "You look very much like your father, Derryth."

Parvys gently hovered his hands over Vala's body, from above her head to below her feet. His expression remained neutral and gave nothing away. He repeated the action in reverse, lingering this time first over Vala's lower abdomen, her chest, and then her head. Parvys gently placed his hands on Vala's head, his thumbs pressing her forehead, and closed his eyes. Elvar and Merridyn watched as a warm glow emanated from beneath his hands. He repeated the action over Vala's chest with one of his hands directly over her heart. When Parvys reached Vala's abdomen, he furrowed his brow, gently touching the area but doing nothing more.

"Vala," Parvys spoke softly. "Please open your eyes now, you are safe."

Vala's eyes flickered open, fixing upon Parvys' face.

"Where am I?"

"You are in my home, Vala," Parvys said kindly. "Your husband and young Master Ashwood here were gravely distressed by your condition. Indeed, you gave them both quite the fright!"

"What's wrong with me?" Vala asked, feeling strangely calm.

"Absolutely nothing, my dear," Parvys assured her. "You had an anxiety attack, a rather extensive one, admittedly, but there is nothing physically wrong with you. However ..."

"What is it?" Elvar asked, feeling uneasy again.

"Vala," Parvys began, "your energy fields are all very healthy again, it is just that the energy over your abdomen is rather unusual. You are not ill, I promise you that. Maybe it is due to your part human physiology or if you are ... no, I am sure it is nothing significant."

"You are positive that Vala is well?" Elvar asked, nervously raking a hand through his hair.

"I am certain," Parvys replied. "Now, what precipitated this anxiety attack?"

"There was a noise outside our beach house," Elvar explained. "It seemed to disturb the animals, but there was nothing to be seen when I went outside to investigate."

"Perhaps it reminded Vala of something traumatic? Maybe something pertaining to the events leading up to the Spindler's demise?"

"That may be so," Elvar replied. "The animals acted in a similar way when the Spindler sent his minions to spy on Vala, and since then we have had another two disturbing encounters, or rather, Vala has."

"A girl," Vala said, "tried to forcibly take me to her mistress. She wasn't ..." Vala could not find the right words and looked to Elvar.

"The girl, we believe, was using a glamour," Elvar said, squeezing Vala's hand. "We have reason to believe she was a Dessicatus and intended to bring Vala to ... it is complicated, but Vala has had contact with Amalia."

"Maybe you can tell me over a nice hot mug of Elisi tea and some of my honey cakes," Parvys said. "I will also teach Vala some calming techniques."

Parvys looked at Vala sympathetically and smiled. "It is important for you to stay calm, Vala. Life is in a constant state of flux, and none of us can ever truly be prepared, but accepting that is part of the battle. I would also advise you not to consume any alcohol or stimulants—they are not conducive to a calm mind."

As Vala climbed off the examination couch, Parvys laid a hand on her shoulder and whispered in her ear, "If there is anything you wish to tell me in private, I will be in the kitchen preparing refreshments."

"There isn't anything," Vala replied softly, puzzled by Parvys' remark.

After spending some time with Parvys, the three of them returned to the beach house.

"Probably none of my business," Merridyn said, his voice a little slurred after his third glass of Linsum, "but what did Parvys whisper to you earlier?"

"You're right, Merri," Vala said, laughing as she sipped her juice, "it is none of your business, though there is not much to tell. He asked if there was anything I wanted to tell him, and I assured him that there was nothing—certainly nothing I am aware of!"

"Hmmm," Merridyn replied, the side of his mouth turning up in a lopsided grin. "I wonder what he was alluding to?"

"I am sure Parvys was merely availing Vala of a little privacy should she so wish it," Elvar replied. "Nothing more."

"Of course," Merridyn said, his eyes a little glazed. "I think maybe it is time for me to take my leave. It has been a delightful—if rather unusual—evening."

As Merridyn stood, he swayed a little, and Elvar held his arm to support him.

"You have been wonderful company, as always, Vala," Merridyn said, pulling her into a fierce hug and surprising her with a kiss on the lips.

"Um, Merri," Elvar said, pulling him gently away from Vala, "that is my wife you are kissing."

"Of course," Merridyn replied, beaming at them both. "My apologies. You, too, have been a wonderful host, Elvar." Merridyn pulled Elvar into a hug. "Though I would rather not kiss you if that is all right?"

"More than all right!" Elvar said, amused by Merridyn's inebriated state. "I will help you home, Merri, we both will."

26

Vala and Elvar woke early the next morning to prepare for their journey home. Vala pulled the pillow over her head, reluctant to get up.

"I am sorry, my love," Elvar said, joining Vala under the pillow and kissing her gently, "but we have a long journey ahead, and we must depart shortly if we are to arrive before dark."

"I know, I know," Vala groaned from beneath the pillow. "I just don't feel like getting up now."

The journey back to Avalonia was thankfully uneventful, and with the exception of their rest stops, Vala slept most of the time. However, their blissful solitude was broken abruptly as they journeyed into the first town on their way into Avalonia. Vala blinked and her heart raced as she was shaken suddenly from slumber to the sounds of raised voices—fast, some shrill, but universally alarmed voices. A wave of terror washed over her, permeating her body and gripping her in its clutches. The discordant cacophony pounded in her ears like a persistent drumbeat.

Vala inhaled deeply and focussed on implementing some of the techniques Parvys had taught her. She filtered out the noise, allowing it to blend into a more muted static sound, like white noise, and centred herself, listening to the cadence of her own breath: in one, two, three, four, five, six, seven—out one, two, three, four, five, six, seven. After Vala had settled her breathing, she allowed her attention to drift back to her surroundings, only this time from a more detached view, becoming aware of all the sounds around her, not just the frightened voices; she tuned into the reassuring birdsong, the soft whickering of their horses, a baby cooing happily, and then ... Elvar's voice.

"Beloved, are you all right?" Elvar asked, his brow crossed in concern.

"I am now," Vala said, feeling much more relaxed, "though I would like to know what's going on."

"As would I," Elvar said. "I will not leave you in the carriage alone, Vala, so would you care to accompany me for a spell of fresh air to find out what all the commotion is about?"

"Definitely!" Vala said, though a feeling of trepidation seeped through her veins as they stepped out of the carriage.

"Elvar!" A young man of about Elvar's age ran up to him and placed a hand on his arm.

"Tristan," Elvar replied, starting to feel anxious himself, "what is it?"

"It is Adair!" Tristan's voice caught, his face white with shock. "He is dead!"

"How?" Elvar asked, bile rising into his throat. He nervously raked a hand through his hair.

"He was found a short time ago in his bed ... his body ... his body was ossified and his eyes—white," Tristan said, his voice and countenance enervated and sad.

"This sounds identical to the incident we heard about whilst in Moredonia, from where we just came," Elvar said, almost to himself.

"It is as though he has returned," Tristan said, his voice trembling. "But you destroyed him, did you not?" Tristan turned to Vala, his voice bordering on hysteria.

"Yes!" Vala retorted. "I can assure you that the Spindler is dead! Whatever is happening is not the work of the Spindler. Perhaps there is another?"

"How can this be happening?" Tristan cried, rubbing his hands over his face. "Adair was our friend, Elvar—this is too much! I have never lost anyone before."

"Nor I, Tristan," Elvar said sadly. "But all we can do now is support each other through this tragedy and find out who, or what, is responsible."

27

It had been several days since the death of Elvar's friend, Adair. Elvar had never lost anyone close to him before, and it had shaken him greatly. Vala had been a source of comfort for him, a refuge, and her support was helping him through his grief.

As an extra birthday surprise, Elvar had organised a surprise party for Vala, inviting their friends, Jelly and Max. Just as Elvar was thinking of them, there was a knock on the door. Even though he had been expecting it, his heart leapt and he rushed to open it.

"Jelly, Max!" Elvar said, genuinely happy to see them. "Greetings! Please do come inside."

"It's great to see you too, Elvar," Jelly said, engulfing him in a bear hug and planting a kiss on his cheek.

Elvar and Max shook hands and attempted an awkward man-hug.

"Oh just hug it out, guys!" Jelly said, laughing. "We haven't seen each other, like forever!"

"What's with all the celebrations outside?" Max asked, raising an eyebrow. "It took forever to get to your place—hordes of people everywhere."

"Oh that," Elvar said nonchalantly. "It is the One-hundred Days Festival: it is an ancient festivity based on mythology, really." "You have to tell us more about that!" Jelly replied.

"Its provenance is from folklore, in which the very first fae received a Divine visitation from an archangel who bestowed them with magical abilities. Before that, the fae purportedly were not very different from humankind. The visitation apparently occurred one hundred days after the fae were created. So, every year on this date, and I have no idea how the date was worked out so please do not ask, we celebrate the One-hundred Days Festival with feats of magic, copious quantities of food and wine, and a spectacular light show at dusk."

"Ooh, I love fireworks!" Jelly gushed. "Magical ones? Now that is something I have to see!"

"Well, you will not be disappointed, I am sure!" Elvar replied.

Elvar's Iridiscus crystal suddenly started glowing, and he ushered everyone into their hiding places.

"She will be here any moment!" he whispered loudly.

A few minutes later, the front door opened and Vala stepped into a darkened room.

"Hello?" Vala called out. "Elvar?"

There was no answer, so Vala called out again. She felt a presence behind her and turned to see Elvar there.

"How ..." Vala started, but was hushed as Elvar placed a finger over her lips.

"Hush, my love," Elvar whispered and covered her eyes, giving a signal to the others.

"Surprise!" Vala's family and friends shouted as Elvar took his hands away.

Vala stared at her family and friends, completely taken aback, her mouth agape.

"Wow! I didn't see this coming!"

Vala's parents, Laoli and Patrick, rushed up to her. Patrick ruffled his daughter's hair and kissed her forehead. Laoli took Vala in her arms and held her tightly.

"I have missed you, Sugar Plum," Laoli said quietly, with her cheek resting on Vala's head. "Elvar tells me there is something you wish to discuss with us later."

Vala turned her head and shot Elvar a look—he shrugged his shoulders and smiled. Vala knew what this something pertained to—she had not yet told her parents about her decision to leave Cambridge, and now Elvar had forced her hand.

"I missed you too, Mama," Vala replied. "We'll talk later."

"Vala, hon," Jelly said, pulling Vala into a tight hug. "It's sooo good to see you, I've missed us all being together like this."

"Me too," Vala said, her eyes tearing up. She had missed her friends immensely.

Jelly eventually released her friend before Vala was swept up into Max's waiting arms. Max lifted her off her feet and swung her around.

"Our little Vala!" Max said teasingly, kissing Vala's cheek. "She's all growed up, Jelly!"

"Shut up, Max!" Vala said, swiping the top of his head.

"We have pressies for you!" Jelly said excitedly, tugging Vala's hand and leading her to a large black box tied with red ribbon.
"These are from both of us."

Vala untied the ribbon and lifted the lid.

"A chocolate hamper!" Vala said. "My favourite type too! OMG, Jelly, it's massive! I'm going to get really fat!"

Max handed her another two packages: one in a gift bag, the other wrapped in black embossed paper, also tied.

"You might want to open those upstairs," Max suggested, whispering in Vala's ear.

Once in her room, Vala delved into the gift bag. Inside was a lacy, silk black negligee and matching briefs, dotted with tiny red roses.

"All washed and ready to wear!" Jelly said, her face lighting up. "And here's the best bit." Jelly took the briefs in her hand and unclipped a couple of poppers on the gusset.

"Easy access flap!" Jelly said, snorting.

"You guys are terrible!" Vala said, nudging Jelly's arm.

"Wait, it gets better!" Max said. "Open the other one!" Vala shook her head, grinning, and opened the present.

"The Kama Sutra!" Vala said, giggling. "You two are incorrigible!"

"Well, we thought you might need some fresh inspiration," Jelly said. "You know, in case you start running out of ideas ..."

"Talking of which," Max said, nudging Vala. "How was your fourday shagathon with Elvar?"

"Max!" Vala said, only half feigning shock. "I can't believe you just asked me that!"

"What he means," Jelly said, punching Max's arm, "but so crassly expressed, is did you have an enjoyable break with your lovely husband?"

"It was amazing," Vala said. "We saw the most fantastic places. I'll tell you about it downstairs so the others can hear."

Vala promptly bounded down the stairs, keen to avoid any more awkward questions from her friends.

Tarrys gently touched her elbow. "It is good to see you again, Sister. I trust that you had a relaxing excursion with Elvar? Gweneira sends her apologies but could not attend your party; she cannot exert herself in these final weeks."

Vala looked deeply into her brother's eyes, and Tarrys, seeing a troubled look darken her expression, pulled her into a tight hug.

"Something is troubling you," Tarrys said softly, stroking his sister's hair.

Vala sighed, comforted by her brother's warm embrace. "There was an incident en route to Moredonia."

"Similar to our earlier encounter with the Dessicatus?" Tarrys guessed. "With the two recent deaths that have occurred, I cannot say it is altogether a surprise."

"It was a girl," Vala said, "though she was using a glamour. She attempted to coerce me into meeting with her mistress, but did not say to whom this referred. When she grabbed my arm, her glamour faltered, and I saw something ... something grotesque. Horrific, like a burnt-out skeleton with glowing eyes."

"And where was Elvar while all this was happening?" Tarrys asked, his brow knitting.

"It wasn't his fault, Tarrys," Vala replied. "He was attending to the horses, and we had no reason to believe that there was any threat at the time."

"You must not venture out alone, Sister," Tarrys said tensely, "nor be unattended whilst outside—not until this diabolical situation is resolved."

"Elvar takes good care of me, Tarrys," Vala said, her head still resting on her brother's chest. "You need not worry about me."

"I have known Elvar many years," Tarrys replied. "He is a good man, and no doubt, a fine husband. But, Vala, you are my baby sister. I will always worry, it is my brotherly duty!"

Tarrys kissed the top of her head. "Come now, we should join the others."

"Tarrys?"

"There is something else you wish to tell me?"

"I had a panic attack," Vala said quietly, an unpleasant feeling rippling through her as she said the words.

"There are many techniques you can employ to relieve anxiety," Tarrys said, his voice barely above a whisper. "However, please if at all possible, get someone to call me if it happens again. I can dissolve it with immediate effect; it pains me to think of you suffering unduly."

"Okay," Vala assured him.

Vala felt a tug on her arm and turned to find Maiwen, her hand linked with Lann's.

"Vala," Maiwen said excitedly, "this is Lann—we are officially courting now."

"I am honoured to meet you, my lady," Lann said, inclining his head and bringing Vala's hand to his lips.

"Good to meet you too, Lann," Vala replied.

To her surprise, when Lann's eyes met hers, he frowned, his face lined with anxiety.

Puzzled by his reaction, Vala felt compelled to ask, "Is something the matter?"

Maiwen looked between them, perplexed by Lann's change of countenance upon seeing Vala.

"It is a private matter," Lann said after an uncomfortable silence, then added as he noticed the confused look on Maiwen's face, "of a medical nature. I am sorry, Maiwen, my love, it is something I can only discuss with Vala and your brother."

"I'll get Elvar," Vala said, disconcerted by Lann's words. Whatever it was, it must be something of grave importance, Vala thought, her stomach filled with a fluttery sensation as she went to find Elvar.

Vala located Elvar carrying a gargantuan pot of Marisali Satura to the table.

"Elvar ..." Vala began, but was interrupted by Essyeult.

"This is a double celebration today," Essyeult announced loudly, capturing the attention of her guests. "Today we celebrate our lovely Vala's birthday, but also the One-hundred Days festivities. The food and drinks are both served now, so please, dear friends and family, be seated, fill your stomachs, and rejoice!"

Derryth, Vala's parents, Jelly, and Max brought through platters of breads, cheeses, Uquilico cream cakes, Silanchi berries, and two large carafes of Velinosa wine. Already on the table were an assortment of cakes, pastries, and nuts. The last time Vala had seen such a grandiose spread was at her and Elvar's wedding. *Well, both of them*, Vala thought, smiling.

"Lann needs to talk to us," Vala said, glancing at Lann who sat opposite Vala—head in hands and lost in thought.

"I have a bad feeling about this," Elvar replied, glancing at Lann's troubled expression. "Let me handle this, Vala, please. I do not want this to spoil your special day."

"If you're sure," Vala conceded reluctantly, as she took a slice of Chavalet cheese and a Mavami bun. "But first, enjoy the meal."

Over the meal, Vala and Elvar recounted the events of their holiday, including the unsettling encounter with the mysterious girl. Vala was finding it increasingly hard to concentrate, though, and ferociously twisted locks of her hair as she wondered what Lann wished to discuss with them.

After the meal, Vala tried to help clear up but was shooed away by Essyeult and Derryth. After a painful wait for Vala, Elvar and Lann walked out of the kitchen together. Lann walked on, his eyes downcast, refusing to meet Vala's gaze.

"We can go to my room to talk," Elvar said, prompting Lann to follow him upstairs.

Vala watched on as Elvar and Lann ascended the stairs. She had developed a headache and a wave of nausea overcame her. She suddenly felt very tired and wished Lann would end the suspense.

Meanwhile, upstairs, Lann wrung his hands together, pacing the room anxiously.

"I have been in such turmoil!" Lann said, running his hands over his face. "I have made a very grave error for which I am very sorry;
I only pray that it has not done any damage."

"For goodness sake, just bloody tell me, Lann!" Elvar snapped.

"That day when you came to collect the elixir, we were having a heated discussion, Elvar," Lann began. "My attention was diverted for a moment, and I gave you the wrong vial. I know this because afterwards, I tested the contents of the other vial just before I was due to give it to another."

"And my elixir?" Elvar demanded angrily. "What potency did you give me?"

"It was one week's worth," Lann said, recoiling at Elvar's sharp tone. "You had already left for Moredonia when I noticed my error and so ..."

"So, we have been unprotected," Elvar finished Lann's sentence, his words sinking in.

"I am truly sorry," Lann replied. "I should have attempted to contact you sooner, but I had urgent examination papers to prepare for and I clean forgot. I know it sounds terrible—and it is! But when I saw the two of you here, I felt it the right time to tell you."

"Do you realise what you may have done?" Elvar retorted hotly, his face reddening.

"I am profusely sorry!" Lann cried. "Here, this is the correct vial!" He thrust a vial of Nonceptium elixir into Elvar's hand. "I can only hope that it is not too late for that!"

*

Jelly sat with Vala on the sofa, a comforting arm around her shoulder. Vala rested her head on Jelly's shoulder and closed her eyes, her breath shuddered—she could not allow her thoughts to dwell on this now, it was too much.

"I can't deal with this right now," Vala said, feeling enervated and despondent. "I'm going to tell my parents about Cambridge— might as well get it out of the way!"

Trying not to dwell on the implications of the information that Lann had just imparted was like the proverbial elephant in the room—Elvar could think of nothing else. His emotions were conflicted: on the one hand, he felt truly terrified of potentially facing something that he was not sure he was ready for, but on the other, he felt an unexpected thrill—a jolt of excitement and wonder over the prospect of creating a new life with Vala. Their baby! He knew that Vala had seen a future vision of them with their child but had imagined it to be a distant event; he wondered now if it might be sooner than they had anticipated.

Laoli was sitting at the bottom of the stairs having heard the heated discussion taking place between Elvar and Lann. She sighed upon seeing her daughter approach and led her to the kitchen to afford them some privacy.

"What is going on, Vala?" Laoli asked, anxiously smoothing down a lock of hair. "It is fortunate that there is a general hum of conversation down here or the others would have heard too."

"Actually, it's a new development and not one I have full knowledge of yet," Vala said quietly. "It isn't what I wanted to talk to you and Daddy about."

"Would you like to tell me about this new development may be before I find your father?"

Vala exhaled loudly and pulled her mother closer, resting her head on Laoli's chest. Laoli gently stroked her daughter's long auburn hair.

28

Patrick sat on the kitchen stool, his elbows propped on the wooden work table, and rubbed his hands over his face, forcibly blowing out a stream of air.

"Why didn't you tell us sooner?" Patrick asked, shocked by Vala's revelation of leaving university.

"I didn't know how!" Vala admitted. "I knew you'd be disappointed and feel like I'd let you both down but ... it is so hard to explain!" Vala felt aggravated by her inability to express her true feelings.

"I *love* psychology," she continued, trying to find the words to express how she felt. "It involves an aspect of healing that I still wish to explore and be involved in. However, when I help someone—save their life even—the feeling is like nothing else. I just know it is my true calling."

"We are not upset with you, Vala," Laoli said, covering her daughter's hand with her own. "We are just sad that you felt unable to tell us this until now."

"I'm sorry," Vala said, sighing and rubbing her temples as her head throbbed. "I just didn't want to face you being disappointed with me."

"Never, Vala, never!" Patrick said, cupping his daughter's face. "We could never be disappointed in you. We are very proud of you,
of the amazing young woman you have become."

Vala hugged both her parents before they returned to the lounge to re-join the others. Vala looked around for Elvar but couldn't see him. Just as she was about to check upstairs, Elvar came down, a stormy expression clouding his face. He glanced at Vala, his expression softening for a moment till he spotted Maiwen laughing with Lann. Elvar's thunderous countenance returned.

"Your boyfriend is an imbecile!" Elvar growled as Maiwen stared at him, openly shocked.

Elvar looked at Vala apologetically. "I am sorry, my love, I need some air. Enjoy your party, I will not be long."

Vala said nothing as Elvar walked out of the house, leaving her with a stunned Maiwen, who now looked at her quizzically.

"You'll have to ask him yourself!" Vala said, at Maiwen's expression.

Maiwen silently nodded her assent as Vala left their company to find Jelly and Max.

"What's up, hon?" Jelly asked, cupping Vala's face. "You're upset."

"Did someone leave the party early?" Max asked, raising an eyebrow. "I heard the door slam."

"That would be Elvar," Vala replied sardonically.

"No way!" Jelly exclaimed. "You guys couldn't have had a fight? Surely not!"

"*We* didn't," Vala replied. "In fact, there was no fight, per se. Elvar was ... no, reword that, *is* mightily pissed off with Lann."

"That's a tad out of character for him, isn't it?" Max said. "I mean Elvar's a pretty chilled guy—it must be something pretty big that's gone down, right?"

"I imagine so," Vala replied, sighing.

"Oh, Vala!" Jelly said, her lower lip quivering. "I wanted this day to be perfect for you. We haven't seen you in ages, and now all this drama with Elvar storming off!"

"He'll be back," Vala said. "And I will be okay. Besides, you two are here with me like old times, so, in spite of everything, I am happy! Why don't we go up to my room with some grub and have a good old catch-up?"

"That would be great!" Jelly replied, pulling Vala into a bear hug, before gathering an assortment of snacks and fruit juices to take upstairs.

They had been talking for half an hour when Vala heard the door open. Truth be told, she had been listening for the door the entire time she had been in Jelly and Max's company. Fast footsteps ascended the stairs and a red-faced Elvar burst into their room, barely registering Jelly and Max, but heading straight for Vala. He knelt down in front of her and took her hand in his.

"Forgive me, Eternal Beloved," Elvar said, his head bowed. "I did not intend to disrupt your celebrations earlier, nor cause you any unhappiness. Can you forgive me?"

"I think the man's shown enough contrition," Max commented, the corners of his mouth twitching.

"Shut up, Max!" Jelly hissed, punching Max's arm.

Vala gazed into the violet depths of Elvar's eyes, darkened by his intensity of emotion. She placed a hand on his cheek and touched her nose to his.

"Yes," Vala whispered, "of course I do, though there's nothing to forgive—you just needed to clear your head—it's fine."

Elvar cupped Vala's face and pressed his lips to hers. She kissed Elvar back fervently, savouring the warmth and softness of his lips, his taste, his intoxicating scent. Vala was so lost in Elvar's embrace that she had forgotten they had company.

"Ahem!" Max said loudly, coughing deliberately.

Vala and Elvar broke contact and looked at Jelly and Max, who had hopped off the bed during their friends' romantic interlude.

"My apologies," Elvar said. "I got a little caught up in the moment."

"No kidding!" Max said, laughing. "I thought you guys were about to launch into another shagathon!"

"What Max means," Jelly interjected, "is that it's really cute how romantic you guys still are. Maybe Max could learn something!" "Hey! I'm plenty romantic!"

*

A few hours later, they all gathered outside to watch the light show. Vala had only seen the light show once before and had been dazzled by the spectacular, magical display. However, though she was excited by the prospect of the light show, an uneasiness gnawed inside of her. She had never really seen Elvar angry before with the exception of their showdown with the Spindler, and from what she had seen of Lann, he seemed very personable—Vala had certainly not sensed any ill will or malice from him. And yet Elvar had been truly enraged. What had happened? Vala's thoughts were soon pulled back to the present as a musical symphony was sung to the cosmos, accompanied by a burst of bright colours that resembled fireworks until each spark of colour converged and arranged itself into an image of a red rose bursting into bloom.

Jelly gasped and squeezed Vala's hand. "OMG! That is amazing!"

"I have to agree!" Max said, clearly awed by the spectacle. "Do you know how it's done?"

"Initially the same principles as fireworks, only once the sparks reach their trajectory, each one is suspended and manipulated into a shape," Vala replied. "True artistry, though—not something I can do!"

The friends watched in wonder and fascination as images of animals, plants, buildings, and a few abstract fractals flashed before them in turn, then faded away like falling stars.

After the show, further celebrations took place: there was dancing, music, magic displays, and tables laid out with a cornucopia of fruits, breads, cheeses, pastries, nuts, and wines. Vala looked on as her friends partook in the festivities; Jelly squealed as Max whirled her around before kissing her warmly on the lips. Elvar had danced with Vala once, but his mood was sombre and there had not been an opportunity for them to talk privately. Elvar sat swirling the last remnants of his Velinosa wine around the glass; it was his third glass, and the alcohol was taking notable affect as his eyes glazed over, his thoughts fogged and hazy.

"Um, Elvar, mate," Max said, eyeing him with a mixture of concern and surprise, "I think you've probably had enough."

"No amount is enough for this," Elvar slurred, his forehead against the table.

"Are you going to tell me what *this* is?"

"Nooo," Elvar replied. "Cannot do that, Max, old buddy."

"Okay!" Jelly said brightly. "Well, since we've established that Elvar isn't going to spill, I think we should get him home."

Vala stared, her hands shaking. She had never seen Elvar like this, and unlike her friends, it disturbed rather than amused her. She stood behind Elvar, who was still seated, and pressed herself against his back, wrapping her arms around his neck. Elvar groaned unhappily and covered his face with his hands.

"Vala," Elvar said, "please, no. Feeling your body against mine makes me want to make love to you and I cannot."

"I imagine not," Max jibed, laughing. "Not that tanked up!"

"Come on, Elvar," Vala said gently. "Let's go home."

Max helped Elvar to his feet and placed his arm around Elvar's back to steady and support him. Vala went to Elvar's other side and placed her arm around his waist. She inhaled deeply; the smell of alcohol mingled with Elvar's scent and the aroma of food—Vala felt her stomach roil. She felt exhausted but it was imperative that Vala get Elvar home, sober him up, and find out the source of his distress.

When they reached home, Max convinced Elvar to take a shower, advising that Vala accompany him to the bathroom, whilst Max waited outside the bathroom door should his assistance be required. Elvar had been keen to avoid his parents seeing him intoxicated and it had been an effort to hurry him up the stairs and into the bathroom without attracting attention.

Elvar emerged from the shower and wrapped a towel around his waist. He was surprised to find Vala sitting on the toilet lid.

"I had forgotten you were here," Elvar admitted, his voice more controlled now. "The shower has helped. I feel less—"

"Drunk?"

Elvar grinned, his happy countenance returning for a moment.

"Are you going to tell me what happened?" Vala asked, getting up to dry Elvar's back.

"I will," Elvar said. "I promise—when we go to bed."

*

Vala rested her head on Elvar's chest as he sighed unhappily. He had not meant to delay in telling Vala what had transpired earlier, but it was difficult. Really, really difficult. Elvar kissed Vala's head, resting his cheek against her. Taking a deep breath, he told her everything. Vala stared at the ceiling, lost for words.

"Are you all right?" Elvar asked, knowing she wasn't.

"Not really," Vala admitted. "You should get some sleep, Elvar. We can talk in the morning, you're looking a little worse for wear right now."

"If you are sure?" Elvar said reluctantly, his brow knitting.

"I am," Vala said softly, turning to kiss him. "Sleep now, beloved."

Elvar closed his eyes, and within a few minutes he fell into a deep sleep.

Vala lay awake as the significance of Elvar's words filtered through the layers of her mind. A dichotomy of terror and elation battled within. Neither won. Accepting the stalemate, Vala allowed her mind to rest and drifted into a deep but troubled sleep.

29

It had been five weeks since Elvar's startling revelation, and Vala had done her best to disassociate herself from the worrying thoughts and feelings, which, in spite of her best efforts, continued to follow her, stalking her and pouncing unexpectedly like a ravenous predator. It was during these quiet moments that Vala felt most vulnerable because when it was quiet, her intuition spoke the loudest. Usually Vala welcomed her enhanced intuitive abilities, but on this occasion, she wanted to silence them, to block her ears from hearing.

Her university life was now officially over, and once Gweneira had given birth, she intended to begin their quest; the mysterious girl that apparently posed a great threat to Vala was still at large, and Vala hoped that they would find her before she found them.

Most of her belongings had already been packed and taken to Elvar's home in Avalonia. Elvar had had to procure another wardrobe just to accommodate Vala's extra clothing, and her toiletries now covered the once-uncluttered surface of his dresser. She wondered if Elvar was truly comfortable with the changes, especially when this was the one area where they were diametrically different. Elvar was very minimalistic and owned few personal possessions, whereas Vala loved clothes, jewellery, books, music, and cuddly toys. Much of her belongings had stayed behind in her parents' home because, until she and Elvar had their own home, there was no space available. Vala didn't know why she was worrying so much about it, as Elvar had given her no cause to believe he was anything but relaxed about their living arrangements. She knew that this anxiety had probably arisen as a diversion to what was really troubling her.

She squeezed a fluffy pink sweater into her carryall and sat on the bed, gazing out of the window. Streaks of fuchsia and vermillion flamed the now-turquoise sky. Vala focussed her attention on the pink-hued clouds that drifted lazily along; employing one of the techniques she had been taught, she visualised all of her anxiety transferring from her body to one of the clouds where the energies could be taken away and cleansed. She felt the tension dissipate and walked away from the window. Feeling fatigued, she lay back on the bed. She closed her eyes and was soundly asleep within minutes. As she slept, unsettling emotions stirred within, accompanied by troubling, confused dream visions.

She was walking away from Elvar's house. Sunlit leaf patterns danced across the pathway and melodious birdsong surrounded her. A gentle breeze carried the soothing scents of lavender mingled with pine. The colours around Vala seemed particularly saturated and bright. It appeared, for all intents and purposes, to be a perfect sunny day and yet something stirred beneath the surface ... something that did not feel right. A feeling of unease assaulted her senses as she continued to walk towards the Avalonian woodland. Suddenly the birdsong stopped—the forest became eerily quiet. Vala felt her heartbeat quicken as the foreboding engulfed her, steadily growing with each step. Footsteps. She started to turn her head. Darkness began to fringe her peripheral vision as a hand holding a damp cloth clamped down over Vala's nose and mouth. A sickly sweet, potent odour overpowered her. And then ... nothing. The blackness started to fade. A blurred face lowered over Vala's prone form. She started to scream.

Vala felt a familiar touch on her shoulder and her dream world shattered, splintering and dissolving into the ether. She opened her eyes.

"Elvar," Vala murmured, still hazy from the nightmarish vision.

"I am here, beloved," Elvar replied, brushing away damp locks of hair from her forehead. "A bad dream?"

"I'm not sure," Vala said uncertainly. "It seemed ... I don't know ..."

"Like the vision you had of my death?" "Yes," Vala said, sitting up slowly.

Elvar lay down next to Vala and encircled her in his arms, planting a kiss on her forehead.

"I have something for you," he said, delving into the pocket of his jeans and handing Vala a small piece of paper.

"With reverence, Celestia, I summon thee; take me to the realm beyond land and sea. Once my business there is done, return me safely to my land of sun," Vala read aloud.

"To invoke the Celestia, you will need to speak that incantation whilst channelling your energies to your Iridiscus crystal," Elvar said. "It is important to keep your intention clear."

"Do you think this is the right time?" Vala asked, sensing that Elvar had intuited her contemplation about making contact with Amalia again.

"Maybe you should tell me about your vision," Elvar said, stroking her hair.

30

It was early evening when Vala and Elvar crossed through the Fernacre Stone Circle into Avalonia. Due to recent events, both Vala and Elvar were quiet, both hyper-alert and attuned to anything in their environment that might be amiss. Vala felt a tingling in her spine and looked to her right towards a house about thirty feet away.

"That is Lann's home," Elvar said quietly, noticing the shift in Vala's energies.

A twig snapped. Vala and Elvar froze. Watching, waiting to see the source of the sound. A girl appeared on the woodland path leading up to Lann's home.

"It is Maiwen!" Elvar said, breathing an audible sigh of relief.

"Maiwen!" Vala called out, waving.

The girl turned and stared in Vala's direction. She said nothing.

Vala was about to call out again, but something in the girl's gaze chilled her. The girl turned away again and continued to Lann's home. Vala and Elvar watched as she disappeared inside.

"That was strange," Elvar commented, his brow knitting.

"Something feels off," Vala said, as an icy sensation spread through her veins. "Why didn't she answer?"

"I do not know," Elvar replied. "We should hurry home, though, maybe something has happened and Maiwen is upset. Perhaps she is trying to resolve an issue with that idiotic boyfriend of hers."

Vala sighed, squeezing Elvar's hand. "Lann is your friend. He made a mistake; it is not like you to bear such a grudge towards someone."

"I cannot help it," Elvar said, his voice catching. "We still do not know the consequences of his incompetence. And the problem is, it is I who would feel responsible!"

"But why, Elvar?" Vala challenged. "How are you responsible? It was just an accident, and you were not at fault."

"Because, Vala," Elvar began, his voice flooding with emotion, "I am responsible for keeping you safe and ... and if I had not distracted Lann with our heated exchange, he would not have made such an error."

"You're angry with yourself," Vala said, pulling on Elvar's hand gently as she stopped to face him. "You can't blame yourself, your anger on that day was understandable. Maiwen's your little sister; it's natural that you feel protective of her. Likewise, you need to stop being angry with Lann—all of it was an accident, and whatever happens is destined to be."

Vala cupped Elvar's face in her hands and stood on her toes to kiss him.

"Your counsel is wise, my beloved," Elvar said, soothed by her words and touch. "As always. I will make amends with Lann in the morning. I do not wish to be the cause of any further discord, especially as he is courting my sister, and their relationship ..." Elvar paused. "If she is going to him so late in the evening, I can only presume that their relationship is serious."

As they reached Elvar's home, Vala's sense of foreboding increased. Not waiting to speak to Elvar, Vala rushed up the stairs to Maiwen's room and knocked on the door. The door opened and Maiwen stared at Vala, confused by Vala's horrified expression. A moment later, Elvar appeared, visibly shocked to see his sister.

"What is it?" Maiwen asked impatiently. "What is wrong with the two of you? Why are you looking at me in such a way?"

"We just saw you at Lann's," Vala answered. "You couldn't possibly be back so quickly—surely?"

"I have not seen Lann since lunchtime," Maiwen said, her face draining of colour. "What do you mean, you saw me there?"

"It wasn't you!" Vala said, voicing her fears. "It was her!"

"Where are Mother and Father?" Elvar said with a sense of urgency.

"They are in the kitchen preparing dinner," Maiwen said flatly.

"We need to get them!" Elvar said, his voice rising. "We have to go now!"

Maiwen nodded, silent tears streaking her face as she ran to inform her parents.

A short while later, the five of them alighted in front of Lann's home. Maiwen pounded loudly on the front door. After what seemed like an eternity, Lann opened the door. He was shirtless, his hair ruffled and his cheeks flushed.

"Maiwen?" Lann said, his eyes widening in surprise. "I was not expecting to see you again so soon!"

"Where is she?" Maiwen demanded, her voice hysterical.

"Where is who?" Lann asked, confused.

"Whoever you were just with," Maiwen answered, barely able to maintain her composure, "it was not me!"

"May we come in?" Essyeult asked calmly.

"Yes, yes, of course!" Lann replied, his face florid as an uncomfortable realisation seeped through him.

Before any of them had had a chance to speak further, Maiwen raced inside and up the stairs to Lann's bedroom. She stared in horror at the rumpled sheets on his bed. Lann raced after her.

"What did you do, Lann?" Maiwen asked, her voice choked as a torrent of tears streamed down her cheeks.

"I thought it was you!" Lann cried, rubbing his hands across his face. "You did not say much, but I thought perhaps you had had a change of heart and ..."

"But I told you I was not ready!" Maiwen screeched. "How could you not realise?"

Maiwen turned as she felt a gentle touch on her shoulder. She looked tearfully at her mother as Essyeult held her tightly in her arms. Maiwen continuing to sob.

"He slept with her!" Maiwen said mournfully, her voice muffled by her mother's shoulder.

"I think it best I take Maiwen back home," Essyeult said, looking directly at Lann. "She has endured a great shock. I imagine the girl is long gone, but we shall take our leave now and leave the three of you to discuss matters with Lann.

Lann looked on helplessly as Essyeult led Maiwen away from him.

"I had no way of knowing!" Lann insisted, looking at Vala, as he felt uncomfortable meeting Elvar or Derryth's gaze.

"This is not an easy situation," Derryth said. "We are not here to apportion blame. We need to find out what happened, beyond the obvious, that is."

"I genuinely thought that girl was Maiwen," Lann said, perspiration beading his forehead. "She said very little, only that she wanted to ..."

"Please, Lann," Vala said gently, touching his arm. "We need to know."

"She removed her clothes and asked me to make love to her," Lann admitted, bile rising in his throat in revulsion.

"And you were foolish enough to believe that my innocent sister would behave in such a provocative way?" Elvar retorted hotly.

"I am so sorry!" Lann said, burying his face in his hands. "I love Maiwen dearly—I was not thinking clearly." "Obviously!" Elvar said angrily.

"Enough!" Derryth shouted. "There is no time for childish bickering. This girl is very likely the one behind the recent murders and poses not only a threat to us all, but has a particular interest in Vala. Lann, I would like you to accompany me to discuss this with Lady Elomia Fernleaf. The council must know of this immediately." "Yes, of course, sir," Lann replied obsequiously.

"You might be needing this!" Elvar said hotly, throwing Lann's shirt at him and storming down the stairs.

"Vala?" Derryth called out as she made her way to follow Elvar.

Vala turned. The palpable tension and discord made her uncomfortable, and she was keen to go home.

"Please tell Essyeult what has happened," Derryth said, "and that I shall be back slightly late for dinner. You are all welcome to start without me, though."

"I'll do that," Vala replied. "I should go talk to Elvar and try to diffuse his anger."

"Until later then, Daughter," Derryth said. "Take great care walking back."

"Likewise!" Vala said, bounding down the stairs to find Elvar.

Vala found him in the lounge, leaning against a wall, his jaw clenched, his gaze fixed on a point outside the window.

Vala looked outside before looking back towards Elvar. Dark shadows danced hypnotically across the room, illuminated by the moonlight. Vala usually loved nightfall in Avalonia. It felt peaceful and romantic, filled with song and sounds from nocturnal birds and animals—the night air infused with the scent of jasmine and Levonaria. Tonight, however, felt ominous and carried with it the fear of an unknown threat.

Vala lightly touched Elvar's arm. Elvar looked at his wife, his gaze softening. She stroked her thumb across his cheek. He looked so vulnerable, and in so much anguish.

"Let's go home," Vala said, lacing her fingers with his.

31

The house was quiet when Vala and Elvar returned home, save the occasional sound of sobbing from Maiwen's room. Hearing the door open, Essyeult appeared at the top of the stairs.

"I presume Derryth has gone to alert the council regarding the girl's presence in Avalonia?"

"Yes, Mother," Elvar confirmed, his voice weary.

"Maiwen is understandably upset," Essyeult said. "Maybe if we delay dinner till Derryth's return, she will be more amenable to eating a bite or two."

"That works for me," Vala said. "Besides, I'm not sure Elvar is in much of a mood for eating either."

Essyeult nodded in agreement. "I will be with Maiwen then."

When Derryth returned, the family, with the exception of Maiwen, sat down to dinner. Elvar had barely uttered a word since arriving home, and he poked his food listlessly, his appetite gone.

"Please try and eat, Son," Essyeult said, sighing. "It is bad enough having one unhappy child. Besides which, we can do nothing more than be extra vigilant."

"I am glad to see that at least Vala appreciates my cooking!" Essyeult commented as she observed Vala hungrily devouring the food on her plate.

Vala felt her face redden in response to Essyeult's comment. Truth be told, she was absolutely ravenous.

"This is really good," Vala said in between mouthfuls. "And I'm hungry! I don't see much point in stressing about the girl, we know I'm going to encounter her sooner or later. I am more concerned about Maiwen."

"I do not understand how you can be so blasé about your own safety!" Elvar retorted angrily. "How can you not comprehend the gravity of the situation?"

"I do!" Vala returned, annoyance creeping in. "I just don't see the point in ruminating over something that we cannot control!"

"And I cannot—" Elvar began, but was interrupted by Derryth, whose Iridiscus crystal was glowing.

"That was Tarrys," Derryth interjected. "Gweneira is in the final stages of labour. I must leave immediately."

"I'm going with you," Vala announced, rising to her feet, feeling a little unsteady but putting it down to the stress caused by the friction between her and Elvar. "I promised Gwen I would assist the birth."

"I will accompany you," Elvar said firmly. "As Mother said, it is imperative that we are all extra vigilant."

"Well, in that case, you need to calm down!" Vala said. Her anger was dissipating as she realised that Elvar's dark mood was due to his desire to fervently protect her from harm. "A tense atmosphere is not conducive to a good birthing experience."

"Vala is right," Derryth said, touching his son's shoulder. "You need to keep your emotions in check—Gwen has already suffered complications. We need to create a relaxed environment to welcome her baby into the world."

Vala flung her arms around Elvar's neck and drew him into a deep kiss. Under normal circumstances, she would not indulge in such an open display of intense affection; however, these were not normal circumstances. Elvar's initial shock over Vala's actions were soon replaced with profuse love and longing. No, he couldn't allow himself to feel like this, not now, not in front of his parents. He broke contact with Vala before his body became further aroused.

"Feeling better?"

"Much!" Elvar replied, grinning at Vala ruefully. "Right, then, we should go now before Vala finds another reason to embarrass me!"

Essyeult reached out for Derryth's hand as they neared the front door.

"Take care, beloved—and my dear children too," Essyeult said, biting her lower lip. "And send felicitations and apologies from Maiwen and me."

"I'll tell her Maiwen and Lann have had a misunderstanding," Vala said, trying to reassure Essyeult, "and that you needed to stay behind to console her. It might be best not to mention demon girl just yet."

Essyeult nodded in agreement and waved them off.

32

Gweneira's face was contorted with pain, perspiration beading her forehead, but she forced a smile upon seeing Vala approach.

"I am so glad you are here, Vala!" Gweneira said breathlessly. "It is good to see you both too, Derryth and Elvar."

"As agreed, Vala will be overseeing the birth, Gwen," Derryth said. "I shall be on hand to assist and instruct where necessary."

Gweneira cried out as another powerful contraction tore through her body. Vala sat down beside Gweneira, placing one hand on her swollen belly and held her hand with the other. The air in the room felt heavy and charged, and for a moment, a vertiginous sensation overcame Vala, causing her to feel faint and nauseated. To Vala's relief, it soon passed and she quickly focussed her attentions back to Gweneira.

"I'm going to decrease the strength of your contractions," Vala said calmly. "But, as you know, I cannot completely remove the pain as you need to be attuned to both yours and the baby's signals."

Tarrys steeped a cloth into a bowl of water, wringing it out lightly before mopping his wife's brow. His face was tense and his jaw set tightly.

As with Elvar, Vala could sense, and ultimately experience, Tarrys' emotions the most potently. The waves of anxiety radiating from him were palpable and struck Vala like tiny arrows of ice, stinging as they hit her skin and penetrated her heart, causing it to beat harder and faster, as frozen shockwaves rippled through her body, chilling her blood.

"Tarrys," Vala said softly, looking up at her brother, "Gwen and the baby are fine. Please, open the window. We need some fresh air in here."

Tarrys did as his sister instructed before returning to her bedside. Gweneira smiled at him weakly.

"I could create a cool air current in the room," Elvar offered, having been silently observing for some time. "I feel quite useless presently."

"That would be lovely," Gweneira replied, her voice fatigued and weak.

Gweneira cried out again as she was gripped by a sharp, burning sensation between her legs.

"Not long now!" Vala said excitedly.

33

Maiwen tiptoed to her parents' room and cracked the door open an inch, peering in. Her mother lay on the bed, her breathing slow and rhythmic; she was asleep.

Not wishing to risk waking Essyeult, Maiwen levitated to the bottom of the stairs, alighting in the porch, where she quietly pulled on a jacket and a pair of boots and stole outside into the night.

Maiwen was accustomed to the Avalonian woodland after dark, as she had often been on post-supper evening strolls with her family. Until quite recently, she and Elvar had gone animal and insect spotting as there were a number of nocturnal creatures: Fintesia butterflies, Vintili moths, and Shandosi—small mammals with luminescent markings that resembled something between a dormouse and rabbit, but with long, glowing bushy tails and ear tips. For many of these animals, the luminescence was a method of attracting a mate.

She looked up at the almost full moon; it cast a glow on the woodland below, and whilst it still held a magical quality to Maiwen, tonight it felt somewhat ominous. Maiwen was unaccustomed to venturing out on her own this late—her previous nighttime expeditions had always been with her family, and the one time with Lann. Lann! Her eyes stung as hot tears surfaced. Lann was the reason she was out here; Maiwen had felt stifled in her room, the air too warm and oppressive. She needed the solace of the woodland, needed to scream and wail without being heard.

Twigs crunched underfoot, the sound amplified and more sinister than usual. Maiwen's head snapped up as the hoot of an owl flying overhead caught her attention and her heart palpitated rapidly. Her eyes and ears became finely attuned to every sight and sound: a rustle in the undergrowth from a pair of Shandosi, dark amorphous shadows on the tree trunks—all of it causing a surge of adrenaline to charge through Maiwen's body, her senses on high alert.

After ten minutes of walking, Maiwen found a tree with a lowlying but substantial bough, and using her hands for leverage, she pushed herself up and sat upon it, leaning her head against the trunk. She exhaled a shuddery breath and closed her eyes.

How could Lann not have known that it was not me that called upon him earlier? The girl, the imposter, whose lips he kissed and whose body …

The thoughts rolled unbidden into Maiwen's mind as fresh tears sprang from her eyes, flowing over her cheeks and onto the forest floor. She wasn't sure how long she had been sitting there before sensing that she was being watched. Maiwen hastily rubbed the heel of her hands over her eyes and waited as they refocussed. A shape, there in the distance between two oak trees stood something or someone. As Maiwen's eyesight sharpened, she saw him: a small boy heading cautiously towards her. Maiwen remained on the branch. Watching. Waiting. When the boy stood just a few feet away, Maiwen leapt down from the branch and looked at him curiously.

"What are you doing out here so late?" Maiwen asked the boy, wondering why such a young child should be wandering the woods at night alone.

When the boy didn't answer, Maiwen prompted him with further questions.

"Where are your parents?" Still no answer.

"Are you lost?"

The boy nodded and reached out tentatively, lightly touching Maiwen's arm. Inexplicably, Maiwen's maelstrom of emotions suddenly quietened and a wave of calm passed over her.

She looked at the boy sympathetically, genuinely disturbed that such a young child be wandering out on his own so late at night. He couldn't be much more than ten years old. She gently took his hand in hers.

"It is not safe for you to be wandering the woodland so late," Maiwen said. "Would you like to come home with me and we can set about finding your parents in the morning?"

The boy looked up at Maiwen. He smiled, nodding his assent.

"Do you not talk?" Maiwen asked the boy, puzzled by his silence and wondered if he had been traumatised in some way.

The boy shook his head.

"Okay!" Maiwen said. "So this might be something of a challenge! No Iridiscus either. Never mind, let us be going. Maybe after a good night's sleep you will find your voice again and I can get you back to your undoubtedly frantic parents!"

The boy remained silent throughout their walk back to Maiwen's home. As she felt his tiny hand clasped in hers, she hoped it brought the poor child some comfort. However, she was more surprised by her own serenity—maybe the distraction from Lann was the source of this newfound calm.

As Maiwen quietly opened the door, the little boy dutifully removed his shoes and followed her inside. Maiwen realised when she looked up at the wall clock, that she had been gone for just over two hours—much longer than she thought. The house was silent; either the others were still with Gweneira, or they had returned and gone to bed. Maiwen took the boy's hand again and led him to the kitchen, intent on making the child a hot chocolate before settling him down for the night in the spare room. Not expecting to see anyone else, she was startled as Vala stepped out of the pantry with a jar of nuts and a wooden canister of hot chocolate. Vala almost dropped the items she was holding as she took in the sight of Maiwen with … who was this child?

"Vala!" Maiwen said, her voice rising slightly. "I was not expecting anyone to be awake."

"I was hungry," Vala said, her gaze fixed upon the child. "Who is this, Maiwen?"

"I found him wandering the woods alone," Maiwen explained. "I could not leave him—he is just a lost little boy."

A cold, prickling sensation needled along Vala's skin, darts of foreboding piercing her heart and causing her to shiver.

"Who is he though, Maiwen?" Vala probed. "Where are his parents?"

"I do not know," Maiwen admitted. "He seems unable to speak. I thought that he could stay overnight and that hopefully Mother and Father will be able to help find his parents in the morning."

Vala frowned. She adored children … and yet … something felt off and her disquietude troubled her.

Where is my generosity of spirit? Vala thought to herself, trying to push her unsettling feelings aside.

"Well, I don't suppose one night will hurt," she conceded. "I was just about to make some hot chocolate—would you like me to make another two mugs?"

"That would be most kind of you," Maiwen replied. "Thank you. By the way, has Gwen had her baby?"

"Yes!" Vala said, her voice brightening. "My first successful delivery! She had a healthy baby girl, weighing in at seven pounds, six ounces. They named her Temiritha."

"Oh, that's wonderful!" Maiwen exclaimed, feeling genuine elation at the news. "I cannot wait to meet her! And you are an aunty now!"

"Indeed!" Vala said, grinning back as she heated the milk on the stove, adding a couple of Chando pods for further flavour.

They sat down at the dining table with their mugs of hot chocolate as Vala attempted to question the little boy, gently, so as not to further alarm him. Like Maiwen, Vala wondered if the child had endured some trauma, rendering him unable to speak. Her efforts were unavailed: he merely nodded or shook his head—all the time fixing Vala with an unrelenting, curious stare.

"Right, well it's been a long day," Vala said, standing. "I'm off to bed."

"Of course," Maiwen responded. "And congratulations on your first successful childbirth! At least you know what to expect yourself now."

"Thanks for that thought!" Vala retorted. "And on that note, I bid you goodnight, but make sure you tell Essyeult and Derryth first thing."

"I will," Maiwen assured her. "I promise. Goodnight."

34

Maiwen felt uncertain of how to proceed on preparing the boy for bed. She didn't have any nightwear that would fit him, so she removed his socks and gave him a toothbrush and washcloth to clean himself with. After he returned from the bathroom, she brushed his hair and tucked him into bed, watching as he stared up at her.

"Close your eyes now and go to sleep," Maiwen said softly as she stroked his hair. "Would you like me to stay till you fall asleep?"

The boy nodded as Maiwen continued to stroke his hair, softly singing a lullaby to soothe the child to sleep. Before long, Maiwen's eyes grew heavy as she drifted into a deep sleep.

*

Vala couldn't settle. She tossed and turned as her feelings of trepidation twisted in her gut. She knew it was because of the strange boy Maiwen had brought home and could not quieten her misgivings about who or what he was. Vala realised that unless she checked in on Maiwen, sleep was a lost cause, and she had been feeling tired enough lately without the added encumbrance of sleep deprivation.

She quietly climbed out of bed and padded over to Maiwen's room, softly knocking on the door, before opening it a notch and peeking inside. Maiwen's bed was empty. Alarmed, Vala quickly made her way to the guest bedroom where she saw Maiwen asleep on the chair next to the bed. The boy was not in the bed! He was standing in front of Maiwen, with one hand hovering over her chest, the other over her head. "Get away from her!"

The boy did not respond, and Maiwen did not waken. As Vala approached the boy, she noticed that his eyes were closed as though in trance. She pulled him away from Maiwen, and the child's eyes bolted open, registering a mixture of fear and surprise. He stood there for a moment as Vala shook Maiwen awake. Maiwen groggily opened her eyes.

"What is going on?" Maiwen asked, her voice heavy with sleep.

"He's one of *them*, Maiwen!" Vala said in alarm. "He's a soul-taker and ..."

The boy was still standing there, seemingly uncertain as to what action to take. He cast one last look, first at Vala, then Maiwen, before bolting from the room.

"But he was just a child," Maiwen said sadly, "and ... and he made me feel ... he made all the bad feelings dissipate."

Elvar appeared behind Vala, his brow knitted in confusion and concern.

"I'm sorry, Maiwen, but he was about to take your soul and," Vala paused, uncertain of how to explain. "There was something more ... when I touched him I felt immense power. He doesn't just take souls, he absorbs and assimilates others' special abilities; he can also influence emotion, which is why you felt so calm around him."

"I tried to chase him," Elvar said. "Who was that boy?"

"Your sister found him wandering the woods and thought it wise to bring him home," Vala said.

"What is all the commotion about?" Essyeult demanded, stepping into Maiwen's room with Derryth, who wearily rubbed his eyes.

"I think that my sister has some explaining to do," Elvar said, pointedly glaring at Maiwen.

35

The following morning after a lengthy discussion at the breakfast table, it was decided that it was imperative that their quest to find Merlin begin immediately. Vala had returned to her family home to inform her parents and contact Jelly and Max.

Vala tightly coiled a lock of hair between her finger and thumb, pulling it taut in frustration, before letting it bounce back again. This was not going to plan.

"But Mama, I already have Jelly and Max to protect, and it's still possible that Elvar and Merri may need my help too."

"We are coming with you, Sugar Plum," Laoli insisted, taking her daughter's hands in her own. "We do not need your protection—it is our job to protect you."

"But what about the shop?"

"We have been prepared for this," Patrick explained. "Uncle Michael, Aunt Elisa, and Aunt Seravyna, are all on a rota to run the shop in our absence. We also have an apprentice herbalist who will be on hand for medical and health guidance."

Patrick put down the jug he had been using to water the kitchen plants and pulled up a stool next to Vala at the breakfast bar.

"Your mother and I will be with you," Patrick said, hugging his daughter. "We will not let you face this threat alone. I will not allow any harm to come to either of you."

"No offence, Dad," Vala said, a flicker of a smile crossing her face. "But I'm not sure how much protection you can use against such a foe."

"I may be able to manipulate her emotional state, make her less hostile, and I can probably aid the Enhanced Barrier Spell too."

"Fine!" Vala said. "I concede!"

"You will understand one day, Sugar Plum," Laoli said softly. "Now, when are Jelly and Max arriving? I have prepared a mixed pea and asparagus tartlet, followed by Silanchi berry crème brulée for dessert."

36

"No, Mother!" Elvar retorted hotly. "There are enough of us already. No harm will befall Vala."

"And while you are all protecting Vala, who will be protecting you?" Essyeult protested.

"I would insist on accompanying you too," Derryth said. "But with Gwen only just having given birth, a chief healer needs to be on hand."

Elvar sighed and shook his head; he knew there was nothing to be gained in arguing his point further. Once his parents had made a decision, it was nearly always resolute, and no amount of discussion would shift their stance on this.

The numbers partaking on this quest were steadily growing; Elvar had already received word that morning that in addition to Merridyn, his friend Gannlyth would also be joining them. Elvar could only hope there would be no more surprise companions on this quest—it was starting to give him a headache.

37

"So we'll really be meeting fae royalty?" Jelly said excitedly as they walked to the Royal Palace.

"Queen Assanli herself, no less," Vala replied, bemused by Jelly's excitement, though truth be told, although she had previously met the queen, she too felt a flutter of nervous excitement.

Vala stopped suddenly, feeling a disturbance in her heart rhythm; it was like nothing she had ever experienced. She bent over, forearms resting on her thighs, and inhaled deeply. The warm air, suffused with the fragrance of meadowsweet and lavender, tickled Vala's nostrils, dancing across her tastebuds and filling her airway with a heady floral aroma. She allowed the soporific scent to soothe her and restore balance to her being.

"Vala," Elvar said anxiously, "what is wrong, my love?"

"Um ... I'm not sure actually," Vala admitted, her rapid heartbeat now much slower. "I just felt a little odd for a moment. I'm okay, Elvar. Really!"

"Vala, your aura ..." Essyeult began, touching Vala's arm.

"It's fine!" Vala interjected. "I'm just a bit tired. Please, let's just get to the palace."

Elvar shook his head but reluctantly agreed.

The colourful array of crystals adorning the palace walls glistened spectacularly in the bright sunlight, casting a full spectrum of colour over its white walls; it was truly a sight to behold, and both Jelly and Max gasped as they stood transfixed by its splendour.

They followed Elvar through a lovely walkway comprised of tall, lush green trees with elongated tear-shaped fronds that interconnected not only with the adjacent trees, but those opposite, creating an elaborate woven effect, almost like a wicker basket; the bark had a shimmery metallic appearance with copper and white stripes. From some of the leaves, long curled tendrils extended, laden with tiny blue bell-shaped flowers with bright pink-and-yellow stamens. They exuded a potent alpine aroma—stimulating and refreshing to the senses.

"This is awesome sauce!" Max exclaimed. "That smell is really invigorating too—just what we need for the long journey ahead."

"These trees are beautiful," Jelly said wistfully, reaching up and letting her fingers graze a trailing cluster of flowers. "What are they?"

"Mystifosa," Essyeult replied, smiling. "The oil from the flowers is used as a stimulant: one of the main components of a tonic for when a little extra concentration and alertness is required." "Wait!" Merridyn called out.

The others turned, startled by Merridyn's sudden outburst.

"I completely forgot!" Merridyn said, his cheeks flushed with excitement. "I solved the riddle!"

"Max and I have no idea what you're referring to," Jelly said, placing a hand on Merridyn's arm. She hadn't consciously meant to touch him. *Damn! Do all fae guys have to be so infuriatingly alluring?*

"Indeed," Max said, frowning as his gaze followed to Jelly's hand, still resting on Merridyn's arm. "Care to enlighten us?"

"Beneath the canopy of palest blue,

The second of three,

The darkest of two,

Within the outer,

It resides in plain view," Merridyn said.

"And?" Vala said impatiently.

"The canopy of blue," Merridyn replied. "It was always assumed that it referred to the sky at dawn, that somehow, whatever it was exactly would be revealed in the morning light. But it is not the sky to which the riddle alludes—it is the Viaspa trees!"

"Do you think that somebody else may have also reached the same conclusion?" Elvar challenged.

"Maybe," Merridyn countered. "But they did not find the ring—I did!"

"You found the ring?" Essyeult said, her eyes widening in disbelief.

"As you are aware, the Viaspan wood is associated with protection; there is a grove of Viaspa trees, a particularly dense cluster on the Alusian cliffs. There are three trees that stand in formation, slightly taller than the others, so I picked the middle one. That is when it all got rather more perplexing ..."

"Merri!" Vala said. "Stop milking it!"

"Milking it?" Merridyn replied, puzzled by Vala's response. "I do not understand."

"Never mind," Vala returned, trying to suppress a giggle, "just continue!"

"Well, as I was saying, the next part was more difficult to decipher, so I started searching in the hollows within the tree—of which there were many, may I add—when I came across two branches with
a familiar marking carved in: the Meridia Absolutas."

"Wait," Elvar said, raising an eyebrow, "both branches had the Meridia carved upon them?"

"Yes!" Merridyn continued excitedly. "However, one was overshadowed by the other—*the darkest of two*. Within that *darker* branch were several hollows. However, the riddle pertained to the outermost one, or at least, that was my theory. Well, it proved correct."

Merridyn partially unbuttoned his shirt and reached inside, producing a light-brown pouch, mottled and weathered by age and the environment in which it had been contained. He reached within the pouch and extracted a gleaming gold ring, untarnished by the ravages of time, which he nested in the palm of his hand for the others to see.

"It looks completely new!" Vala said, gazing upon it in wonder. "May I?" She looked up at Merridyn, hoping to hold it for a moment.

"Yes, of course, Vala," Merridyn said softly. "It is yours, I found it for you, to keep you safe."

Vala carefully took the ring from Merridyn's outstretched palm and held it between her fingers to examine it more closely.

"Look," Vala said, "it is engraved with the Meridia Absolutas."

"You must wear it, beloved," Elvar said, closing his hand around Vala's. "It is infused with considerable power; it will help protect you from whatever awaits us."

"No," Vala said softly, "I can't."

"But you must!" Merridyn replied, his voice trembling. "I found it for *you*, Vala, to protect you from that girl—the soul taker."

"I can protect myself," Vala insisted. "Jelly and Max cannot, they are defenceless. The problem is there is only one ring." "Then Jelly should wear it," Max said firmly.

"No!" Jelly protested. "What about you, Max? You're no safer from her than I am!"

Silence befell the group and Merridyn turned away from the others, his face cupped in his hands. Vala knew she had injured his feelings and felt terrible in doing so, but what choice did she have?

"Wait!" Essyeult said. "I have a solution, or at least, a partial one. The ring will protect not only the wearer, but whoever is in physical contact with the ring."

"So if Max and I are holding hands," Jelly said, understanding immediately, "which we already do, then we will both be protected!"

"But what about at night?" Max said. "Or, um, certain *personal* bodily processes that entail a degree of privacy?"

"I doubt she'll attack you on the toilet, Max!" Vala said, laughing. "Even crazy soul-sucking psycho girls presumably have some sense of decorum!"

Max's cheeks burned and he looked at Vala squarely, "And when we sleep?"

"We were not asleep in Amalia's vision," Vala answered. "So which one of you wants to wear it?"

Max took the ring from Vala and placed it on Jelly's middle finger. "She will!"

Jelly sighed and shook her head, but she decided not to pursue it further.

"All right," Essyeult declared loudly. "Enough squabbling! We must hasten our steps—Queen Assanli is expecting us."

The group fell into silence again, following Elvar's lead as he continued through the leafy walkway, which took them around the side of the palace to a domed antechamber. Vala hazarded a glance at Merridyn—he looked completely crushed. His disappointment was palpable and it struck through Vala's heart, causing a tidal wave of sorrow to flood her being.

As they approached the door to the antechamber, Elvar placed his hand over the keyhole and murmured an incantation; the door opened. Vala and Elvar stepped through the doorway first, with the others trailing closely behind. Vala had been to this part of the palace only once before, when Queen Assanli had requested an audience with her after she had defeated the Spindler, but the grandiose chamber still took her breath away, and she smiled as she heard pleasurable gasps and excited whispers from Jelly and Max. Gannlyth revealed that he frequented the palace on many an occasion to play for the fae royalty. Even Merridyn, who was still very sullen, looked up at the wondrous sights surrounding him.

Although the exterior of the chamber had the appearance of fine opaque alabaster, the interior had the appearance of faceted frosted glass, embedded with a multitudinous array of crystals in many different colours and hues, all expertly and magically arranged like a mosaic to depict ever-changing scenery, which Vala explained to Jelly and Max was representative of the four kingdoms of Candalia. They watched for a while, mesmerised, as forests gave way to lush green valleys, which morphed into snow-capped mountains that transposed into seascapes: each of the scenes alive with motion and carrying a redolence of that landscape.

Essyeult glanced at Elvar and nodded, she held her Iridiscus pendant and closed her eyes. Within moments, Queen Assanli was standing before them. She was of average height with flowing waves of golden hair and sparkling azure eyes.

"Vala, Elvar, and my dear friends, Essyeult," the queen said warmly, laughing as she welcomed them inside. "It is wonderful to see you all again, and I see you have quite the entourage!"

"We are honoured to meet with you again, Queen Assanli," Vala said, inclining her head and kissing Assanli's hand. Elvar did the same. "My parents send their apologies—they have had an unexpected delay and will join us later."

Removing their shoes in the antechamber, they stepped into an even larger domed hallway with a high ceiling adorned with the sky frescoes characteristic of so many fae interiors. The walls depicted the palace gardens, all with animated imagery of birds, butterflies, bees, and other wild creatures. A bouquet of floral scents suffused the air, creating a relaxing atmosphere.

"It is good to see you too, Queen Assanli," Essyeult said, inclining her head and bringing the queen's hand to her lips.

"Come now, Essyeult," the queen replied, "there are no formalities between us—we are old friends."

"Indeed we are," Essyeult replied warmly.

Vala and Elvar introduced their friends to the queen before following her through the hallway into an airy, capacious room, filled with natural light. The walls were a pale blue with wispy white clouds ambling gently through the painted sky, changing form and density as an imaginary breeze carried them along. A large croissant-shaped sofa lined in pale-blue damask and scattered with cream silk cushions took pride and place in the centre of the room with a vantage point of the gardens, which could be viewed through the concave glass wall in front. Vala's feet had grown hot during the walk to the palace, so she had taken the opportunity to remove her socks, which she had stuffed into her shoes earlier. She wiggled her toes in the plush cream carpet underfoot—it was blissfully soft and soothing to her tired feet.

"Please be seated, my honoured guests," Queen Assanli said, gesturing towards the sofa.

Jelly huddled up close to Vala, feeling rather overawed by their current circumstances. Max's attentions, however, were fixed on the delectable array of pastries and other culinary delights set out on a large, curved Viaspan wood coffee table.

"And help yourself to food and refreshments," the queen added. "There is chilled Alushi nectar on the table, but if another drink is desired, please do not hesitate to request it."

Max needed no further prompting and piled his plate high with pastries, nuts, and various berries.

"Thank you for agreeing to assist us, Queen Assanli," Vala said, as she reached for a plate.

"I am greatly honoured to be in a position to help you this time, Vala," the queen replied. "I and all who reside in Candalia are indebted to you for your great bravery and interminable courage. As you know, it is my sacred duty to protect my subjects from harm, but more than that, I want to be *useful* this time. You faced the Spindler without the aid of my protection. This time, I would at least like to be of service and contribute towards your mission in finding Merlin and protect you from this new abomination, whoever she is."

"We are very grateful, my Queen," Elvar said, squeezing Vala's free hand.

"Please," Queen Assanli said, "just call me Assanli, and, for a while, let us take a brief interlude from such grave matters and en-
gage in more light-hearted discourse."

Assanli looked towards Jelly and Max, smiling warmly.

"It is good to see you enjoying fae cuisine so much, Max," Assanli said, laughing.

Max smiled back at her ruefully, cheeks aflame. Jelly gave him a sharp nudge in his side, startling Max as he swallowed a few pastry crumbs prematurely and started to cough. Jelly mouthed an apology and quickly handed him a glass of Alushi nectar, which he hastily gulped down.

"With the exception of Vala, whom I did not press at the time for such information, it has been a long time since I have had the opportunity to converse with another about what is happening in the human realm," Assanli continued. "Please, Jelly and Max, enlighten me! Nothing too melancholy—I do not wish to hear about wars and suffering. What interests me greatly is your human technology and the arts."

"Well, you're in luck there," Jelly replied, grinning. "Max is a tech-head and knows all things science; he's studying astrophysics. And me, I'm at drama school, training to be an actress; Vala here knows more about the visual arts."

"Well," Max said, removing his phone from his jeans pocket and handing it to the queen, "this is a smartphone, though if you have spoken to Vala previously, you may already be familiar with it?"

"Yes!" Assanli returned excitedly. "Vala showed me ... what do you call it? Ah yes, a *video* of her and Elvar's wedding ceremony and photos and music! Yes, a wonderful invention indeed! We fae also have ways of capturing both static and moving images, but it is greatly different to this. Do tell me more, though! What other functions does this phone have?"

"Oh, lots," Max said, beaming at Assanli. "I'll show you some more of what this baby can do, though I'm a little limited without an Internet connection. However, there are now these visors that can be worn, featuring all the functionality of a phone, but beamed directly in front of the eye to create a holographic projection. Oh,
and in case you were wondering ..."

Max's enthused science and technology rhetoric continued for the next half hour, before Jelly nudged him again, allowing her, Vala, and the others a word in edgeways.

"It has been a wonderful morning with perfect company!" Assanli announced. "But before I take you to the pendants, I have a final request."

The queen looked directly at Gannlyth and inclined her head, a flicker of a smile crossing her face, almost imperceptibly, but the warmth of the gesture reaching her eyes.

"It would be a great pleasure before we part ways to hear you play, Gannlyth."

"I would be delighted to, my lady," Gannlyth replied. "However, I do not have my instrument with me."

"I know it is not quite the same," Assanli replied, "but I can provide you with a Chantaris if you are agreeable?"

"Of course, my lady," Gannlyth answered, bowing his head.

"Jelly and Max," Assanli said, "you are in for quite a treat!"

38

"That was ..." Jelly began. "I'm speechless!"

"That would be a first!" Max said, snorting.

Jelly jabbed him sharply in the ribs; he responded with a yelp.

"Damn it, Jelly!" Max looked at her, frowning. "You are seriously going to crack a rib if you keep elbowing me!"

"Sorry," Jelly said, genuinely shocked that her actions may have been causing Max pain. "It's a bad habit, I didn't realise it hurt you."

"Okay," Max said, his tone softening, "it kind of does sometimes, but you know now, and besides, I should have said something sooner."

Max kissed the top of Jelly's head. "I forgive you."

Assanli stood, the corners of her mouth twitching as she watched Jelly and Max. She was about to speak when she noticed her Iridiscus pendant glowing.

Smiling, her eyes met with Vala's. "I believe your parents are ready to join us, Vala. I will usher them through; you are all welcome to wait here."

A short while later, Assanli returned with Laoli and Patrick. Vala rose to give them both a hug. Assanli convinced Laoli and Patrick to sample the delicious spread she had laid out and to refresh themselves with a large glass of Alushi nectar, in spite of their protestations.

"Thank you kindly, Assanli," Laoli said, smiling at her host, "that was quite wonderful. I do miss Avalonian cuisine."

"Well, now that your daughter has returned to live amongst us, I dare say you will be visiting more frequently?" Assanli ventured.

"Yes," Patrick confirmed, "we will. At least it's easier to get here than it is to Cambridge!"

Assanli smiled, her azure eyes twinkling. "If you care to follow, I will take you to the pendants and Merevina's bracelet."

They followed Assanli back out into the domed hallway and into yet another hallway, this one smaller and tubular, with creamy chalk walls decorated with animated reliefs of halcyon countryside: lambs frolicked on rolling hills, rabbits hopped in and out of view, butterflies fluttered in the sky settling occasionally on a flower, and leaves swayed in an imaginary, yet redolent breeze.

Towards the end of the hallway and carved into the wall was what looked like a large window, curved at the top. The queen incanted a few words and walked through the wall, inviting the others to do the same.

Max and Jelly, not having experienced this before, stood for a moment, hesitant. Tentatively, Max reached out and touched the wall; his fingers passed through. He looked at Jelly to gauge her reaction. She nodded, and the two of them walked through together.

Vala looked around her; she had seen much of the palace, but never this part. They were standing on a wide marble platform with curved corners, which led to a long flight of steps. The marble was not cold underfoot as Vala had expected, but comfortably warm. She glanced down at the floor and noticed that it was embedded with thousands, maybe millions, of tiny coloured crystals, many of which looked familiar. The banisters of the stairway were elaborately and realistically carved into an interconnecting vine of branches, many with blossoming flowers, tiny buds, and clusters of leaves.

"This is our antiquities room," Assanli explained. "It is an archive of artefacts, relics, and ancient books."

The antiquities room was considerably darker than the other rooms in the palace and was filled with shelves, cabinets, and bookcases. Vala thought it had an *old library* kind of smell, which she found rather pleasing. At the end of the room was an indigo-coloured sofa, lined in silk and scattered with cream and duck-egg coloured cushions; in front of it sat a Viaspan wood coffee table. A little farther along sat a huge, majestic marble table, its legs curved and boasting the same interwoven branch vinery as the stairway.

"This is fantastic!" Merridyn exclaimed. "What I would not give to explore all of this!"

"You are very welcome to, Merridyn," Assanli responded, "once you have returned from your quest, that is. It will take quite some time to peruse all that is there. However, my son, Andrys will assist you; his historical knowledge is extensive."

"Thank you, my lady," Merridyn replied, his face flushed with excitement. "I am most honoured."

Assanli walked over to a painting hanging on the wall. The painting was of a forest setting: an ornate wooden bridge ran over a babbling brook, surrounded by a copse of lush green, white, and purple trees; the verdant grass below was blanketed in tiny white flowers. Vala, Jelly, and Max watched transfixed as Assanli reached into the painted stream and retrieved a box, her fingers dripping with sparkling droplets of water. She knelt before Vala and presented her with the box. The box was constructed from a clear crystal that emanated a pulsing purple glow; it was fairly minimalistic in appearance, with carved curlicue edging and a simple rose relief in the centre. Vala held it reverently in the palm of her hand, hesitant. She waited for whatever would come next.

"Press your fingertip to the rose, Vala," Assanli said softly. "The box will open."

Vala did as instructed, and the lid slowly opened. Inside were two Iridiscus pendants and a child's silver bracelet with an oval Iridiscus crystal embedded in the centre. One of the pendants was fashioned into a star-shaped flower, the other a crescent moon—each of them threaded through a silver snake chain.

"The moon-shaped one is Merlin's," Assanli explained. "The flower is Nimeva's, and of course the bracelet—"

"Merevina's," Vala finished Assanli's sentence. "How old was she when it happened?"

"Just a little girl of seven," Assanli answered sadly. "I am not certain if you know this, but if you do come within close proximity of the wearer, their Iridiscus will glow brightly."

"I have tiny wrists," Vala stated. "I'm pretty sure Merevina's will fit me." She carefully fastened Merevina's bracelet around her wrist.

"Elvar," Vala said, turning to him, "why don't you wear Merlin's. And Nimeva's …"

"May I wear it?" Jelly asked in a small voice, afraid of being turned down.

"Of course you can!" Vala replied, smiling. She fastened the pendant around Jelly's neck.

Vala returned the box to Assanli and thanked her.

"There is one final gift I can bestow, which might afford you all some extra protection," Assanli said, walking over to an alcove in the far side of the room.

Within the alcove lay a trunk composed of a dark-purple marbled crystal with vine leaf edging and decorated on top with a sculpted sleeping fae child curled into a foetal position. The child was made from a pale-pink crystal that emanated a soft pink glow.

Assanli ran her hand over the child's back and the chest opened. "Nine of you," Assanli said, casting a glance at the group.

Reaching into the chest, she gathered nine cloaks; made from a fine iridescent gossamer, they glistened, throwing off sparks of light as the queen walked towards them.

"These are light-refraction cloaks," Assanli explained. "They afford the wearer the protection of invisibility. Although you can see them now, once worn, their chemical structure is altered by the wearer's body heat, and all light is bent around the wearer and then recombined without distorting the image of what is behind them."

"Um," Max said, mouth agape, "that shouldn't be possible!" "Oh, but it is, dear Max," Assanli said, amused by his reaction. "Why not try it and see for yourself?"

She handed a cloak to Max, who took it from her and excitedly pulled it over his head.

Jelly gave a small shriek.

"Max, my dear," Assanli's voice shook with laughter, "pull the hood over, you look like a disembodied head!"

Max's face flushed with embarrassment, and he hastily pulled the hood over his head.

"This is friggin' awesome!" he shouted, causing Jelly to shriek again as he pinched her bottom.

"Well, as you can see," Assanli said, handing a cloak to each of them, "as Max has demonstrated, these do provide quite the opportunity for mirth, and they do serve a very useful protective function."

After each of them thanked Queen Assanli for her help, they began their journey to Cavania, the home from which Merlin and his family were last sighted.

39

The warmth of the afternoon sun felt rejuvenating and blissful to Vala as she held out her bare arms, absorbing the rays—a rain of precious gold goodness falling gently upon her. She allowed her mind to quieten as she focussed on the warmth of Elvar's hand within hers, the softness of his skin, and the little sparks of electricity that flowed between them. Something felt different to Vala, as though an irreversible change had passed. She could feel it, whatever *it* was, on the periphery of her consciousness, but for now, it remained elusive—just out of reach.

"You seem rather pensive, Vala," Jelly remarked, gently touching her friend's arm. "Is everything okay?"

"Yes!" Vala said, smiling at Jelly. "I feel really good right now, which may seem at odds with the gravity of our mission, but I've just got a good feeling about this."

"Considering Amalia's vision," Elvar said, "I cannot say I share your positive mentality. However, you are deeply intuitive, my love, so perhaps there is a good reason for your optimism."

"Come on, bro," Max said, placing a hand on Elvar's back. "Don't put a damper on your girl's positive vibes! I agree with Vala, this is going to be an awesome adventure!"

"I'm with you on this one, Elvar," Jelly said. "OMG Max! Do you not remember the Tenebrae Lands, Krazgrits, Drouzers, the Spindler. Oh, and my personal favourite—Keela's lovely hallucinogenic potion!"

"We won't be travelling near the Tenebrae," Max argued. "The Krazgrits are no match for Vala, and I doubt they'll come near her again anyway; you saved us from the Drouzers last time; the Spindler is dead; and Keela is out of the picture."

"Hmmmph!" Jelly replied, but surprised Max by kissing him on the cheek. "I think you're a little crazy, Max, but I do love your eternal optimism. It makes me feel ... happy, I guess."

As they approached the forest, Vala felt a flutter of nervous anticipation and tightened her grip on Elvar's hand.

"I will keep you safe," Elvar said, intercepting her thoughts.

"I know you will," Vala said, resting her hand on Elvar's arm and yawning.

"Are you tired, my love?" Elvar asked, tipping Vala's chin up to look into her eyes.

"What is wrong, Sugar Plum?" Laoli said, reaching out and grasping her daughter's arm.

"Nothing!" Vala said, pulling away from her mother. "Please, stop fussing, we have a long way to go before nightfall."

"Vala," Patrick said softly. "We are worried about you. You do not seem quite your usual self."

"And then of course there was that funny turn you had in Moredonia ..." Merridyn interjected.

"What funny turn?" Laoli and Patrick asked in unison.

"Are you sick, Vala?" Jelly asked, placing her hand across Vala's forehead.

"Would you like me to scan you, Vala?" Essyeult offered. "I have learnt some advanced diagnostic techniques from ..."

Essyeult was cut off by a frustrated scream from Vala. Vala grimaced; she had probably screamed a little *too* loud, as a flock of birds perched on a nearby tree were frightened away.

"Please, all of you," she said in a calmer tone, "I am fine. I just haven't been sleeping too well."

"But what about this *funny turn* that Merridyn is referring to?" Laoli implored.

"I fainted," Vala stated simply. "I just ... there's been a lot on my mind as I'm sure you can all appreciate. It's affected my sleep."

"If you are sure it is nothing more?" Essyeult said, her voice weighted with concern.

"Honestly," Vala answered, repeatedly twisting the same lock of hair around her finger. "I would know if something were wrong."

"I think we all need to give Vala some space," Max said, surprising Vala with his sudden show of support. "Would you like to walk with me a while, Vala? I've had some thoughts on how that *living* painting might work."

"I would love to, Max," Vala said, releasing Elvar's hand and linking her arm through Max's.

"I think I'll leave you two to it," Jelly said. "Not much in the mood for scientific debate."

"Would you like to walk with me, lady Fairfield?" Gannlyth asked, a warm smile lighting his face. "I hear that you partake in the dramatic arts—I would love to hear more about it. I have created a number of compositions for various productions, including incidental music; it would be most interesting to hear how you feel music contributes, and is overall, instrumental in creating atmosphere in a dramatic performance."

Jelly's mouth quirked as she caught Max's scowl, and with a triumphant smile, she sauntered off to Gannlyth's side, linking her arm through his.

"I would love to talk to a fellow artiste," Jelly said, flicking her long blonde hair back and grinning flirtatiously at Gannlyth.

Gannlyth's face reddened, and Jelly shot a glance back at Max, raising her eyebrows and smiling widely as he scowled back at her.

With the general buzz of conversation, it was almost missed; an almost imperceptible warbled, whistling sound.

Max frowned as Jelly clutched Gannlyth's arm, but cast his gaze up to where the sound appeared to originate from. A rustle in the brush. Silence.

"Hush, everyone," Essyeult whispered. "Be still."

"What is it?" Jelly whispered back anxiously, the tiny hairs on her arm raising. "Please tell me it's not something bad?"

A light breeze stirred, catching several strands of Jelly's hair in the updraft. Jelly let out a frightened squeal, quickly covering her mouth with her hand.

"It is all right, Jelly," Gannlyth said to her calmly in a hushed tone and placed an arm around her. "There is nothing to fear, it is just a Cowlat."

Gannlyth placed a finger on Jelly's lips and pointed upwards. There, sitting on a tree branch, was a furry animal, a little smaller than a squirrel. It had pale bluish-green and cream striped fur that framed its tiny face, a face with big pale-blue eyes dotted in the centre by a large black pupil, a tiny pink nose, and a small mouth, currently rounded into an 'O' shape, as it emitted the whistling noises that they had heard earlier. The rest of its body was covered in a silky-soft downy fur, dappled in the same colours as its crest, and its long bushy tail was ringed in the same contrasting colours.

Jelly watched in wonder as the Cowlat used its tiny fingers and opposable thumbs to peel the husk of a vine fruit before eating it.

"Aren't they amazing?" Vala whispered in Jelly's ear as she and Max stood next to her.

"They're adorable!" Jelly whispered excitedly in return.

"Wait till you see them fly!" Gannlyth added quietly.

"They do not fly, Gannlyth," Elvar said softly. "They glide." They did not have to wait long to see the Cowlat's gliding prowess.

Jelly squealed in delight as the Cowlat sailed several feet over their heads onto a branch of an adjacent tree.

"No, you can't have one," Max said, affectionately bumping his head to Jelly's and laughing.

"We are close to the river crossing," Essyeult said, pointing to a clearing between the trees.

"And how are we getting across?" Max asked, his curiosity piqued, as he wondered by what *miraculous* means they would travel across the river.

"Just a good old-fashioned boat, Max," Patrick said, clapping his hand on Max's shoulder. "Sorry to disappoint."

"No, that's fine!" Max replied. "I love boats. My Uncle David has a longboat moored at Wrexham, he used to take us on riverboat cruises along the Broads when we were younger."

Vala sighed contentedly as the sparkling aquamarine water came into view. She loved being surrounded by a large body of water; there was something calming, almost hypnotic about the mesmerising action of the waves, even a small ripple.

As Vala was gazing out, she felt a small tingle of electricity around the skin of her left wrist—the wrist that carried Merevina's Iridiscus bracelet. She looked down and noticed a soft indigo glow from the crystal. Vala was about to speak when a large flock of birds noisily took flight from a number of nearby trees. Vala placed a hand over her racing heart. Suddenly, there was silence: no animal sounds, no talking amongst the group, nothing but the quiet sound of breathing.

"Um, guys," Vala said, barely above a whisper, "my bracelet is glowing."

In the few seconds since Vala had first noticed the glow, it had now grown much stronger, emitting a powerful violet glow.

"Merevina!" Laoli and Essyeult said in unison.

A twig snapped behind them. All heads turned towards the sound. A Cowlat scurried into its burrow, seemingly as afraid as they all were. Elvar pulled Vala close; Laoli hugged Vala on the other side. Patrick stood in front of his daughter, and Merridyn, directly behind. Essyeult and Gannlyth ushered Jelly and Max between them. They stood silently. Waiting. Another twig snapped. Another Cowlat. Vala heard Max curse under his breath. The tension felt like a stream of thick resin had been poured over them: cloying, sticky, oppressive, and utterly immobilising.

Merevina's bracelet began to thrum as the source of the energy drew ever closer.

"Lady Vala Oakley-Pendragon, I presume?" said a disembodied female voice.

"We should form a circle around Vala, Jelly, and Max, and activate the Enhanced Barrier Spell," Essyeult said in a hushed tone.

"Futile! There is no need for all of you to be harmed," the voice said again, followed by a tinkling laugh. "My business is with Lady Pendragon, I have no quarrel with the rest of you."

Seemingly from nowhere, a girl appeared. Vala's eyes widened in terror as they met with the girl from Amalia's vision. The girl had long waves of glossy ebony hair, indigo eyes, and a flowing blue gown. Secured around her waist was a bejewelled scabbard, which revealed the unmistakable tip of a gleaming golden hilt. The girl smiled, but no warmth reached her eyes.

"Vala," Elvar whispered in her ear, "the Barrier Spell!"

Vala squeezed Elvar's hand first, then her mother's, nodding to Merridyn who still stood behind her, as they surreptitiously initiated an invisible barrier around their group.

"Goodness!" the girl said, laughing again. "Where are my manners? I have not introduced myself: I am Athanasia."

Athanasia stepped towards the group, touching the invisible barrier with her index finger. A small spark bounced off, which seemed to further amuse Athanasia. She uttered a few words under her breath, brought the palm of her hand just under her mouth, and gently blew. Tiny gold sparks bounced off the barrier as it began to dissolve. Athanasia laughed harder.

"Really?" Athanasia said incredulously. "Do you not know with whom you are dealing?"

Athanasia made a sweeping motion with both of her arms, incanting, "I commit thee to the air, where unseen chains shall bind thee, till to the earth I return thee."

Vala felt Elvar and her mother pulled from her grasp, as the entire group, with the exception of Vala, were suspended in mid-air.

"What do you want from me?" Vala shouted angrily.

"You really are rather slow, Lady Pendragon," Athanasia said disdainfully. "Have you honestly not figured out who I am?"

"This Iridiscus bracelet," Vala replied, pointing to her wrist, "indicates that you are Merevina, daughter of Merlin."

Athanasia's brow furrowed, a flicker of uncertainty crossing her features.

"I am Athanasia!" the girl bellowed. "You killed my father!" "Merlin?" Vala returned.

"Stop trying to confuse me!" Athanasia yelled. "I do not know of whom you speak. I am Athanasia, daughter of the Spindler."

"The Spindler killed my husband!" Vala yelled back angrily.

"Well, he seems quite alive at present, does he not?"

"I revived him," Vala replied, adrenaline coursing through her veins.

"Yes," Athanasia said, her voice dripping with venom. "Unlike my father! However, I do not underestimate your power, Lady Pendragon, but fortuitously your body's energies are channelled elsewhere now, leaving you maybe just a *tad* more vulnerable?"

"I don't know what you mean," Vala answered, her voice trembling.

"You are with child," Athanasia said in irritation. "Please, you really did not know?"

"No!" Laoli cried out as Patrick gripped her hand.

"Do not harm her, Athanasia," Elvar shouted. "We will give you whatever you want! Just leave my wife, and my child, alone. Please."

"And what do you think you have that could possibly be of interest to me?" Athanasia replied with scorn.

"It is ironic: it is I who was trying to conceive a child, but *she*," Athanasia said, spitting the word out, "has unintentionally conceived a child with you. Goodness, a tad *careless* of you, Master Oakley!"

"Does this have something to do with those poor young men?" Essyeult called out, trying to keep Athanasia engaged in conversation.

"Collateral damage," Athanasia replied coldly. "They failed to impregnate me, so I took their souls."

"You tricked them!" Vala said, glaring.

"Only some of them," Athanasia answered. "The others were quite content with my natural form."

Vala was about to speak again when Athanasia cut her off.

"Enough of this!" Athanasia snapped. "I will not let the prophecy come to fruition, nor will I leave my father's death unavenged. That baby of yours is an extra boon—its blood will be most useful indeed."

"No!" Elvar screamed, flailing in the air helplessly. "Please, I will give you *anything*. Take my life in lieu of Vala's."

Essyeult put a hand on her son's shoulder, hot tears streaking her face.

"Don't take my daughter!" Patrick cried out. "If it is Pendragon blood you want, take mine!"

"No!" Laoli begged. "There must be something, Athanasia. Please spare my daughter!"

"I have access to many powerful antiquities," Merridyn called out. "I can procure for you anything that you desire."

"This banter is getting tiresome!" Athanasia growled. "I do not desire anything from any of *you*—now be silent!"

Athanasia's hand went to the bejewelled scabbard and she unsheathed the sword. The sword was truly a magnificent sight, the metal unlike any Vala had seen: the blade was a marbled gold and platinum colour with embossed red and white roses and verdant leaves trailing along it. The hilt, a rich gold had what looked like Latin lettering engraved upon it.

"Excalibur!" Vala and Patrick said together.

"Yes," Athanasia replied. "I had heard that it would be instantly recognisable to those of the Pendragon bloodline. Rather ironic, do you not think, that this will be the blade to kill you."

Vala started the soul-mirroring incantation but before she could finish it, Athanasia lunged at her with Excalibur. Instinctively, Vala reached out and grabbed the blade—the blade that should have lacerated her palm and plunged into her chest. Only it didn't. Excalibur hovered just above an exposed area of skin as though held there by an invisible forcefield.

"Vala!" Elvar yelled.

"I'm all right!" Vala replied, not breaking eye contact with Athanasia who stood silently, staring at Excalibur in shock.

Vala took advantage of Athanasia's inertia and finished the soulmirroring incantation in her head.

A look of pain crossed Athanasia's face as she crumpled to the ground, clutching her head. Her hold on Vala's family and friends abruptly stopped, and they drifted back to terra firma surprisingly gently. Athanasia's anguished screams pierced the air. Vala watched with baited breath to see what affect her soul-mirroring would take. At the exact moment Vala had grabbed Excalibur's blade, a series of images and emotions flashed through Athanasia's mind forming a sequential blur of her life, all of her life: from the moment she was born to her abduction by the Spindler at seven years of age, to everything that had happened since.

Elvar interwove his fingers with Vala's. No words seemed appropriate. Laoli engulfed her daughter in a hug, sobbing quietly as Patrick placed an arm around both of them.

A feral snarl escaped Athanasia's lips as she lunged for Vala— hands viciously coiled around Vala's neck. It happened so quickly, none of the others could react in time to prevent it.

Elvar immediately tugged at Athanasia's hands, trying to prise her fingers from their vice-like grip, whilst Patrick and Laoli flanked Athanasia on either side, desperately trying to pull her arms away from their daughter.

In desperation, Athanasia dug her fingers in tighter. Vala's air supply was now so constricted that dark spots started to cloud her vision—a strangled, wheezing sound escaping her lips as she attempted to draw in breath. Panic set in as Vala felt her life ebbing away. She reached up, closing her fingers around Athanasia's wrists and dug her nails in as Elvar finally succeeded in bending back Athanasia's fingers. Athanasia released her hold on Vala, screeching angrily as Laoli and Patrick seized her arms, pinning them behind her back.

Vala frantically gasped for oxygen, swallowing large lungfuls of air through her burning throat, till the darkness in her vision retreated and her breathing began to normalise. Jelly silently passed Vala a bottle of water, which she gulped down as Elvar scooped her into his arms.

Athanasia's screams abruptly stopped as her body started to convulse.

"What have you done to me?" Athanasia cried, falling to her knees. "I do not understand. What is happening?"

"No, no, no!" she shouted, shaking her head wildly as her eyes rolled back.

"What *is* happening?" Vala rasped, watching in horror at the scene unfolding.

"I do not know," Elvar replied softly, looking on.

"Help me!" Athanasia whimpered, no longer sounding like the fierce girl of a moment ago. "I am ... Mother, Father, where are you?"

Athanasia's eyes closed as she fell backwards, crashing into Patrick's legs. She was breathing, but apparently unconscious.

"What should I do?" Patrick asked uncertainly, her head resting against his knee.

"Set her down," Essyeult said. "Here." She removed her shawl and placed it on the ground for Athanasia to rest her head upon.

They stood watching, waiting for any sign of change in Athanasia's prone form. Minutes passed. Nothing. After what seemed like an uncomfortably long time, Athanasia made a small mewling noise and her eyelids flickered open.

"It's all right, Mama," Vala said quietly, disentangling herself. "Just a moment, please."

She tentatively stepped towards Athanasia, whose undulating wailing of a moment ago had subsided into soft weeping. She moved back and forth in a disturbing rocking motion.

As Vala approached her, she looked up as though seeing Vala for the first time.

"Who are you?" Athanasia whispered. "Where are my mother and father?"

"What do you remember?" Vala asked, crouching down to meet Athanasia's eye level. "Do you know who you are?"

"I am Merevina," the girl replied, glancing at Vala's wrist. "Why do you have my bracelet?"

"I was keeping it safe for you," Vala said, removing the Iridiscus bracelet and handing it to Merevina.

"I was taken!" Merevina said. "By the Spindler. Mother and Father too, though we were separated. I did not see where he took them, do you know where they are?"

"No," Vala said. "Though we will help you find them in time. I am Vala Oakley-Pendragon; the others are my family and friends. We are all here to help you."

"I believe ... I have done terrible things!" Merevina wailed. "Things I do not understand. He did something terrible to me!"

"The Spindler?" Vala ventured.

Merevina nodded.

"I want to go home!" Merevina cried, her voice quivering.

"You can come home with us for now," Vala answered, tentatively reaching out to touch Merevina's arm.

"Vala?" Laoli said, her eyes wide with shock.

"It's fine," Vala said, turning to face the others. "She is no threat now, the Spindler's malevolent hold on her is broken."

"Did you say your name is *Pendragon*?" Merevina asked, looking up anxiously at Vala with red-rimmed eyes. "Are you related to King Arthur?"

"I am indeed!" Vala said, smiling at Merevina and holding her hand out. "Please, come with us, Merevina."

Merevina took Vala's hand and rose to her feet, looking at everyone in turn.

"I am Elvar Oakley," Elvar said, protectively placing an arm around Vala.

"These two here," Elvar continued, gesturing towards Merridyn and Gannlyth, "are our friends, Merridyn Ashwood and Gannlyth Pyrisi."

"Hello, Merevina," Essyeult said, slowly approaching the girl. "I am Essyeult Oakley, Elvar's mother."

"We are friends too," Jelly said, stepping forward. "I am Jelly to my friends, aka Katherine Fairfield, and this is my boyfriend, Max Orsini."

"That leaves us, I guess," Patrick said, ruffling Vala's hair and smiling. "We are Vala's parents: Patrick and Laoli Pendragon."

"I am afraid," Merevina's voice trembled as another stream of tears slid down her cheeks.

"I can help with that," Patrick said, taking another step towards Merevina. "I won't hurt you, I promise."

"I can do this remotely," Patrick said, now standing directly in front of Merevina, "but it is more effective if I have physical contact with you. I will just need to touch your head."

"You did say that you are Uncle Arthur's kin?" Merevina asked in a shaky voice.

"Yes, Merevina," Patrick replied in a soothing tone, "we are—Vala and I."

Merevina nodded her consent and Patrick placed his hands over her head, his thumbs gently pressed against her forehead. Gradually Merevina's fearful expression gave way to one of peaceful serenity. Patrick released his hands from her and smiled.

"Merevina," Essyeult said, "we have a spare room at our house; you may stay there until we locate your parents."

"What if they no longer want me?" Merevina said, biting her thumb. "I cannot remember everything, but I have done terrible, heinous things. The Spindler erased my childhood memories, my true identity, but when Vala ..."

This time it was Merridyn who stepped forward. He had been quietly observing the scene until now, but felt compelled to comfort this strange girl, who had only moments ago tried to take the life of the girl he had unwittingly fallen in love with.

"Your parents could never reject you, Merevina," Merridyn said, touching her shoulder. "You were under the Spindler's enchantment. All that you did—it was not you, it was his insidious influence. You are free now, you are Merevina once more."

Merevina looked up at Merridyn and smiled shyly, her cheeks aflame. "Thank you, kind sir."

To Vala's relief, Merevina walked in between her parents, holding each of their hands, as Patrick's calming influence continued to keep her at ease.

Although she knew it could not be avoided for long, it gave Vala a brief reprieve from their questioning about her pregnancy. If she were being truly honest with herself, Vala had known she was pregnant for some time: her body felt different somehow—no longer completely her own, and after Elvar had confided that Lann had mixed up the Nonceptium Elixir, giving them the short-term one, it confirmed her suspicions. Of course, Vala had missed her period, but had initially put it down to the extra duress she had been under. However, the concept had been so beyond anything she felt prepared for, Vala had pushed the feeling away. She rested her head on Elvar's arm and sighed.

"We knew this was a possibility, my love," Elvar whispered. "Although it is quite an undertaking, I truly believe we are ready for this, as ready as we will ever be, that is! We can do this—together."

"We're only nineteen, Elvar," Vala whispered back. "Though we did marry young too, and that's turning out pretty well if I do say so myself!"

"I love children," Vala continued. "I just wasn't expecting to be a teen mother."

"You will be nearer twenty when the baby is due," Elvar whispered, his lips grazing her ear and sending shivers down her spine. "And of course—" Elvar was interrupted by a slap on the back from Max.

"Nice one, mate!" Max said. "No doubt the result of that trip ..."

"Shut up, Max!" Jelly said, placing her hand over his mouth. "Are you okay, Vala? I thought something seemed a bit different about you. Did you know?"

"I suspected," Vala admitted. "I just didn't want to confirm anything till I knew for sure."

Max frowned and looked at Vala dolefully. "I'm sorry, I did not mean to be so insensitive—it's just super exciting news! Um, at least I hope you are both excited about it. Are you?"

"You know Max means well, Vala," Jelly interjected. "He just has a case of foot-in-mouth disease on occasions."

"Well, it's crazy scary!" Vala admitted. "But it is, as you put it, Max, *super exciting* too! A lot to get my head around, though, for both of us, I guess?" Vala glanced at Elvar to gauge his reaction.

"I can only hope that I will be at least half as good a father as mine has been to me," Elvar said, rubbing Vala's belly affectionately and grinning. "Honestly, though, I could not be more ecstatic; that our love has brought forth a new life is nothing short of miraculous. It feels incredible!"

"We are very happy for you both," Jelly said, placing an arm around Vala's shoulders and hugging her.

Max ruffled Vala's hair and planted a kiss on the back of her head.

"Elvar, Vala," Gannlyth said, grinning broadly as he approached them. "Congratulations! Marvellous news indeed! I am sure you will both make wonderful parents."

"Yes," Merridyn said, his face unreadable. "Congratulations to you both on this most joyous occasion." "Thank you, guys!" Vala replied.

"Of course, you do all realise that our quest to find Merlin must wait for a time, now that Vala is with child?" Elvar stated firmly.

"Do you intend to continue after baby Pendragon is born?" Max asked eagerly.

"We will have to find a way," Vala said emphatically. "Merevina needs her parents too. Besides which, something big is brewing and we'll need all the help we can get."

"What do you mean, *something big*?" Jelly asked. "Another premonition?"

"Not a premonition as such, just the usual presentiment—I can feel it in the air. Maybe if Merevina's memory returns fully, we'll have some clue as to what we're up against."

"She mentioned the blood of your unborn child," Merridyn said, touching Vala's shoulder, "when she was still Athanasia."

"I know, I'll ask her about it later," Vala said, exhaling deeply. "I just hope Merevina's living with us won't be too problematic." "Why would it be problematic?" Merridyn probed.

"Because only yesterday Athanasia used a glamour in the guise of Maiwen and slept with Lann, Maiwen's boyfriend."

"Oh," Merridyn replied quietly. "Yes, I can see why that might be a tad awkward."

"Well," Elvar said, drawing his fingers through his hair, "only one way to find out!"

40

"You cannot be serious!" Maiwen screamed. "This is the girl who tricked my boyfriend into bedding her, and I am supposed to accept her living with us!"

"Maiwen, dear," Essyeult said, "she is not the same girl—the girl that did those things was under the enchantment of the Spindler. This is Merevina, daughter of Merlin."

"Do not expect me to interact with her!" Maiwen said, clenching her jaw tightly, before running up the staircase to her room.

Merevina flinched, taking a step back towards the front door.

"I should not be here," Merevina cried. "I only cause pain and discord!"

"No, Merevina," Vala said, placing her hand on Merevina's arm, "your soul is pure. If it were not, the soul-mirroring would have destroyed you as it did the Spindler."

"Vala," Essyeult said softly, "why not escort Merevina to her room. Help her wash, and select a dress from my wardrobe for her to change into."

"Come," Vala said, holding her hand out to Merevina. "Mama and Jelly, maybe you should come too."

Merevina silently took Vala's hand and followed her up the stairs to the guest room. The guest room was very simple in design, with soft white walls decorated by a solitary oak tree, its leaves rustling gently in an imaginary breeze, and a setting sun, which would soon morphose into a crescent moon with the gently ambling clouds giving way to sparkling stars. There was a Viaspan wood dresser with a mirror, and a simple Viaspan wardrobe. Gauzy butter-hued curtains framed an oval window, and a large bed covered with a patchwork quilt rested in the right side of the room.

Merevina was considerably taller than Vala, but she moved behind her, clutching Vala's hand tightly and burying her face into the nook between Vala's shoulder and neck. Vala could feel the girl shaking, and in spite of what had transpired earlier between them, she felt a rush of sympathy.

"I am afraid," Merevina said, her voice catching as hot tears rolled over her cheeks.

"Everything will be fine," Vala assured her. "We'll run you a hot bath with lavender, rose and Pyrisi wood oils—it's my special blend—to help you relax."

"Would you like us to help you undress, Merevina?" Laoli asked gently.

"That is most kind of you," Merevina said quietly. "Thank you."

"Um," Vala said hesitantly, "I know this may not be the most appropriate time, but may I hold Excalibur?"

"Oh!" Merevina replied, her hand reaching for the scabbard before unfastening her belt. "As you are Uncle Arthur's kin, it should be in your possession until it can be returned to him."

Jelly shot Vala a surreptitious look, arching her eyebrows slightly.

'*I know,*' Vala mouthed back, shrugging her shoulders.

As Vala took Excalibur from Merevina and unsheathed it from the scabbard, the blade emitted a bright bluish-white glow. Vala and Jelly gasped.

"It is because you are of Pendragon blood," Merevina said.

"Dad will love this!" Vala said as she skimmed her fingers lightly over the flat of the blade.

"Oh!" Vala said, as her fingers traced over engraved letters on the blade. "It has an inscription—I didn't notice that before."

"*Amor victor verus est etiam nostrorum cordium*: Love is the true victor and conqueror of our hearts," Laoli read out as she examined the sword.

"I have to get a picture of this!" Jelly said excitedly. "Max'll go nuts!"

"He can see the real thing later," Vala replied, grinning. "However, right now I'm going to run Merevina's bath. Put her clothes in the laundry basket and bring her through, she can borrow my bathrobe."

As Vala waited for her mother and Jelly to bring Merevina through, she stood in profile in front of the full-length bathroom mirror, lifting her top and examining her belly. If she looked closely enough, Vala could see a small protuberance over her usually flat stomach. She rubbed her hand over it, marvelling that her and Elvar's tiny baby lived within her, and was startled when Laoli and Jelly walked in with Merevina between them, clutching their hands.

Laoli closed her eyes, letting out a shuddery breath.

"Later, Vala," Laoli said as she closed the bathroom door behind her.

Vala turned away from her mother, irritated that she was being reprimanded like a naughty child.

"You'll feel a little better after this," Vala said, smiling at Merevina.

Laoli helped Merevina disrobe, Vala and Jelly holding her hands as she stepped into the bath. Merevina smiled for the first time as she immersed herself in the fragrant water.

"Thank you," Merevina said. "You have all been very kind to me. And, Vala, apologising to you seems wholly inadequate, but I am truly sorry for trying to harm you."

"I know it wasn't really *you*, Merevina," Vala said, "though I'm curious—how did you know I'm pregnant?"

"I do not know for sure," Merevina answered sadly. "Large parts of my memory are missing, but I have a vague recollection that I have always been able to sense certain aspects of a person's being, like when someone is unwell and what is ailing them precisely." Merevina sighed, swirling the water around with her finger.

"I am sure that at least some of your memories will return over time," Laoli said as she used a jug to pour water over Merevina's hair. "You need time to heal from this trauma."

"Maybe it would be better if some of them did not resurface," Merevina said. "It is confusing for me ... the Spindler ... I know he did terrible things, committed great atrocities, but I do remember that he ... he was always caring towards me ... he looked after me, taught me, read me stories, played games with me ..."

"We understand," Vala said as she lathered shampoo into Merevina's raven locks. "Do you remember, Merevina, what you said about my baby's blood being useful?"

Merevina closed her eyes, her brow furrowed in concentration.

"I am sorry," Merevina replied. "All I know is that a drop of a child's blood is instrumental in a spell my father—I mean, the Spindler—asked me to perform just a few weeks before he died, but the details are hazy."

"You don't know what the spell pertains to?" Jelly asked.

"No," Merevina answered. "Though his most trusted followers were also privy to this information, in case for whatever reason, I was not be able to carry out whatever it is I was supposed to do. I do know that he was hopeful that I would conceive a child to continue our heritage, but the blood ... I can feel it at the edge of my consciousness, but I just cannot ..."

"Don't force it, Merevina," Vala said. "As Mama said, maybe it will come back to you in time."

Merevina remained quiet as they finished bathing and dressing her, before taking her back down to the living room, where Essyeult and Derryth were waiting.

"Elvar and Patrick have taken Max, Gannlyth, and Merri to guest lodgings," Essyeult explained. "They were rather fatigued and thought it best not to overwhelm Merevina."

"We thought you might be hungry, Merevina," Derryth said, stepping towards her, hand extended. "We have not yet had the pleasure of meeting: I am Derryth Oakley, husband of Essyeult and father of Elvar and Maiwen."

Merevina took Derryth's hand in hers and met his gaze as he kissed the top of her hand.

"It is an honour, sir."

"And yes," Merevina continued and smiled shyly, "I am very hungry indeed!"

41

After lunch, Merevina retired to her room to rest, leaving Vala, Jelly, and Laoli, with Essyeult and Derryth.

"Vala," Essyeult said gently, "we just want you to know that we are both delighted for you and Elvar—a little shocked perhaps—but a baby is a blessing, and we will help you both in any way we can."

"And of course, we would love for you both to continue living with us," Derryth added, "until the time comes when you and Elvar are able to have a home of your own."

"Thank you," Vala said, taking a sudden interest in her hands. "We didn't mean for this to happen."

"We know, Vala," Derryth replied. "Elvar explained what happened whilst you were bathing Merevina. I shall be having a serious conversation with Lann regarding his careless actions, though I dare say he is more than aware of the gravity of the situation."

"This is not something I am yet aware of," Laoli interjected. "How is this connected to Lann?"

"Elvar and Lann had a disagreement," Vala explained. "He had just discovered that Maiwen and Lann had become ... um, romantically involved. He was angry and it must have affected Lann's concentration as he was labelling the serums. Lann gave us the wrong one by mistake."

"Forgive me, Sugar Plum, for my terse tone earlier," Laoli said, a tear rolling down her cheek. "I did not realise ... I thought maybe ..." "Maybe what?" Vala challenged. "That we actually planned this?" "Vala," Jelly said, placing her hand on Vala's arm, "this is a lot to process. I'm still really shocked, I can't imagine how your mum must be feeling."

"What about how I'm feeling?" Vala said, pushing herself up from the sofa. "I'm the one who's having the baby!"

Vala turned away from the others, racing up the stairs to her room.

"I should go after her," Laoli said, wiping her cheek with the heel of her hand.

"Wait a while," Jelly suggested, rubbing Laoli's back. "It will be all right. Vala's tired, shocked, and no doubt hormonal. Give her some time to calm down."

"Yes," Laoli said, patting Jelly's hand. "You are a wonderful friend to Vala; she looks upon you and Max as her brother and sister."

"We feel the same way," Jelly said. "And we will always be there for her, even if we can't always be physically present."

"Thank you, Jelly," Laoli replied, squeezing her hand. "I think I might just have a rest myself, it has been a long day."

"And on that note," Jelly said, standing, "I think I shall get back to Max now. Thank you, Mr and Mrs Oakley for a lovely lunch. Tell Vala we will come and see her in the morning."

"I will escort you to the guest house," Derryth said, smiling warmly. "It is not a long walk."

"Thank you, Mr Oakley."

"Come, Laoli," Essyeult said. "I shall bring up a tray of tea to your room."

"That would be lovely," Laoli answered as she made her way upstairs. "Thank you, Essyeult."

42

Elvar returned home to find Vala curled into a foetal position on their bed; her eyes were closed.

"Beloved," Elvar whispered, lightly touching Vala's shoulder. "Are you asleep?"

Vala shook her head and glanced up. Elvar sighed, lying down beside her and cupping her face in his hands.

"You have been crying," Elvar said, taking in Vala's blotchy face and bloodshot eyes.

Vala stroked her fingers through Elvar's hair, kissing him lightly at first, then more fervently as her tongue found his.

"We should talk, Vala," Elvar said breathlessly as he reluctantly broke away.

"Not now," Vala pleaded. "Please. I just don't want to think anymore today—I just want to be held. And to sleep, I'm so tired."

"That I can do," Elvar said softly, holding her in his arms. "Just sleep now, beloved."

43

Whorls of dense mist coiled around Vala's bare ankles like hungry snakes, the grass cool and damp beneath her feet. The purple sky seemed darker than usual, the atmosphere more ominous. Vala shivered, partly from cold, partly trepidation. In spite of her unease, Vala felt a surge of exhilaration at her success.

I've done it! I successfully summoned the Celestia. Now how do I find Amalia?

"Amalia?" Vala spoke quietly.

There was a blur of colour and movement as Amalia stood before her.

"Vala!" Amalia said, smiling as she embraced Vala. "It is so good to see you!"

"And you too, Amalia," Vala replied, taking Amalia's hand. "There is so much to tell you. And so much to ask you."

"I am honoured that you seek my counsel," Amalia said. "Let us talk somewhere more private."

"Where are we going?" Vala asked as Amalia led her along a cobbled crystal path.

"To my home here," Amalia answered. "It is modest in comparison to the accommodation I occupied when I was living, but it is cosy and I like it!"

Vala took in her environment as they walked. Silver trees glistened in the moonlight, their leaves and branches swaying in an imperceptible breeze. Some of the branches bore pear-shaped fruit, but unlike earthly pears, they had a prismatic metallic sheen.

"What are those?" Vala asked curiously, pointing to the fruit.

"Fructus arci," Amalia replied, plucking one from a nearby branch and holding it out to Vala. "Rainbow fruit."

Vala took the fruit, turning it in her hand to study it. She had never seen anything quite like it, and as far as she knew, it bore no resemblance to any fruit on the earthly plane.

"It is safe for you to eat," Amalia assured her. "Do not worry, I have checked!"

Vala sniffed the fruit, which exuded a rose-like aroma and felt icy cold to the touch, as though it had been in refrigeration. Tentatively, Vala took a bite. The texture was crunchy at first like an apple or pear, but once it mingled with the warmth of Vala's mouth, it seemed to melt into a fondant-like texture before evaporating. The taste was unusual at first, like rose-scented caramel, then strawberries, Uquilico, Silanchi berries, Chando pods, and finally, chocolate.

"That was ... um, unexpected!" Vala remarked, grinning. "But lovely, thank you."

"Elsorriden is certainly ... *different* and charming in many ways, though I would love to see sunlight again," Amalia said wistfully.

"And you will," Vala said, squeezing Amalia's hand and smiling.

A thatched cottage stood just a few metres away. It had a chalkywhite façade, its walls embedded with a myriad of crystals, and the straw thatch that lined the roof seemed to emit a golden glow. To Vala it seemed like a fusion between fae and human architecture. An immaculate lawn graced the front of the cottage, dotted with hundreds of tiny glowing flowers in various hues of blue, pink, yellow, white, and purple. A small white picket fence edged the perimeter of the garden, with a gate that opened as Vala and Amalia approached. They walked up a cobbled path to the front door of the cottage: simple oak with a red rose etched into the wood.

"Do come inside," Amalia said warmly, gesturing for Vala to go in.

Vala stepped into the front room, her feet warmed by the plush soft cream carpet beneath. The décor was more akin to that of the human realm, with its white walls, wooden beams, and a woodburner stove situated a short distance from a small cream sofa partially covered by a Furlomyn throw.

Vala relaxed back onto the sofa and waited for Amalia to join her.

"You look cold," Amalia said, frowning. "Let me fetch you a blanket and some slippers to warm your feet."

Amalia returned with a soft heather-coloured knitted blanket and Furlomyn slippers, which she slipped onto Vala's feet, whispering a short incantation as the slippers conformed to Vala's size and shape.

"Thank you," Vala took Amalia's hand, gesturing for her to sit.

"Just a moment," Amalia's eyes twinkled as she walked into the kitchen.

A few minutes later, Amalia returned carrying two steaming mugs of something resembling very creamy milk.

"Camali," Amalia said, handing Vala a mug. "It is a milky drink, sweetened with Camaris Seed extract. It is very soothing and good for ..."

Amalia tilted her head, smiling coyly, and placed a hand on Vala's belly.

"You know," Vala said, meeting Amalia's gaze.

"I could sense the baby's life-force, its aura," Amalia admitted. "And now that you are seated, I can see quite clearly that you are with child! When is your baby due?"

"In just seven months," Vala replied, rubbing her hand over her very slight baby bump. "Of course, I'm ... I'm happy. I love Elvar so much, and this baby is a natural extension of that love, but—"

"You are a little afraid," Amalia finished, stroking Vala's hair softly. "That is to be expected. Bringing a child into the world is the biggest undertaking possible, but one I know that you and Elvar will truly excel in! Your child will be very lucky indeed to be raised by a couple so deeply connected and in love as you and Elvar."

"There is something more," Vala said, placing her hand over Amalia's. "We found Merevina."

Amalia's eyes widened as she took in the news.

"My little Merevina!" Amalia exclaimed. "How? Was she in suspension?"

"Not exactly ..." Vala began hesitantly. "When we found her, she didn't know who she truly is. The Spindler had abducted her as a young child and somehow suppressed her memories. Merevina is an adult now, she has been for a very long time, but—"

"No!" Amalia said, interrupting Vala. "The only way for her to have survived for so long is if she ... no, it cannot be!"

"She learned to take and assimilate souls," Vala continued. "The Spindler had raised her as if she were his own daughter. Amalia?" Amalia had covered her face with her hands, quietly sobbing.

"Amalia," Vala said, reaching out to take her hand, "it is not all bad. Merevina was in possession of Excalibur; when I realised she was about to attack me, I started soul-mirroring. As she plunged the sword towards my heart, I instinctively reached out and clasped the blade, however, it could not penetrate my flesh. It was **as** though it was held back by an invisible barrier. Excalibur, it seems, cannot harm a Pendragon, so my hand too, remained unscathed.

"The moment my hand touched Excalibur, I was besieged by a rush of Merevina's memories, and the soul-mirroring must have reversed whatever hold the Spindler had over Merevina. She was no longer Athanasia, the Spindler's name for her, she was Merevina again."

"And now?" Amalia's voice quivered as she wiped an errant tear away with the heel of her hand.

"She is pure of heart again," Vala said, covering Amalia's hand with her own, "but she is very troubled by what she did during her time as Athanasia, and she is of course missing her parents. Merevina is staying with us presently, my brother is going to help her."

"And what of Nimeva and Merlin?"

"We don't know," Vala answered. "Merevina remembers being taken in the night. I presume the Spindler took Nimeva and Merlin first, then came back for Merevina."

Vala passed Amalia her mug of Camali, which had remained untouched.

"Drink some, Amalia," Vala said softly. "A hot drink always helps."

Amalia reclined back onto the sofa, tilted her head, and sighed. Several minutes passed in silence as Vala allowed Amalia to process this new information.

"Vala," Amalia looked at her with a hopeful expression, "this may seem like an unusual request, but would you permit me to place a hand over your womb?"

"Yes, of course," Vala replied, her brow knitting, "but it is too early to feel any movement."

"I am not attempting to detect movement," Amalia explained, "but your child has a very strong aura. I am gifted at reading others, much like yourself. I know the baby is extremely tiny, but ..."

"Go ahead!" Vala said, beaming at Amalia. "See what amazing powers my super-baby has!"

Amalia gently placed her hands over Vala's belly and closed her eyes. A curious expression crossed her face as the corners of her mouth turned up. Amalia gave a soft laugh, then opened her eyes.

"My goodness!" Amalia said. "Your child ... I have never seen anything like it! Firstly, though, would you like to see your tiny miracle?"

"Yes, of course!"

Amalia placed her hands over Vala's temples, and they both closed their eyes.

At first, Vala could see only darkness. A resonating, pulsating sound, filled her awareness—the steady cadence lulling her—so very calming and safe. Slowly, as her eyes adjusted, the darkness became more diffuse, giving way to a deep red chamber filled with a network of red, blue, and purple strands branching out in all directions. *Blood vessels!* Vala thought.

She felt tranquil and content, cushioned in a comforting oasis of safety and warmth. But then, Vala felt something different, something not yet discernible, yet there nonetheless: it was like an electric charge had started to build from the centre of the chamber—her womb. Vala had not even seen it at first, the tiny foetus, her and Elvar's baby. As Vala watched her baby, she was overcome with an outpouring of love, and somehow, almost impossibly, Vala felt that love reciprocated. Vala's fingers started to tingle as the sensation quickly spread throughout her body, and then came a feeling of serenity and peace. From within the baby's tiny heart, a pure white light was emitted, effusing Vala's womb with a brightness that grew ever stronger, till it was so bright that Vala had to open her eyes.

At that moment, Amalia too, opened her eyes and glanced at Vala.

"That was mind-blowing!" Vala squealed excitedly. "I'm lost for words!"

"You sensed the baby's powers though, yes?"

"Yes," Vala said quietly. "I can't quite put my finger on it, but I did feel something ... I don't know quite how to describe it, but I felt a surge of love and peacefulness. I could feel the baby's love for me!"

"Vala, there is a matter of great importance that I must discuss with you," Amalia began. "This may not seem like the best time, but I need to impart this to you nonetheless."

"O-kay," Vala replied nervously. "This sounds serious. I'm not going to like it, am I?"

"Indeed you may not," Amalia admitted. "When your child is of an appropriate age, I implore you to resume your mission to find Merlin and my dear sister, Nimeva. I have been having visions again that—"

"Whoa!" Vala said. "Back up a little! There is no way I am leaving my baby behind!"

"No," Amalia said, placing her hands over Vala's. "You misunderstand me: I wish for your child to accompany you. In fact, it is imperative for the mission!"

Amalia paused for a moment, exhaling deeply before continuing.

"Vala, I believe that your child is the prophesised one—or at least one half of the prophecy," Amalia explained. "In my visions, although the word *vision* is something of a misnomer, there is complete darkness, I am witnessing something terrible—an abomination. I can feel it, hear it, but I cannot see—there is nothing but blackness. Within the darkness, a great evil is about to be released. But there is even greater good present. The vision starts fading there, but before it does, a beautiful glowing mandala forms. And then I awaken."

"And you really believe my child is the key to overcoming this ... evil?" Vala furrowed her brow, savagely twisting a lock of hair tightly around her finger. "I will not place my child in danger."

"I truly do not believe that your child is in any danger," Amalia replied. "The prophesied pair shall possess a power that will be unsurpassed. I just wonder who the other might be?"

"You absolutely believe in this prophecy?" Vala asked, a prickling sensation needling at her spine.

"Emphatically," Amalia said, her unwavering confidence evident as she leaned forward and placed her hands on Vala's shoulders.

"There is another child," Vala began hesitantly, "with a similar bloodline to mine. Perhaps—"

"Indeed!" Amalia interjected excitedly. "Who is this child that you speak of?"

"The child of my brother, Tarrys, and Gweneira, Elvar's cousin," Vala answered. "She's beautiful! Her name is Temiritha."

"This is exciting news indeed!" Amalia enthused. "For now, though, go back, rest, and enjoy your pregnancy. Then, when the time is right, return to me and we can formulate a plan."

44

After summoning the Celestia, Vala felt a falling sensation, followed by an abrupt jolt. Her eyes shot open, and she pushed herself up into a sitting position, perspiration beading her forehead and trickling down her back. Her heart was racing and she gulped in mouthfuls of air; travelling back had almost been like being sucked into a vacuum, or walking at high altitude. Whatever it truly was, it left Vala feeling breathless—breathless and extremely nauseated.

Elvar stirred and sat, woken by Vala's apparent respiratory distress.

"What is wrong?" Elvar asked, pulling her against him.

"I, um," Vala screwed her face up and put her hand to her mouth.

She ran to the bathroom, her head bowed over the toilet bowl as she heaved and vomited until her stomach was empty. Elvar crouched behind her, holding her hair back. He brought a glass of water to rinse her mouth and helped Vala back to the bedroom.

Elvar was about to speak when there was a soft knock on their bedroom door.

"Come in!" he called out.

Laoli took a seat beside her daughter on the bed.

Vala looked up wearily.

"Mama," Vala said, grasping her hand.

"Sugar Plum," Laoli responded, pulling her daughter into a hug. "I had terrible morning sickness with Tarrys, but I was absolutely fine with you."

"Not reassuring," Vala replied.

"It has been suggested that male babies cause worse sickness," Laoli said. "But as awful as it is at the time, it does not last long. I always found sweet ginger and Haylip tea very soothing." Vala groaned and covered her face.

"I shall make you some, beloved," Elvar said, getting up to leave.

"Wait!" Vala called out as he reached the door. "The sickness ... something precipitated it. I visited Amalia."

"She called upon you again?" Elvar asked, his brow knitting. "No," Vala said, "I called upon *her*."

45

Vala was awoken by a gentle touch to her shoulder. She instinctively placed her hand there, presuming it to be Elvar, though upon making contact with the hand beneath, she quickly realised it was Jelly.

"Hey there, sleepyhead!" Jelly said, brushing back Vala's hair from her face and smiling at her friend.

"Hey," Vala replied, yawning. "What time is it?"

"Just gone eleven," Jelly said, glancing at her wristwatch. "We were wondering what you might like to do today?"

"Well, I thought that maybe you and Max would like to meet baby Temiritha?" Vala suggested. "And perhaps Merevina could accompany us—it might be good for her."

"Your gorgeous new niece!" Jelly squealed. "We'd love to! In that case, though ..." Jelly reached inside her jacket pocket.

"I ought to do this—babies *always* go for my hair!" Jelly pulled her long blonde hair back into a ponytail, securing it with a hairband.

"At least our children will be close in age," Vala pondered as she pulled back the comforter and placed her feet on the floor.

"Are you really okay with it all?" Jelly asked, sitting at the bottom of the bed.

Vala sighed and twisted a lock of hair.

"I'm still getting used to the idea," Vala admitted. "Though I am happy about it, it's just a hard concept to grasp that Elvar and I have created this little life growing inside me. I already feel a profound sense of love for my baby."

"Just a little scary, I guess," Jelly said, staring at Vala's abdomen as Vala lifted her nightdress over her head.

"Goodness, Vala!" Jelly said, grinning as she placed a hand over Vala's slightly rounded belly. "You already have a tiny baby bump. How adorable!"

Just as Vala was fastening her bra, there was a knock on the bedroom door.

"Girls, what are you doing in there?"

"Go away, Max, Vala's getting dressed," Jelly called out.

"I'll be down in ten, Max," Vala answered.

Vala quickly washed and dressed before knocking gently on the door to Merevina's room. There was no answer, so Vala made her way downstairs where she was greeted by a roomful of friends and family. Amongst them, sitting between Laoli and Essyeult, was Merevina, who, in spite of her height, looked like a frightened child. She glanced up as Vala walked into the room, smiled politely, and inclined her head. Vala smiled back warmly, scanning the room for Maiwen.

"Where's Maiwen?" Vala asked to no one in particular.

"She left early," Elvar replied, standing behind Vala and wrapping his arms around her waist. "Lann asked her to meet with him; he very much wishes to salvage their relationship."

"Okay then," Vala said, addressing the room. "Since all of you are here, sans Maiwen, I need to ..."

Vala paused suddenly, distracted by an aroma drifting in from the kitchen. She sniffed the air, a rich chocolate scent bombarding her olfactory senses and dancing upon her tongue.

"Sorry!" Vala said, racing to the bathroom.

Elvar chased after her, holding Vala's hair back as she dry heaved before vomiting stomach acid and bile. Her stomach was still empty from the night before.

"I don't want you to see me like this!" Vala groaned.

"Vala," Elvar said, in an all too jovial tone, "it does not bother me in the slightest, and besides," Elvar filled a glass of water, passing it to Vala, "I have seen you indisposed twice before."

"Don't remind me!" she rasped, wiping her mouth with a tissue.

"I am in complete awe of you, beloved," Elvar said, bending to help Vala to her feet. "You are growing and nurturing a new life in there—a life we created together! Besides, babies create plentiful quantities of vomit and waste products of their own, so I may as well get used to it!"

"Elvar!" Vala threatened. "I swear, if you make me upchuck again I'll ..."

"Just what *will* you do to me?" Elvar teased, pulling Vala close and grinning.

*

After Vala had updated the others on her latest encounter with Amalia, she, Elvar, Merevina, Jelly, Max, and Merridyn made their way to Tarrys and Gweneira's home. Gannlyth had chosen to return to Moredonia to spend some time with his family, promising to return once they were ready to resume their quest.

"Merri, you've been very quiet today," Vala said, touching his arm.

"Have I?" Merridyn replied. "I suppose I have been somewhat pensive."

"There's something different about you," Vala continued, "since yesterday."

"Respectfully, Vala," Merridyn returned, "it is not something that I wish to discuss presently."

"Okay," Vala said, turning away.

Merridyn placed his hands on Vala's shoulders, forcing her to face him.

"I am sorry, Vala," Merridyn said sadly. "You have done nothing wrong, it is a private matter and something I need to work out in my own head first, but I promise you that when I have more clarity, I will tell you."

"Vala?" Merevina said, her voice barely above a whisper. "I fear that I may have been responsible for your earlier disposition, I am profusely sorry."

Vala looked at Merevina, confused by her statement.

"Why would you think that?"

"The aroma you smelt," Merevina explained, "I was making chocolate rose cookies with Chando pods with your companion, Jelly. I was informed that these are your favourite, and I just wanted to ..."

"Merevina," Vala said, squeezing her hand, "it was a very kind gesture—thank you. For the record, you did nothing wrong, it's just morning sickness, part and parcel of being pregnant, I guess."

"Morning sickness?" Merevina replied, her brow furrowed. "I do not know of this sickness. My father, I mean the Spindler, ensured that I received a full education, but there are obviously matters of which I am not so learned."

"Well, not every pregnant woman suffers from it," Vala said. "It's thought that it's connected to high levels of hCG and oestrogen, although in my case it would be a different form of hCG, being as I am only partly human and my baby is mostly fae."

"hCG is human chorionic gonadotropin, in case you were wondering," Jelly interjected, seeing the confused expression on Merevina's face.

"Ah yes!" Merevina exclaimed, a smile lighting her face. "It is similar in fae physiology, known as fCG, so maybe yours is fhCG!"

Merevina laughed, feeling a temporary reprieve from her sorrow.

"You have a beautiful laugh," Merridyn said, daring a furtive glance at Merevina.

Merevina gazed back at Merridyn, her face reddening.

Vala cast a glance between the two of them, keen to break the tension.

"So, um, I kind of digressed from what I meant to say. Thank you so much, Merevina and Jelly, for the cookies; they are my favourite, and I'm sure I will be able to enjoy them later today!"

When the company reached the house, Tarrys welcomed them all in, clearly excited to show off his new baby. They walked into the living room, where Gweneira sat on the sofa nursing Temiritha.

"So I hear Temiritha is due to have a little cousin soon?" Gweneira said, beaming at Vala and Elvar.

"Um, yes!" Vala confirmed, a light blush colouring her cheeks. "May I introduce Merevina and Merridyn—aka Merri—he's a friend we met on our visit to Moredonia."

Tarrys inclined his head, took Merevina's hand in his, and kissed it lightly. "It is both a pleasure and honour to meet you, Merevina."

Merevina inclined her head in return, giving a cordial but genuine smile.

"A pleasure to meet you too, Merridyn, or Merri, if you prefer?" Tarrys said, taking Merridyn's hand.

"Likewise," Merridyn replied. "And Merri is fine, thank you."

"I would stand to greet you," Gweneira called out, "but as you can see, I am otherwise occupied! However, welcome to our home, it is an honour to meet you both."

"And how is my little niece today?" Vala asked, sitting next to Gweneira.

She held her finger out to Temiritha, who grasped it tightly and looked intently at Vala. Vala laughed in delight.

"Hungry!" Gweneira said, laughing. "Very hungry!"

Gweneira raised the baby's shawl to afford her some modesty as she removed Temiritha from her breast.

"Would you like to hold her?"

"Yes. Absolutely!" Vala answered, taking the baby from Gweneira's arms.

"You are all welcome to have a cuddle!" Gweneira said warmly. "Please do be seated either on the sofa or the floor if you want to be closer to Temiritha."

Max, Merridyn, and Merevina chose the sofa, with Merevina hesitantly sitting next to Merridyn; an unexpected tingle shot through her body, causing her face to heat and redden.

As Merridyn made himself more comfortable, his little finger brushed against Merevina's, and a bolt of electricity surged through him. He quickly apologised and moved his hand to his lap.

"She has unusual eyes," Elvar observed, as he held Temiritha in his arms. "Beautiful, though, the mix of violet and green."

"Goodness!" Tarrys announced suddenly. "Where are my manners? I have been remiss in my hospitality! May I offer anyone refreshments? I do apologise, but we are rather sleep deprived!"

"I can take care of that," Elvar offered, as he passed the baby to an eagerly awaiting Jelly.

"Why don't you both take a nap?" Vala suggested. "We can handle things for a while."

"That is a very kind offer, Vala," Gweneira replied, "though it seems rude to leave our guests."

"Go!" Jelly said. "Temiritha's fine with us. Aren't you, gorgeous?" Reluctantly, Gweneira and Tarrys retired to their bedroom, whilst the others remained in the living room with Temiritha. Temiritha turned her head and watched as her parents ascended the stairs, then turned back, cooing happily in Jelly's arms.

Temiritha looked up at Jelly and touched her cheek, smiling.

"OMG! Did you see that?" Jelly exclaimed. "She smiled! How is that even possible? That was definitely not a *wind* smile, it was an actual smile!"

Vala stroked Temiritha's head, enjoying the sensation of the baby's fine silken hair beneath her fingers.

"Yes, she did," Vala agreed. "Temiritha's a special baby." "So it's not just some fae thing?" Max asked.

"No, Max," Elvar answered. "There is something different about Temiritha."

"You look like you'd like another turn, Elvar!" Jelly said.

"Yes please!" Elvar said, taking the baby from Jelly and cuddling Temiritha in his arms.

Temiritha locked eyes with Elvar and smiled at him too, reaching up to touch his face. Elvar stroked her tiny fingers with his own and kissed her forehead.

"You are indeed a remarkable little lady," Elvar murmured, pressing his cheek gently against Temiritha's head.

"Wow, mate!" Max said. "You certainly are a natural with babies. A good thing, really, considering."

"I am sure you too will experience the joys of fatherhood!" Elvar said, a feeling of complete elation washing over him.

"Um, yeah!" Max replied hesitantly. "No offence, but not for a while, thanks!"

"Okay!" Elvar said. "On that note, may I offer anyone a drink? Here, Max, why not hold Temiritha while I go to the kitchen."

Elvar gently passed Temiritha to Max. Temiritha waved her arms about gleefully, gurgling and reaching out to touch Max's face as he took her from Elvar. A feeling of perfect serenity passed over Max, and he regarded Temiritha with a mixture of awe and curiosity.

"Why don't you just bring in a pitcher of Alushi nectar?" Vala suggested. "I think everyone's too besotted with Temiritha to even care what they drink."

As Elvar returned with the refreshments tray, Max passed Temiritha to Merridyn. Merridyn lifted her into the air, carefully supporting Temiritha's head. She squealed with delight, her tiny fingers curling around Merridyn's index finger. The moment Temiritha's skin made contact with his, he was overcome with a sense of levity, and he laughed out loud as Temiritha continued to babble and squeal.

Merevina watched in fascination, entranced as the others were by Temiritha. Temiritha was suddenly quiet and stretched her arms out towards Merevina.

"I think she wants you to hold her now," Merridyn said.

"I ... I do not know what to do," Merevina replied nervously.

"Just support her head," Merridyn said, smiling reassuringly.

Tentatively, Merevina reached out to take Temiritha from Merridyn, securing her safely within her arms. For a moment, both Temiritha and Merevina were quiet, Temiritha's gaze locked with Merevina's. Merevina inhaled Temiritha's baby scent and sighed contentedly. She lowered her head towards Temiritha, stroking the baby's velvet soft cheek. Temiritha cooed and gurgled, as though impatient to form coherent words that she was not yet capable of. Never breaking eye contact with Merevina, Temiritha placed one hand on Merevina's forehead and the other, just above her left breast. A flash of images, memories, flooded Merevina's mind. She gasped and smiled, tears welling in her eyes and spilling over onto her cheeks.

"Are you all right, Merevina?" Merridyn asked, lightly touching her arm.

"Yes. Thank you," Merevina answered, her voice choked with emotion. "I remember now."

"What exactly do you remember?" Vala asked, her curiosity piqued.

"Everything that I was before the Spindler abducted me," Merevina said. "When you soul-mirrored me, Vala, I remembered who I truly am, remembered who my parents are—snippets of childhood memories. But now, it has all returned. I recall everything up to the part when I was abducted."

Merevina looked down at Temiritha, who was now amusing herself with Merevina's hair.

"Temiritha," Merevina continued, "there is something ..."

"Very different about her," Vala interjected. "I think each of us have felt it, not to mention her advanced development."

Merevina softly stroked Temiritha's head, lightly planting a kiss on her forehead. Temiritha smiled, then yawned, turning her head towards Merevina's breast and closing her eyes.

Merevina watched, mesmerised as she listened to Temiritha's breathing, the rise and fall of the baby's stomach as it gradually slowed and Temiritha fell sound asleep.

"She has certainly taken a liking to you," Merridyn said, his hand touching Merevina's forearm.

Merevina stared at Merridyn's hand, it had caused that tingling sensation again and stirred unfamiliar feelings within her. Merridyn glanced down at his hand, still resting on Merevina's arm. This time he neither apologised nor moved his hand away.

Merevina looked up at Merridyn surreptitiously, her cheeks aflame. He caught her gaze, an affectionate smile lighting his eyes. Within that one look, Merevina felt such a sense of acceptance, belonging, kindness, and something else. Merevina's eyes widened— it was love! Merridyn was radiating such a sense of love—for her, Merevina! Her heartbeat fluttered and quickened. What should she do? She felt confused and conflicted. Merevina's most recent memories of her time as Athanasia were still fresh in her mind; there were almost a handful of men with whom she had had relations, but only for the purpose of procreation, and then she had killed them, all except one. How could this kind and gentle man love her, knowing what terrible crimes she had committed? How could she possibly be worthy of him?

Merevina looked away sadly. She had not been truly herself when she had lain with those men. She had certainly not loved them. She'd had perhaps a fleeting attraction, but nothing more. Merevina had not even enjoyed the act itself: it felt hollow and empty—a means to an end, her duty to the Spindler to continue their insidious legacy. And yet, her feelings for Merridyn were inexplicably powerful, as though a magnetic force were pulling them together.

"Is something troubling you, Merevina?" Merridyn asked, boldly stroking her cheek.

Jelly and Max were engaged in conversation with Elvar, too preoccupied to notice. Feeling fatigued, Vala had closed her eyes for a few minutes but had just opened them in time to see Merridyn's intimate gesture with Merevina. It was clear to her in that moment that Merridyn's affections had transferred to Merevina. Merri was besotted, and even through Merevina's timidity, Vala could see that she felt the same way about him. They were twin souls, like she and Elvar.

"Other than rediscovering who I am and coming to terms with all the atrocities I committed as Athanasia, you mean?" Merevina replied mirthfully, a smile breaking through.

"That was a rather stupid question!" Merridyn said, covering his face with his hands.

"No," Merevina returned, "it is not—I was just teasing! There is something else ..."

"I know," Merridyn said in a hushed tone. "Perhaps we could take a walk together later ... alone."

"I would like that," Merevina said, smiling.

Temiritha stirred in Merevina's arms, murmuring in her sleep. Merevina rocked her gently, humming a tune remembered from her own childhood.

An hour later, Gweneira and Tarrys awoke, and making their way down the stairs, they were greeted by a truly wonderful scene: their baby daughter soundly asleep in Merevina's arms.

"She has been asleep for a while now," Merevina said as Gweneira approached her.

"You have quite the maternal touch," Gweneira replied, smiling warmly at Merevina. "Temiritha has certainly taken a shine to you!"

"Temiritha is a very special baby," Merevina said, "and a very beautiful one."

"She is that," Tarrys said, kneeling down beside Merevina to stroke Temiritha's head. "Just like her mother."

"Holding Temiritha," Merevina said, "I do not know how to put it into words, but she makes me feel more at peace; as though a tumultuous sea has been stilled."

"Vala," Tarrys said, "why not take Temiritha for a moment? You will certainly be needing the practise now."

Merevina gently passed Temiritha to Vala, careful not to wake her.

"Merevina," Tarrys said quietly, "may I have a word with you in private?"

Tarrys noticed an anxious expression cross Merevina's face.

"Do not be worried, you have done nothing wrong," Tarrys assured her.

Merevina followed Tarrys into a glass-walled study, looking around the room with interest.

"Please, be seated," Tarrys said, gesturing to a cream sofa, scattered with orange silk cushions.

Tarrys sat opposite Merevina on a matching cream armchair.

"I work as a listener," Tarrys explained. "Obviously this is an exceedingly difficult and confusing time for you, but I would be honoured if you would permit me to help you, if you are amenable to the idea, or maybe you would like some time to consider it?"

"That is most generous of you," Merevina replied. "I do not need time to consider it—I would be very grateful for any help received."

"Thank you, Merevina," Tarrys replied, beaming. "I will endeavour to do my very best for you. And remember, anything you say to me is in complete confidence, unless of course there is a perceived threat to either yourself or another."

"I understand," Merevina said. "Thank you, Tarrys. You have been very kind to me—you all have."

"Can you drop by tomorrow at ..." Tarrys paused, leafing through his diary, "at 11 a.m.? You can join us for lunch after if it is not too great an imposition on your time."

Merevina exhaled a shuddery breath, her eyes brimming with tears.

Tarrys got up and knelt beside her, placing a hand over hers. "It will be all right." Tarrys passed her a tissue.

"All of you," Merevina said, her voice catching, "the clemency and compassion shown towards me, even after the terrible atrocities I have committed ... and I tried to kill your sister ... I do not understand how I am deserving of ..."

"Merevina," Tarrys interrupted, "the acts committed were that of a persona that no longer exists. It was not *you*, Merevina, it was a phantom: an illusion created by the Spindler, no more than a clever enchantment. *You*, Merevina, are innocent of all the crimes you blame yourself for."

"Thank you," Merevina whispered, looking directly at Tarrys and smiling weakly.

"Let me make you a cup of Belsip tea," Tarrys offered, getting to his feet. "It will help soothe you. I will also show you some techniques to alleviate anxiety and help centre yourself."

There was a soft knock on the door as Merevina sipped her tea. Gweneira poked her head around the door.

"Vala is heading home now," Gweneira said. "She is feeling tired."

"Then I will escort Merevina back to the Oakley's," Tarrys said, overhearing. "I need to spend a little time with Merevina first."

46

Merevina's hand rested comfortably in the crook of Merridyn's arm. They had both been walking in silence since leaving Gweneira and Tarrys' home.

"I had forgotten just how beautiful Avalonia is," Merridyn remarked, reaching up to touch a heart-shaped purple leaf.

"Where are you from?" Merevina asked, casting a surreptitious glance at Merridyn.

"I hail from merry Moredonia!" Merridyn replied, chancing a brief look at Merevina.

"The coastal region," Merevina said, "I frequented it often with my family as a child. I ..."

Merevina was cut off as Merridyn placed his hands on her shoulders, turning her to face him.

"We are engaging in polite pleasantries," Merridyn said, his heart racing, "which, whilst very um ... pleasant, is not the reason I wanted to talk with you."

Merevina sighed, resting her head back against a large ancient oak tree.

"Merri," Merevina began, boldly taking his hands in hers, "I have a terrible past: I have taken lives, lain with men whom I did not love. You are a good, kind, and gentle man, you deserve someone better than me."

"I do not care about your past!" Merridyn stated firmly. "It was not you anyway! We are twin souls—I know you feel it as I do."

"I do not know what I should do," Merevina said, her anguished voice rising an octave.

"Be with me!" Merridyn exclaimed. "I love you."

Merevina placed her hands on Merridyn's cheeks and gazed deeply into his eyes. She moved her face closer to his till their noses were touching.

"I need to take this slowly."

"As slow as you like," Merridyn answered, his breath warm and tantalising on her lips. "But right now, I really, really want to kiss you."

Merevina pressed her lips against Merridyn's. Slowly, their lips moved together. Merevina inhaled sharply as Merridyn drew her lower lip inside his mouth, and she found her hands tangling in his dark curls. Her heart was pounding so hard she felt sure Merridyn could feel it resonating against his chest, and as his tongue met hers, the rest of the world just melted away.

47

Vala stretched and felt a sharp kick from within. She smiled and placed her hand over her distended belly.

"Good morning to you too, Kidley Bean," Vala said, yawning and rubbing the sleep from her eyes.

Beside her, Elvar yawned and smiled, his hand moving to Vala's face as he softly kissed her.

"Good morning, beloved," Elvar said, rubbing his hand over Vala's belly. "And good morning to you too, Kidley Bean."

Elvar laughed as a tiny foot protruded from Vala's belly, delivering him a healthy kick, followed by a series of smaller ones.

"I can't believe it's only two weeks to go," Vala said, placing her hand over Elvar's, which still rested upon her belly. "At least I hope it's only two because I look like a whale on growth hormones!"

"You look beautiful as always," Elvar replied, as he gently lifted one of Vala's engorged breasts, "though I can no longer cup one of these in just one hand!"

"You might want to be careful handling those," Vala said laughing. "I've started lactating."

Elvar cupped Vala's face, kissing her lightly, first on the lips, then leaving a trail of kisses down her neck, over her chest, and stopping upon reaching her belly. He gently rested his head and hand on Vala's baby bump, closed his eyes, and listened. Colourful patterns composed of earthy warm hues of red, orange, yellow, and green danced beneath his eyelids, accompanied by the fast cadence of their baby's heartbeat. Elvar opened his eyes briefly and looked at the clock, closely watching the second hand.

"One hundred and forty-two beats per minute," Elvar said, kissing Vala's belly before closing his eyes again.

"Fast, but normal, I'm told," Vala replied, stroking Elvar's hair.

Elvar felt a slight tingle on the cheek that was pressed against Vala's abdomen: a warm sensation seeped through his veins and spread throughout his body like a soothing balm, ebbing away little knots of tension in his body that he had not been previously aware of.

"I could stay like this all day," he said lazily, enjoying the perfectly relaxed feeling permeating his body.

"Only you can't because you have lessons to get to," Vala said, twisting a lock of Elvar's hair in her fingers.

"Unfortunately true," Elvar answered, sighing. "Would you like me to bring breakfast to our room? We could get in a little more *alone* time, and you can get some rest afterwards—you look tired, my love."

"That would be lovely," Vala agreed. "And you'd be tired too if you were carrying a baby whale in your belly!"

48

After Elvar left, Vala snuggled under the comforter, humming a lullaby to their unborn child, lovingly stroking her belly. The magnitude of love she already felt for their child was all consuming and like nothing she had experienced before. Just as Vala was readying herself for further sleep, a soft knock sounded at the door.

"Come in."

"Good morning, Vala," Maiwen said, standing at the doorway with an apprehensive expression. "I hope I am not disturbing you? I can come back later ..."

"It is fine, Maiwen," Vala said. "Come, sit down, something is obviously weighing heavily on your mind."

Maiwen closed the door behind her and sat on the end of the bed, pulling her knees to her chest, resting her head on them.

"I know we have had a very similar conversation before," Maiwen began, "but I think that the time is right now."

"Maiwen, maybe it's my baby-brain fogging my thoughts, but you are being a little cryptic."

"I want to ..." Maiwen said hesitantly. "Lann and I have grown very close and I ... um ... I ..."

"Want to sleep with him?" Vala ventured.

"Um yes, I guess so," Maiwen answered. "No, I mean, I do! I was just wondering how you knew when the time was right and how much ... um ... pain to expect?"

"Well," Vala said, taking Maiwen's hand, "you just need to trust your intuition: if it feels right, it is. And with regards to the pain, yes, there is some pain to start with, but it is fleeting and should soon be replaced by far more intense ... pleasurable sensations."

"Thank you, Vala," Maiwen replied, enveloping her in a hug.

"Anytime," Vala said, smiling warmly and brushing away a lock of hair from Maiwen's eyes. "Just make sure he takes the Nonceptium elixir or you'll end up like me!"

"Everyone else is out at the moment," Maiwen said. "I am more than happy to spend the day with you, but I was wondering if you might like to help me shop for alluring undergarments?"

"I can't believe I'm turning down the chance to shop!" Vala said groaning, "But I just don't have the stamina for anything more than a short walk. Anyway, where's Merevina?"

"She is out celebrating with Merri—he surprised her! She received word this morning that Merri has been offered a position by appointment of Queen Assanli, as curator of their personal collection of Avalonian antiquities. Apparently the royalty have decided to open it up for public viewing, in small parties of course," Maiwen answered.

"That's amazing!" Vala exclaimed, grinning broadly. "It will be good to have Merri here, especially for Merevina. Long-distance relationships are rather challenging to say the least."

Vala paused, contemplating her next words carefully. "Are you completely at peace with what happened between Lann and Merevina? Your relationship with her seems to be a lot less strained."

Maiwen sighed and smiled sadly. "I fully accept that neither of them was to blame; Lann thought he was making love to me, and Merevina ... well she was not Merevina at the time. To be completely candid, it is rather hard not to like her: she is so thoughtful and kind."

Vala stretched, curling and flexing her toes several times to boost the circulation in her chilly feet.

"And she's come such a long way with the help of my brother and that amazing baby niece of mine! Spending time with Temiritha seems to have healed her somehow—perhaps even brought back buried memories," Vala said. "Even when I'm with Temiritha—"

"She makes you feel at peace," Maiwen finished. "I think she has helped me heal too. It makes me wonder if perhaps the prophecy might be realised very soon—that Temiritha and—"

"No!" Vala interrupted, covering her ears. "I'm sorry, Maiwen, but I can't get my head around it right now. I'm two weeks away from giving birth and scared enough about that, let alone entertaining the notion of my baby being a prophetic chosen one!" "Point taken," Maiwen said ruefully.

"So," Maiwen continued, swiftly changing the subject, "as you are not accompanying me on my little shopping expedition, shall I escort you to Gwen and Tarrys' or will you be alright by yourself for a short while?"

"Go, Maiwen!" Vala replied, shooing her away. "I'll be absolutely fine."

"As long as you are sure?" Maiwen said, ambivalent about her decision. "I really am happy to wait for you to wash and dress, then escort you to your brother's."

"Really, Maiwen!" Vala said in mock exasperation. "I'll be okay—I'm pregnant, not unwell or incapacitated. I can take care of myself!"

"Okay then," Maiwen responded, "I shall go, but I will be as quick as possible."

"Go already!" Vala shouted, laughing. "And have a good time!"

"I shall try," Maiwen said as she got up to leave. "See you later, wish me luck!"

49

Vala splashed her face with cold water and brushed her teeth. Even the smallest everyday tasks seemed to require extra effort, and the added weight she now carried often left her tired and breathless.

Every morning, after breakfast, Vala liked to quietly commune with her unborn child. Often this would take the form of a short walk through the woodland. If Elvar was home, they would go together, but quite frequently Vala would walk alone and talk softly to the baby, feeling subtle shifts in its energy as it responded to her voice.

After a meagre meal of a Savima bread roll and a glass of milk, Vala dressed into a loose, flowing white dress paired with a shellpink cardigan, before stepping outside. It was a typical, gloriously warm Avalonian October morning, and Vala closed her eyes, turning her face skywards, allowing the rays of the sun to energise and rejuvenate her. She inhaled deeply and smiled before exhaling and opening her eyes to continue her walk. Earthy, alpine, and lavender aromas infused her senses, and she felt deeply relaxed.

"Are you all right in there, Kidley Bean?" Vala asked, rubbing her belly. "It feels as though you might be sleeping."

Vala continued walking, the sunlight flitting between leaves, casting dancing shadows upon the ground like golden paint splashed across an ever-changing canvas. She watched in wonder as a Cowlat with a baby attached to its back scurried up a tree, disappearing into a hollow. The woodland was replete with the sounds of birdsong, chattering, and scampering animals, though there was no one else in sight.

After fifteen minutes, Vala decided to rest for a short while on a bench, sheltered by a tall canopy of Viaspa trees. She sat back, stretching her legs out and closing her eyes. Abruptly, the atmosphere changed: birds cawed and screeched, taking flight, and the forest grew silent. Vala's eyes bolted open as she protectively wrapped her arms around her bump. She started to push herself up. Something closed over her nose and mouth: a piece of padded gauze. Vala let out a muffled scream, watching in horror at the fingers holding the gauze over her, but she could not turn to see who it was. She desperately clawed at the fingers pressing the gauze to her face, trying not to inhale the sweet, ether-like aroma, which crept in nonetheless. Defiantly, Vala dug her nails into her assailant and swung her elbows back. She heard the tear of fabric as a second, smaller pair of hands caught one of her sleeves before securing Vala's wrists with rope. Again, Vala tried to scream, resisting the pungent vapours as best she could, though her head was feeling woozy and vertiginous as large blue blotches appeared in her rapidly diminishing field of vision. She felt a tug on the chain holding her Iridiscus pendant in place, temporarily regretful that the ring no longer fitted her slightly swollen fingers. And then Vala's world fell into darkness.

50

"Beloved, I have a surprise for you!" Elvar called out, racing up the stairs and into his bedroom.

Not seeing Vala, he called out again, but instead of his wife, he was greeted by a distraught, tear-stained Maiwen, tightly clutching a note in her hand.

"What has happened?" Elvar asked, an icy-cold chill piercing his heart.

"I do not know!" Maiwen cried. "I got back a half hour ago and found this note."

Elvar took the note from his sister's hand and read it.

"She says she has gone for her usual post-breakfast walk and will be back within the hour," Elvar said, his voice rising in alarm. "It is three o'clock, Maiwen! Why did you not call me as soon as you realised Vala was missing?"

"I was too busy trying to find her!" Maiwen retorted. "She is not with Gwen and Tarrys, or in the first hundred yards of woodland, though I did notice something strange."

"What?"

"The animals," Maiwen said softly. "They are skittish—something feels amiss."

"I have to go," Elvar said, his voice catching. "I need to find Vala. Now!"

"Go!" Maiwen replied. "I shall alert our family and friends—we have a better chance of finding Vala quicker the more there are of us looking. And, Elvar?"

Elvar nodded for Maiwen to continue.

"She is not responding to her Iridiscus."

51

Elvar let out an anguished cry as he slammed the front door behind him. *Where is Vala? Is she hurt? Scared and alone somewhere? Or has something more insidious befallen her?*

"Vala?" Elvar called out at the neck of the woods. "Vala?" There was no answer. He ventured further into the forest. Maiwen was right, the atmosphere felt wrong; too quiet, with just the occasional scamper of a woodland animal or the occasional flutter of bird wings.

Elvar clasped his Iridiscus pendant and called out to Vala. Nothing. He kept on walking. A twig snapped behind him. Instinctively, Elvar turned. It was Tarrys, accompanied by Maiwen and Lann.

"Sorry," Tarrys said. "We did not mean to startle you, Brother."

"Mother and Father have gone to meet Vala's parents in person," Maiwen explained. "They felt it best ... to be there for moral support. They should not be long. Merevina and Merri are on their way too."

"Maiwen and Lann," Tarrys said, "maybe the two of you could conduct an aerial search—it will enable us to cover more ground quickly. Elvar and I will remain on terra firma and meet you back at this point in an hour, unless we find Vala before then."

"That sounds like a sensible idea," Lann concurred. "We will find her, Elvar."

Lann placed his hand on Elvar's shoulder and ascended into the air with Maiwen.

"Tarrys," Elvar said, his voice quivering, "something is very wrong. I can feel it."

"I can too," Tarrys replied sadly. "But she is alive—that much I am certain of."

52

A high-pitched ringing sounded in Vala's ears, followed by muffled voices. Forcing her eyelids to open was effortful, but Vala persevered. Blurred shapes appeared in her vision, but as she continued to concentrate, her world came back into focus. It was then that Vala noticed the pain, and something else, a dampness beneath her. Her inner thighs were wet! For a moment, Vala wondered if she had lost control of her bladder whilst unconscious, but then she realised what it was. Her waters had broken!

She looked up groggily. A woman was looking over her, a child clutching the woman's hand—a boy, the same boy whom Maiwen had brought home that night. Vala's heart started to race, a cold trickle of fear slaking through her spine. Her stomach churned and bile rose in her throat. She started to wretch.

The woman made a mournful noise, releasing the child's hand and hurrying back with a bowl, which she held under Vala's chin. Vala evacuated her stomach contents as the woman knelt beside her, calling out to the boy, who returned with a mug of water in his hand. She passed the mug to Vala. Hand shaking, Vala reached out for the mug and rinsed her mouth out.

"Get him away from me!" Vala screamed, pointing at the boy. "Who are you? What have you done to me?"

The woman whispered to the boy, who ran off into another room. Vala started to raise herself from the bed she was lying on, but another wave of pain took hold and she fell back onto the pillow.

"I am deeply sorry, Lady Oakley-Pendragon," the woman said. "I mean you no harm. *We* mean you no harm. The boy, he is my son, Fenrar. We were under instruction that should the original plan fail, we were to take you and ..."

"Under instruction from whom?" Vala demanded as another surge of pain tugged at her womb.

Before the woman could answer, Vala cried out—the pain was intensifying, the contractions becoming more powerful and frequent.

"I need Elvar!" Vala sobbed. "Please, I need my husband!"

Vala reached for her Iridiscus pendant, only to find her neck was bare.

"Where is my pendant?"

The woman sighed and shook her head regretfully.

"Lady Oakley-Pendragon," the woman said calmly but firmly, "I again apologise profusely for the predicament I have put you in, but it is imperative that you calm down for the sake of your baby ... and yourself. With your permission, I would like to change you into fresh clothes, change the bed linen, and prepare you for the birth. You will also be dehydrated, I can give you fresh water with Pereniquim tincture. It will ease the severity of your contractions."

Vala nodded, realising the futility and danger of further agitation, but she started to sob. She wanted Elvar. She wanted her mother.

"I'm only nineteen," Vala rasped, her throat raw and dry. "I can't do this on my own!"

"You are not alone, my lady," the woman replied, reaching for a folded white cotton nightgown on a nearby dressing table. "My name is Sylvinia Broadleaf. I am at your service. My son will also assist in any way he can—and, yes, we are Dessicati, but we are not a threat to you or your child. I knew as we were bringing you here that our actions were unconscionable, but by then we were close to our home and your amniotic sac had ruptured. I felt it safer to bring you here and return you both after the birth. Oh, and if you are curious as to why our appearance is normal, it is because we have been nourished with extra souls. So, unlike most other Dessicati, we remain youthful."

"But why?"

"Why what, my lady?" Sylvinia answered.

"Why are you helping me now, when just a short time ago ... and why have you been fed extra souls when other Dessicati look ... well ..."

Sylvinia sighed.

"It is complicated," Sylvinia began. "For the sake of brevity ... it began many centuries ago. I had been married for eight very happy years, to a human man, Yvain, the very best of men and one of King Arthur's most trusted knights. We met when he accompanied Arthur and Guinevere to Avalonia for relocation; having sworn fealty to Arthur, he felt honour-bound to protect them, even in the fae realm. I was working as a healer at the time in the royal court.

"Anyway, we were happy—all three of us. Fenrar loved his father fiercely, so when he was taken from us ..."

Sylvinia's voice quivered, her chest heaving as she brushed away a tear with the heel of her hand.

"Yvain had a brother in the human realm, which at that time, was constantly embroiled in skirmishes with the Saxons. His brother, Benedict, had been captured, as the Saxons believed him to possess military knowledge that would help them. As soon as Yvain received word of Benedict's imprisonment, he set out to rescue him; Yvain was successful in freeing his brother and intended to bring him back to us in Avalonia. However, just as they reached the portal, Yvain was struck down by an arrow. Benedict managed to pull him through and brought him to me, but it was too late—Yvain had been pierced through the heart and had lost too much blood. He died in front of us, in front of Fenrar."

"I'm so sorry," Vala said, at a loss and in too much pain to say anything else.

"Fenrar became extremely fearful, terrified by the prospect of losing me too. He changed from being a happy, carefree child to being withdrawn and tearful, often refusing food and confining himself to his room, sleeping for much of the day. After six months of employing all manner of techniques to help Fenrar with no noticeable sign of improvement, I became desperate. I asked Fenrar what would help, what would bring him back to me. He said that he wanted me to never leave him; never, for the two of us to remain together forever.

It was not an easy decision, but I travelled with Fenrar to the Tenebrae—to the Spindler—and assured him our loyalty in return for immortality. He agreed, and Fenrar and I were treated with considerable favour. The Spindler secured our continuing youth with an abundance of souls; he treated us with kindness, gave us a home, and provided Fenrar with a full education alongside his daughter, Athanasia.

After his death, a select minority of his followers were entrusted with explicit instructions. It is complicated, as I said earlier, but your capture was one of them.

"I felt obligated to him, my lady, and even though I knew it was wrong, I stole you away. In the end, though, I could not do what he asked of me. Would not. I want Fenrar and I to be as we were—to do good again, to redeem our own souls. No more soul harvesting. No more wrong-doing."

Sylvinia helped Vala onto a wooden chair by the foot of the bed, while she expeditiously changed the bed linen. For the first time since regaining consciousness, Vala looked around at her surroundings. She was in what appeared to be a bedroom, modest in size and simply furnished, with a mirrored dressing table, a Viaspan wardrobe, and a cream Furlomyn rug covering the wooden floor. The walls were comprised of unadorned Viaspan wood panels, with a long oval window on the side wall above the bed.

"Fenrar?" Sylvinia called out. "Can you please bring a pitcher of water and a vial of Pereniquim tincture. Oh, and some fresh towels."

Vala wilfully tried to calm her breathing and relax as much as possible; given the gravity of the situation she was in, it was not an easy endeavour. Her mind was spinning—who had instructed these Dessicatus to abduct her? She needed answers, now!

Fenrar arrived with the pitcher, a mug, and the Pereniquim tincture, which he set on the dressing table before returning with a bale of towels.

"Sylvinia?" Vala asked, wincing as another contraction took hold. "I need to know who ordered you to abduct me and why."

Sylvinia exhaled loudly and poured Vala a mug of water, adding three drops of Pereniquim tincture.

"Please, drink this first," Sylvinia pleaded. "It will take the edge off your pain."

Vala took the mug and slowly sipped—the water instantly soothing her burning, parched throat.

"The Spindler sent us, my lady," Sylvinia answered finally, a tear rolling down her cheek.

"But the Spindler's dead!" Vala replied, her heart rate accelerating again, her breathing fast and shallow. "It's not possible—I killed him myself!"

"Yes, my lady, you did."

53

Elvar clutched his stomach as a wave of nausea roiled through him. Something had caught his eye—a swatch of pale pink fabric. Elvar carefully removed it from the bush it had become ensnared in and showed it to Tarrys.

"This is from Vala's cardigan," Elvar said before turning away to vomit behind the bush.

Tarrys comforted Elvar as he broke down in Tarrys' arms. Elvar felt the soft touch of a woman's fingers stroke his hair; he knew without looking that it was his mother.

"Come here, sweet boy," Essyeult said soothingly as she took her son in her arms.

As Tarrys moved away from Elvar, he saw something glinting in the bush in which Elvar had found the swatch of fabric. He knelt down to examine it. It was Vala's Iridiscus pendant; the chain had snapped. He dislodged it from the foliage and placed it in his palm to show the others.

"Vala's pendant," Tarrys said quietly, only just noticing his parents standing there, silent, too shocked to speak and their faces whitened by the trauma of the situation.

"We will find Vala, Mother," Tarrys said, taking Laoli's hand.

Tarrys had to be strong—it was his job to help others keep it together. Most of the time, this was well within his skillset, a professional mode he could just slip into. Tarrys closed his eyes, unfallen tears stinging their surface. He had no choice: if his family was falling apart, it was up to him to keep them together. They all needed to be strong and focussed if they were to have any chance of finding his sister.

54

Sylvinia eased Vala back onto the bed, her head supported by a stack of plumped pillows, enabling Vala to be less supine and more comfortable. Vala was exhausted, physically and emotionally, her energy spent. The pain had diminished a little, and she could feel her eyelids growing heavy, longing to close, to shut all of this out and drift off into a peaceful abyss.

"My lady," Sylvinia said, "I was once a healer—will you permit me to examine you?"

Vala nodded her assent, and Sylvinia gently pulled up Vala's nightgown before kneeling down to examine her.

"You are three centimetres dilated, my lady," Sylvinia observed, lowering Vala's nightgown once more. "Try to get some sleep. In the meantime, I will send Fenrar to notify your family of your whereabouts."

Vala settled back into the pillows, praying that Elvar would be here before she gave birth. Sylvinia left the room briefly, returning with a dark glass bottle. She poured a small amount of the contents into her palm, dabbing her fingers into the aromatic pool that had gathered there.

"This is lavender and Mysterium oil, it will help relax you. It is very soporific," Sylvinia explained, as she rubbed the oil onto Vala's temples, neck, and behind her ears.

Vala nodded numbly. Her mind was still reeling from Sylvinia's shocking revelation, and all Vala wanted to do now was sleep.

55

"We need to reach the Sycamore Rest Lodge before sunset," Derryth urged the others.

"I will not stop looking for my baby!" Laoli shouted. "I will look all through the night if that is what it takes! You can all do as you wish!"

"And I will not cease either!" Patrick said, placing an arm around his wife.

"Laoli," Derryth said gently, lightly touching her arm. "You will be of no use to Vala exhausted and sleep-deprived. You must take care of your own needs to be truly there for your daughter when we do find her."

Laoli shrugged Derryth's hand away.

"And how much sleep do you think I will get knowing my daughter is who knows where with who knows what, in the throes of childbirth? Alone!"

"You can sense it too," Tarrys said to his mother.

Laoli nodded back, hot tears coursing over her cheeks, leaving them red and blotchy.

"Please, can we just stay focussed on finding my wife!" Elvar yelled, silencing them all.

"Of course," Tarrys replied. "At least we have her pendant now so we will know if we are on the right track."

At that moment, Maiwen and Lann alighted in front of Elvar, Maiwen pulling her brother into a hug. Elvar stood there motionless as his sister tried to comfort him. Although he had not spoken at the time, Elvar agreed with Laoli—he intended to keep looking. He would search till he dropped dead of exhaustion if it came to it; he would not live without her.

"I am sorry, Brother," Maiwen said, touching Elvar's cheek. "We have, however, managed to cover a wide expanse of the forest and believe we will have better luck splitting into two parties; we need to search north-east and south-west of here."

"I will stay with Elvar," Tarrys said. "I have Vala's Iridiscus pendant; maybe Mother and Father would like to join us?"

"Yes," Patrick confirmed, "we will."

They all turned, as crisp autumnal leaves crunched behind the group.

"I am sorry for our late arrival," Merevina said, her fingers laced with Merridyn's. "I spent some time alone trying to lock onto Vala's energy signature, though unfortunately to no avail; she must be too far."

"The good news, though," Merridyn began, "is that Merevina believes she still might be able to track Vala's energy trail once we are closer to her whereabouts and lead us to wherever she might be."

"We must go now!" Elvar said, his voice raised, as he impatiently raked his hands through his hair. "Please, Merevina, I would appreciate your assistance."

"Of course," Merevina replied. "Merri and I will gladly accompany you."

"Lann and I will go with Mother and Father," Maiwen said, snuggling under Lann's arm. "Which direction would you like to take, Merevina?"

"I will attempt to locate Vala's energy source again ... though I cannot promise I will be successful."

Merevina closed her eyes as everyone fell silent, allowing her to concentrate. A soft breeze skimmed over her bare arms—a reminder that dusk was setting in. Other than the odd bird call, there was very little sound to filter out: the occasional rustle of leaves in the wind, a snapping twig, her own breath. She focussed on Vala and pictured her in her mind, concentrating on her essence—Vala's very soul. Merevina's brow furrowed as she desperately tried to tap into Vala's energy ... and there it was! Faint, but there, definitely there!

"I can feel her," Merevina spoke softly. "It is not a powerful connection, but it is there nonetheless."

"Merevina," Tarrys said quietly, "I have an idea; we could all join hands, see if it intensifies the connection to Vala. If all our energies
are combined, we may have greater success."

Merevina and the others agreed and joined hands, forming a circle.

"I can see what Vala saw!" Merevina exclaimed. "But then it all goes black. Nothing."

"Which way?" Elvar asked her.

"North-east, till we reach a bifurcated path; we then take the right fork to an avenue lined with Firimin trees. It is further on where the path curves to the left, and then left again, amongst a canopy of Viaspa," Merevina answered.

Taking Merevina's lead, the others followed. The sun drew lower in the sky, tinting the clouds pink; the blue of the sky was now painted with mauve streaks and splashes of golden-orange. Elvar usually loved Avalonian autumns: still temperate but not too hot, the musky aroma of fallen leaves and damp tree bark sprinkled with morning dew, and the colours ... the colours were truly spectacular! Reds, oranges, yellows, purples, greens; silver-and-white leaves scattered across the woodland floor, blanketing it in a cornucopia of vivid colours. Today, however, Elvar did not notice. The leaves crunching underfoot held no interest to him— all he wanted in that moment was to find Vala.

They were just approaching a bench beneath the Viaspa trees when a rush of air swirled around them. A small boy alighted a few feet in front.

"Get away from him!" Maiwen shrieked. "He is a Dessicatus! He tried to kill me!"

The boy took a few steps back, his face sorrowful.

"Please," said the boy, holding up his hands in what he hoped was a conciliatory gesture. "I mean you no harm. I am here to take you to Lady Oakley-Pendragon. I know where she is!"

5 6

Vala wasn't sure how long she had been asleep when she was rudely wrenched from slumber by a sharp pain tearing through her body. The contractions were coming now every two minutes, and she whimpered as her womb convulsed violently.

"I am here, beloved," Elvar whispered in Vala's ear, clutching her hand in his.

"We all are, Sugar Plum," Laoli murmured, sitting on the side of the bed and taking Vala's other hand.

"She is very close," Sylvinia said. "There are too many of you in here, please, some of you should wait in the living room."

"I want my husband and mother," Vala said through gritted teeth.

"I am a healer," Derryth stated. "I should be here to assist with the birth."

"As once was I," Sylvinia replied sadly. "I shall leave you in Mr Oakley's capable hands."

"No!" Vala called out as Sylvinia approached the bedroom door. "Stay. Please, I need you both!"

Sylvinia ushered the others out and closed the bedroom door.

"Your brother was all set to vanquish me!" Sylvinia said, approaching the bed. "But he had a change of heart. Your friend, Merevina—daughter of Merlin, no less—is quite a persuasive young lady. I would be interested in learning more of her history later."

Derryth discretely lifted Vala's nightgown to assess her progress. Vala cried out as a sharp pain shot through her abdomen to between her legs, followed by an intense burning sensation.

"The head is crowning," Derryth said calmly. "I need you to push Vala. On the count of one ... two ... three ... push!"

Vala bore down and pushed hard. She was tired and was concerned that her heart rate was faltering; it had slowed, and it thudded in her chest dramatically, as though each beat was becoming increasingly burdensome. Perspiration pooled down her face and back, stinging her eyes. Elvar gently dabbed a fresh towel to Vala's face and kissed her lightly.

"You can do this, beloved!" Elvar said excitedly. "You are amazing! I am so proud of you."

Vala's body shuddered as she readied herself to bear down again.

Laoli squeezed Vala's ankle and smiled at her encouragingly.

"Almost there, Sugar Plum!" Laoli said, tears brimming in her eyes. "He or she certainly has a full head of hair!"

Sylvinia left the room momentarily, returning with a jar of balm.

"I apologise," Sylvinia said. "I should have brought this earlier, it has been a while."

"Elastium?" Derryth asked, opening the jar lid.

"Yes," Sylvinia answered. "There is still time."

Sylvinia carefully applied the balm between Vala's legs.

"This will help the tissue stretch without tearing."

Vala screamed as a fiery explosion of pain detonated between her legs. Elvar wrapped his arms around her, pressing his head to Vala's.

"I can't do this!" Vala sobbed. "It's going to kill me!"

"No, Sugar Plum," Laoli said, her voice choked with emotion. "You are almost there; the baby is nearly out."

"Okay, Vala," Derryth said, patting her leg. "Another big push ... now!"

Vala growled in pain as the baby's head slipped out.

After a further small push from Vala, the baby was eased out into Derryth's hands. A shrill cry pierced the air—a welcome sign that all was well.

"Would you like to meet your new son?" Derryth asked, his voice heavy with emotion.

Vala silently nodded, completely overcome with intense feelings of love and euphoria as the tiny infant was placed into her arms. She unbuttoned her nightgown and placed the baby on her chest, cradling him to her and kissing his head. Elvar fought back tears, a lump forming in his throat as he leaned over to kiss his baby son. A surge of powerful emotions coursed through him, suffusing his entire being with profound love and the need to protect his new family.

"In a moment, we will need to cut the umbilical cord," Derryth said. "Will you be doing the honours, Elvar?"

"May I hold him while you do it?" Laoli asked excitedly, watching as Elvar held his tiny son in his arms.

"I think he's cold," Vala said, gazing lovingly at her newborn.

Sylvinia placed a small blanket on the bed, and Elvar gently set his son upon it, wrapping him lightly before carefully handing him to Laoli.

"Okay," Derryth said, clamping the baby's umbilical cord. "Elvar, take these and cut here."

The moment Elvar cut the cord, the baby began to cry again.

"Have I hurt him?" Elvar asked anxiously, soothingly stroking his son's head.

"No," Sylvinia answered. "But I think he wants his mother."

Laoli caressed the baby's head and tenderly passed her grandson back to Vala, kissing her daughter's cheek as Vala gathered her baby son in her arms. She gently rocked her baby as he continued to cry.

"Maybe he's hungry?" Vala suggested as she guided her breast to the baby's mouth.

The baby nuzzled against his mother, latching on immediately and suckling hungrily as Vala watched him in fascination, awestruck by his beauty and perfection. Elvar huddled closer, placing his finger in the infant's palm and grinning in delight as his son tightly grasped it with his own tiny fingers. Suddenly, Vala was overcome by another strong contraction and whimpered.

Laoli held her daughter's hand. "It is just the placenta. Do not worry, it will be over very soon."

By the time Vala had finished feeding her newborn, the birthing process was over. Derryth and Sylvinia checked that the baby was fully healthy before weighing and cleaning him. In the meantime, Elvar and Laoli attended to Vala, washing her and giving her a change of clothes and bed linen.

"Just before we invite everyone in," Vala said excitedly, "I need to have a quiet word with Elvar, so if you wouldn't mind stepping out for a moment—say for five minutes?"

Epilogue

Elvar joined Vala on the bed, perched at the edge with their newborn son nestled between them. He felt a tremendous sense of pride as he announced their son to their family and friends.

"My amazing wife here," Elvar announced proudly, "has bestowed upon me the greatest gift ever! I would like to introduce you all to baby Arthur Patryth Oakley-Pendragon, weighing in at a healthy seven pounds, ten ounces."

"Daddy," Vala said, turning to her father, "would you like a cuddle with baby Arthur?"

Patrick hugged his daughter before taking his new grandson into his arms.

"He's beautiful, Vala," Patrick said. "Just perfect, and his eyes …"

Patrick gently stroked baby Arthur's cheek, as Arthur cooed in delight, looking directly at his grandfather.

"His eyes—they are like Temiritha's—that same unusual mix of violet and green … and look!"

Everyone stared transfixed as Arthur smiled.

"That was a genuine smile!" Patrick remarked.

"Please," Essyeult interrupted, "may I have a hold?"

By the time most of Vala and Elvar's family and friends had held baby Arthur, he was ready for a second feed. All of them, except one, had cradled the baby. Merevina remained at the back of the room, pensively staring in Vala's general direction, but not at her. Merridyn could plainly see that Merevina seemed distant and distracted, but was uncertain if he should say anything now or wait for a private moment.

"Merevina," Vala said, noticing the faraway look in her unseeing gaze, "is something wrong? Would you not like to hold Arthur?"

"Oh!" Merevina started. "Yes, of course! There is just something that I cannot quite … a memory … never mind for now, I would love to hold him!"

Merevina knelt by Vala's bedside as she carefully placed Arthur in Merevina's arms. Merevina was overcome by a sense of profound peace—the same peace she had felt holding Temiritha, but this time something else was happening, something unexpected. Arthur's tiny fingers coiled around Merevina's index finger as images flashed through her mind, fast and incoherent at first, but as she concentrated, they slowed down, playing out like a movie within her mind. Merevina gasped, looking down in shock at Arthur, hot tears spilling over her cheeks.

"I remember!" Merevina exclaimed. "What hc plans to do—all of it!"

"Who?" Elvar asked, a knot of dread twisting in his stomach as he stared at Merevina, his heart already knowing the answer.

"The Spindler," Merevina replied, her voice quivering.

"No!" Laoli shrieked, stricken with the same sickening dread that now spread to each of them. "He's dead, he's dead! Vala vanquished him!"

"Yes," Merevina replied sadly.

Arthur had begun to cry, and she passed him back to his mother's waiting arms.

"For now," Merevina continued. "He had made plans for his demise. It was almost as though he could sense it coming. The Spindler left explicit instructions with his most trusted followers—and me of course—that in the event of his termination, we obtain a small quantity of an infant's blood."

"I know this much," Vala interjected as the others turned to her in shock. "Sylvinia told me that this had been the reason for my abduction, that the blood of a child was necessary to resurrect him."

"What?" Elvar said, his voice raised. "Why did you not tell me this, Vala? And Sylvinia, *you* could have told us this. Why did you keep it concealed?"

"She didn't," Vala confessed. "I asked her not to. I didn't want our joyous event marred by something so ugly."

"I am also sorry to cast gloom over such a wonderful and momentous occasion," Merevina said. "But we must be extra vigilant. The Spindler was hoping that I would conceive a child—he believed it would be more fitting, a way of continuing his legacy. However, he stipulated that should this not occur, that we use the blood of any infant, and should Vala conceive, that it be her child. On the advent of the next total solar eclipse, he asked us to gather at the summit of Mount Cavalis with the vial of blood and wait for darkness to fall; at the moment of the eclipse, we were to pour the vial of blood over a marked spot—it is where his ashes are buried."

Merevina covered her face and began to sob, her body shuddering as she recalled the memory. Merridyn gathered her into his arms, stroking her hair.

"It is all right, my love," Merridyn whispered softly, his breath warming the top of her head.

"Once the blood had been dispersed," Merevina exhaled deeply, "an incantation would be chanted; a powerful spell invoking the Spindler to arise from the ashes."

"Arise?" Patrick said in disbelief, reeling from the preposterous news.

"Yes," Merevina confirmed. "The Spindler is set to return, and I do not know of a way to stop him."

Lovers, by Carmen Willcox

There once was a girl whose skin smelt of rainwater. She placed her hands onto the boy's young shoulders. And at dusk, wove flowers of belladonna into his sleeping hair.

In the seamless hours, their dreams would float together.

And though never touching, their fragrant glances would collide. Above the rooftops, their trailing voices, their cool skins, bled the same rich scent. Two flowers born out of one stem.

And when all of their dreaming was over. And when all of their gazing was done. They would take the night's stray, tongue-slick anointings, and blush and gush at what they had known.

Down by the hermit's cave, by the old pine's cliff slide, they would awake on their bed of damp earth. Entwined arms, dawn-moist and curving, they sprinkled petals upon their bodies to make themselves warm. And the amber clouds of the morning fled silently, as a monk unshod.

There once was a girl whose skin smelled of rainwater.

And she plucked the flowers of the belladonna to weave and bind them into her awaking lover's hair.

Dear Reader,

Thank you for reading Reawakened!

This is my second novel, and I sincerely hope you've found it to be a fun read.

As you may know, online reviews are the lifeblood of an author. Please take a few minutes to place an honest review on Amazon.

Please follow my characters' progress or just drop me a line at my website:

www.eternaluk.com

If you would like to know when I publish my next book you can sign up to receive an email alert at my website. By the way, if you would like an advance pre-publication review copy of the next book in The Eternal Trilogy, when it is ready, please contact me via the web form on my site.

Alternatively, stay in touch via Facebook, Instagram, Pinterest, Twitter or LinkedIn.

Love and light,

Denise

Denise is a Young Adult Fantasy novelist, with a special interest in Arthurian legend, the Fae and history. She lives in a picturesque, riverside town in Cambridgeshire. A beautiful son and four fur-babies keep Denise on her toes and bring her unlimited joy and oodles of love! She loves communing with nature, adores animals, loves reading, creating art, concocting culinary wonders, listening to beautiful music, watching great TV and film, and seeing what road her creativity leads her down next...

www.ingramcontent.com/pod-product-compliance
Lightning Source LLC
Chambersburg PA
CBHW020318160726
47992CB00004B/1596